P9-DWJ-360

THE SECRET KEEPER

By Beverly Lewis

HOME TO HICKORY HOLLOW
The Fiddler • *The Bridesmaid*
The Guardian • *The Secret Keeper*

THE ROSE TRILOGY
The Thorn • *The Judgment* • *The Mercy*

ABRAM'S DAUGHTERS
The Covenant • *The Betrayal* • *The Sacrifice*
The Prodigal • *The Revelation*

THE HERITAGE OF LANCASTER COUNTY
The Shunning • *The Confession* • *The Reckoning*

ANNIE'S PEOPLE
The Preacher's Daughter • *The Englisher* • *The Brethren*

THE COURTSHIP OF NELLIE FISHER
The Parting • *The Forbidden* • *The Longing*

SEASONS OF GRACE
The Secret • *The Missing* • *The Telling*

The Postcard • *The Crossroad*

The Redemption of Sarah Cain
October Song • *Sanctuary (with David Lewis)* • *The Sunroom*

Amish Prayers
The Beverly Lewis Amish Heritage Cookbook

www.beverlylewis.com

THE SECRET KEEPER

BEVERLY LEWIS

BETHANYHOUSE
a division of Baker Publishing Group
Minneapolis, Minnesota

© 2013 by Beverly M. Lewis, Inc.

Published by Bethany House Publishers
11400 Hampshire Avenue South
Bloomington, Minnesota 55438
www.bethanyhouse.com

Bethany House Publishers is a division of
Baker Publishing Group, Grand Rapids, Michigan

Printed in the United States of America

Library of Congress Cataloging-in-Publication Data

Lewis, Beverly.
    The secret keeper / Beverly Lewis.
       pages cm.—(Home to Hickory Hollow)
    Summary: "Jennifer Burns has always had an 'old soul,' but joining the
Amish world will challenge her spirit—and her heart—in ways she never ex-
pected"—Provided by publisher.
    ISBN 978-0-7642-1148-5 (cloth : alk. paper)
    ISBN 978-0-7642-0980-2 (paperback)
    ISBN 978-0-7642-1149-2 (large-print paperback)
    1. Amish—Fiction. 2. Lancaster County (Pa.)—Fiction. 3. Domestic fiction.
I. Title.
    PS3562.E9383S45 2013
    813'.54—dc23   2013014889

Scripture quotations are from the King James Version of the Bible.

The poem quoted in chapter 18 can be found in its entirety under "Morning Thoughts"
in the June 1859 copy of *The Friend of Youth and Child's Magazine.*

Cover design by Dan Thornberg, Design Source Creative Services
Art direction by Paul Higdon

13 14 15 16 17 18 19   7 6 5 4 3 2 1

For
Jackie Green,
with love.

And . . .
for all of my devoted reader-friends
whose heart's cry is to live more simply—
if not Amish,
then a more peaceable life.

Prologue

Today's the day I'll tell them.

I parked my car beneath the brilliantly red sugar maple tree at the impressive Connecticut estate—my childhood home. It was a yearly custom for my parents to throw a dinner party to celebrate my October birthday.

Twenty-five and still trying to fit in . . . somewhere.

I glanced at the console and spotted a pile of mail tucked away there, including a card from Marnie Lapp in Lancaster County. *May this be the best birthday ever, dear Jenny!* she'd written beneath her name.

A chance meeting several years ago while on vacation, and curiously enough, Marnie and I had become friends. Despite being Amish, she was one of my closest confidantes.

Getting out of the car, I drew a deep breath and strolled toward the formal entrance. At the grand double doors, I paused to muster up the required poise, straightened my breezy floral skirt, and pushed back my shoulder-length auburn hair. Ready or not, I reached for the gleaming handle and stepped inside the two-story foyer.

My older sister, Kiersten, greeted me, her brown-eyed gaze lingering with unconcealed disapproval on my high-necked blouse and open-toed sandals. "Happy birthday, sister," she said, waving me into the intimate gathering room near the dining room. "Mom's knocked herself out, as usual." Then, pausing as we passed through the doorway, she added, "Oh, and I should warn you. Robb brought along a colleague from work. His name is Frank." Her eyes communicated the message *Not my fault!*

So my brother-in-law, Dr. Robb Newburg, was obviously as concerned as Mom about my single state.

I cringed. Now what? How could I possibly reveal my plans?

Attempting to conjure up some enthusiasm, I smiled as Robb rose from his comfortable perch and rushed over to extend his hand. He turned to introduce a good-looking, very tall blond man.

Frank gave me an engaging smile. "It's great to meet you," he said, all charm.

"Thanks for joining us," I replied politely even as my heart sank. I didn't like the idea of postponing my inevitable news. This was supposed to be the night I actually dared to be honest with everyone.

"My sister's something straight out of the nineteenth century," Kiersten declared. "In case you wondered, Frank." She punctuated her remark with foolish laughter.

Ah . . . Kiersten. True to form, interlacing her banter with shards of truth. She glanced coyly at Robb, who smiled back at me, apologizing with his blue-gray eyes.

"Um, what's so special about *this* century?" I asked, glancing over at my brother, Cameron, and his girlfriend, Tracie Wells. "High-tech gadgets aren't everything."

Kiersten simpered as she fingered her diamond earring.

"Does this mean you *still* don't have a cell phone?" asked Cameron, feigning pain when Tracie poked him.

"Life is far less complicated without one," I replied.

My own family. After all these years, they still didn't know what made me tick.

In the corner of the room, our father was hunched over one of his many research books, oblivious to the undercurrents. *All the better. Wouldn't want to spoil things for Mom.* Such parties translated to fun and socializing for her—the more, the better. Dad, however, preferred to immerse himself in his work as a research scientist for a pharmaceutical company, more at home with books than with people.

I went over to say hi. "What're you studying, Dad?"

He glanced up as if just realizing I was there. He blinked at me, a vague look on his face, apparently still deep in thought about his book. So typical of my cerebral father. "Hi, Jenny."

Not "Happy birthday, honey."

Then Mom appeared in the dining room archway, impeccably coifed, pretty eyes smiling. She was ready to serve dinner and motioned gracefully without a word, contentedly leading the way.

The chandeliered space was adorned with silver streamers, and matching candles flickered across the gleaming table. We'd celebrated numerous birthdays here in Mom's favorite room, yet I'd never stopped feeling out of place.

Once we were all seated, I tried to make conversation with my mother, but she was eager to talk about an upcoming gala instead.

The prime rib was wonderful. But with Frank seated next to me at the table, it wasn't easy negotiating our forced meeting. *Really, Mom?* The uncomfortable pauses between Frank's upbeat comments—and his attempt to ask me out—were the last things I needed at my final dinner party in the modern world.

And sitting there with my family gathered near, I wondered, *If I were to disappear, would they even notice?*

After dinner, my mother produced a spectacular chocolate layer cake and lit the birthday candles. Kiersten studied me like a lab tech with a specimen while Mom coaxed me to blow out my candles, as if I were still six. "The evening's not perfect without a birthday wish. Make it a good one, Jenny."

Making wishes was the easy part. It was the end result that was iffy. Despite that, I closed my eyes to appease her, knowing all too well my *mother's* dearest wish—that I'd settle down and marry. The sooner, the better.

I puffed out the candles, but my wish had nothing to do with a man—not that I was opposed to marriage and a family of my own. More times than I could count, I'd imagined what it would be like to live in a simpler era, when people actually *listened* to one another.

The ideal world . . .

But there would be no announcement tonight. Hours after the superb meal, we parted ways and I drove to my modest condo on the outskirts of Essex. Inside, I hurried to my bedroom and sat on a chair to reread Marnie's card. Remembering the serene Pennsylvania setting that was her home, I savored the thoughtful birthday greeting, then scanned the sparsely furnished room where I'd hatched my secret plan.

Not even my closest friends had seen my room. Not that they were missing much by their standards. My cherished decorating style was essentially Early Attic.

I breathed out the number of my years, "Twenty-five," and rose to reach for my scuffed antique silver brush on the simple dresser. I pulled it vigorously through my hair, eager to lose myself in something other than my parents' decked-out home or frivolous table chatter. I stared into the antique oval dresser mirror, recalling how Kiersten *always* introduced me: "My *sister's an old soul. . . .*"

Absolutely, I agreed. *I was born too late.*

Turning from the mirror, I strolled to the cozy window seat and opened its top. Inside were scores of clippings from my subscription to a Lancaster newspaper, arranged by categories I'd labeled more than a decade ago. I recalled the first time I'd heard of the Amish. I was only eleven when I was transfixed by a TV documentary.

People actually live and dress that way?

Mom hadn't known how to react back then; my fascination with the simple life perplexed her. "*What can they be thinking—no cars, no electricity, and even some outhouses?*" she'd mused aloud.

Regardless, by the time I was fourteen, I'd devoured everything written about the People, including novels with Amish settings. I yearned to know why the Plain folk continued to live as though they were locked in time. Several years later, my first road trip had led me to Lancaster County, where I had returned each summer thereafter, walking barefoot along the dusty byways and stopping at roadside vegetable and fruit stands, relishing the way the sweet, juicy peaches split right open. What fun it was to make small talk with the more outgoing Amish girls. I met Marnie Lapp at one such stand, and she agreed to exchange letters with me, apparently curious about why an Englisher girl was so taken with all things Plain.

Oh, hers was such a gloriously peaceful world, one firmly grounded in the past. I sincerely desired the stability of Amish tradition and hoped my own personal issues might simply disappear in such an established, dependable community. I'd held that hope within me for years now—I'd even committed it to prayer. *After all, God gives His children the desires of their hearts.*

If only my earthly family—my parents, especially—had taken the time to really try to understand me.

"Bloom where you're planted," Mom had often insisted while I was growing up, but what if you were planted in the wrong soil? What then?

I was very sure I knew the answer. And I was willing to give up everything to follow my dream. Never had I felt so free.

Chapter 1

Rebecca Lapp felt so numb and stiff she could scarcely move. It was past three o'clock in the morning according to the wind-up clock on the small table near the headboard. Breathless from the harrowing dream, she worried, *Is it a warning?*

Slowly, lest she awaken Samuel, she inched her way up to a sitting position, her eyes wide against the darkened room. But her heart was a lump of lead. She pondered her dream in a stupor, wishing she could release the misery.

Minutes ticked by, and at last she inched out of bed, creeping to the dresser a few feet away. She probed the area with her fingers in search of the box of matches. Clumsily, she managed to light the small kerosene lantern. The wing of flame faltered, then blazed brightly.

Just a silly dream, she assured herself. *Everything's fine—I haven't been found out.* Besides, most dreams had no particular meaning; she knew that.

Samuel's snoring was familiar and steady, even comforting, as Rebecca reached for her warm bathrobe on the wooden wall peg and wandered down the hall to Katie's former bedroom.

She stepped inside and perused the vacant room by lantern light. Breathing deeply, she felt sure there was still a hint of Katie's lilac-scented potpourri. Mrs. Daniel Fisher had been blissfully married now for six years and kept busy with four-year-old Samuel Dan, known mostly as Sammy, and his baby sister, Kate Marie, eighteen months old next week. Other than her blond hair—so like her *Dat's*—little Kate was the spitting image of her pretty *Mamma*, though Kate Marie wasn't the most Amish-sounding name Katie might have chosen.

Close enough, Rebecca mused.

She still could not shake the notion that the dream might be prophetic. Samuel and their sons—Elam, Eli, and Benjamin— would surely think so. After all, she *was* pushing the boundaries of the *Bann,* going over to see shunned Katie and the children now and then these past few months. *If I'm caught, I'll be accused of hindering the effect of* die Meinding, Rebecca thought. She didn't want to stand in the way of God's work in her wayward daughter's life, yet Katie's was the harshest shunning in all of Lancaster County. Rebecca was terribly conflicted—wanting to obey the church ordinance while also heeding her heart's cry to see Katie and the grandbabies.

She set the lantern on the end table and tiptoed to the neatly made bed and knelt there. Goodness' sake, there was plenty to pray about, considering that her niece, twenty-one-year-old Marnie Lapp, had dropped by unexpectedly last week, all rosy cheeked and talking up a storm, *babblich* as ever. It seemed she had befriended an out-of-state *Englischer*—a young woman named Jenny Burns—and written her letters for several years. Oddly, the outsider had sold off near everything she owned somewhere in Connecticut—even her car. To top things off, she was coming to live in Lancaster County as an Amish seeker and needed a place to stay for a while, till the bishop acknowledged her as a convert. *"I was wondering if she might rent one of your empty bedrooms,"* Marnie had suggested, her blue eyes ever so hopeful.

Another one of Marnie's rather ferhoodled *ideas . . .*

Marnie had clasped her hands as she stood fidgeting in the utility room just beyond the kitchen, a fallen gold leaf stuck to her black woolen shawl like a curious posy. From the look on her niece's face, there was not a doubt in Rebecca's mind that Marnie was thrilled about the prospect, outsider though Jenny Burns was.

Rebecca had never known any of the People to open their homes for the purpose of giving a stranger time to learn the Old Ways and *Deitsch*, too—certainly not with the hope of joining church. When she'd mentioned the idea to her husband after Marnie left, Samuel was not keen on the idea, though in the end he'd taken up the matter with Bishop John Beiler.

Presently, she bowed her head and pressed her hands together. Rebecca hardly knew what to pray. "Almighty God, grant divine guidance and grace in this peculiar matter," she whispered. "And help us know how to proceed. We want to do the right and wise thing, to glorify thy name."

The day following her birthday, Jenny had given her two weeks' notice at Always Antiques, where she'd worked as an appraiser since college graduation. While neither her job nor her home state of Connecticut had any real hold on her, she would miss her friends, especially Pamela and Dorie Kennedy, two sisters she'd known since childhood. It was a significant blessing that her condo lease was finally up. She would also miss Woodbury—the antiques capital of Connecticut, about forty minutes away—and beautiful Essex. Her parents' estate was located a mere block from the Connecticut River. *Rushing . . . like time's own swift current*, she thought while making a list of things to pack.

Her soul was starving for a sensible, more solicitous life. Since her first visit to Lancaster County years ago, Jenny had decided to make it her home, but she hadn't seen her way clear until now. Thanks to Marnie's working behind the scenes, finding her a place to live, she was finally able to move ahead. The Amish life offered what Jenny longed for: more time to savor each moment, slow the torrent of time, and grow as a child of God. She was ready to embrace a unique people, one set apart.

Perhaps one day her own family would come to accept this near-constant yearning in her bones. Up until now, they'd barely endured her obsession with the past, frowning at her frustration with ever-changing modern society.

But now Jenny was sure she had the ultimate answer. "Hickory Hollow," she breathed.

In the diffused autumn light, she caught herself staring at the old pine desk in the corner of her bedroom, where she'd stored a beloved album from the past. The memory of creating it tugged at her, as did the thought of leaving it behind. But her heartache of that time had since mended—the split had come more than two years ago. She had moved forward, glad to have more than survived the demise of her first love. *I'd do everything differently, given the chance*, she vowed.

She went to the desk and removed the cherished scrapbook. Taking her time, she memorized each page of the romance represented there. Every picture, every memento—the movie stubs, photos of flea market events, and visits to the Mystic Aquarium . . . the bits and pieces of two remarkable years.

She headed to the living room and built a blistering fire in the quaint fireplace. Without another thought, she tossed the album into the flames. "Good-bye, Kyle Jackson," she whispered. "Good-bye forever."

Jenny could hear the beating of her own heart. That small, fragile sound made her wish for peaceful Lancaster County more than ever. *Heaven on earth,* she thought, counting the days until she could finally move.

She watched the moon rise and settle into the trees beyond her living room window while the familiar question persisted: *Can I really do this?*

Suddenly, Jenny remembered what Marnie Lapp had penned in a recent letter: *My dear friend, there's only one way to find out!*

Chapter 2

T hat's right, Hickory Hollow," Jenny Burns repeated for the cab driver outside the Lancaster train station. The short, balding cabbie looked completely baffled, so she opened her purse and located the house address on Hickory Lane.

Tired from the long trip, Jenny recalled the cell phone joke her brother had made two weeks ago at her birthday party. Surely the cab driver had a smartphone, or at the very least, a GPS. He shuffled to the trunk of the cab and opened it, then *thwomp*ed her large suitcase inside. He glanced at her as if to say, *"Whatcha got in there, Missy? An elephant?"* Then he closed the trunk and waved her toward the backseat. "I'm sure if it's in the area, we'll find it."

Carrying her purse and smaller bag, Jenny slipped inside the cab. She could have happily described the golden vale of a place—the fertile, sheltered hollow bounded on the north by the Old Philadelphia Pike and on the south by the Lincoln Highway.

Jenny buckled up and realized she'd only visited here in summertime. Presently, the air was swollen with the scent of sun-drenched autumn and, unmistakably, manure. "It must be harvesttime," she murmured.

"Excuse me?" the cabbie said.

"Uh, nothing."

"Ah, here we are." The cabbie pointed to the small screen on his dash. "You were right. That's Hickory Lane, over there to the east."

Soon they were off, heading toward Bird-in-Hand. Along the way, they encountered a number of gray horse-drawn, box-like buggies, with two carrying young children who peered out the back. One young girl squinted at them, her eyes smiling when the cab passed the carriage on the left. The little girl's white cap was tilted askew on her head.

"Welcome to Amishland," the cabbie grumbled. He shook his head with something close to disgust. "I don't get it, and I never will."

"I think theirs is a noble way of life," Jenny said, surprised by his attitude and feeling defensive.

"Are you kidding? Can you imagine living Amish? I mean, seriously."

"It works for them," she replied. "Has for more than three hundred years."

He muttered something. Then he said more audibly, "I know an Amish fellow who got fed up with the church and left." He looked at her in the rearview mirror. "Know why?"

Miffed, she merely shook her head.

Mr. Cabbie tapped his forehead. "Told me he wasn't permitted to think for himself."

Some fit in and some don't, she thought.

"He wanted a high school education—a no-no for Amish. When he left, he got his GED and went on to college. Wanted to be a lawyer, I guess. An odd career for an Amishman."

"Well, this country could use some *honest* attorneys." She smiled at herself.

"Last I heard, he had a nice big house over near Eden— opposite direction from where we're headed." The cabbie nodded his head. "This fellow just wasn't cut out to be Plain." He glanced at her in the rearview mirror. "Know much about the Amish?" he asked.

"I've met a few Plain women . . . bought tomatoes and cukes at their roadside stands."

The highway narrowed as they headed through Smoketown, then entered Bird-in-Hand proper, past the Old Village Store on the left and the farmers market on the right.

"All I know is that they make my job harder, clogging up the roads," he said. "Why they don't just get cars, I'll never understand."

"How much farther?" Jenny was ready to end the stream of criticism.

"Not too far. By the looks of it, Hickory Hollow's east of Intercourse Village."

She made herself relax. Thankfully, the cabbie was less keen on chattering now. Jenny enjoyed the sun's warmth as she watched the landscape whiz past, thinking ahead to riding in a horse-drawn carriage with Marnie. She was captivated by the eight-mule teams and the Amishmen working the fields, sporting straw hats, their suspenders crisscrossed against dark blue, green, or gray shirts.

Like in the books I've read . . .

From what Marnie Lapp had said, her aunt Rebecca was the ideal person to mentor Jenny, at least until she found her own place. *"You'll like her,"* Marnie had predicted in the last letter. *"For sure and for certain."*

Jenny's own resolve still surprised her, particularly the sale of her car a few days ago, after having already sold most of her household possessions and dispensable personal effects at area consignment stores following her birthday. She only regretted not being more specific with her parents, especially her mother, although as it turned out, her mother seemed as distracted as her father, most likely finalizing her latest gala. Mom had looked up from her list, her mind seemingly miles away. *"Where are you going again?"*

Jenny had hesitated. *"I'll get in touch once I'm there."*

Mom's frown was inscribed on Jenny's memory; she could see the confused expression even now. *"Well . . . whatever you think is best, dear."* She paused, fixing Jenny with a look of concern. *"Is everything okay?"*

Jenny opened her mouth, wondering if she shouldn't just come clean, but before she could answer, her mother suddenly remembered something and reached for her cell phone, raising her finger. *"Hold that thought."*

It occurred to her not for the first time that it might be weeks before her mother even realized she was gone.

Kiersten had been indifferent, more concerned with Jenny's supposed snub of Frank, her husband's *"really wonderful associate"*—she'd seemed more anxious than usual to get off the phone. And Cameron had just assumed Jenny was taking an extended vacation. *"Must be nice . . ."*

And while she'd tried to tell him it wasn't that at all, Jenny believed in her heart that saying anything more would be a mistake. They would just try to talk her out of moving to Amish farmland, abandoning the materialistic English world. *Their beautiful world.*

When the cab made the right turn onto Cattail Road, Jenny's skin prickled, and she wondered how close the Lapp farmhouse might be. She saw what looked like a waterwheel near a creek. For an instant, she wished for her camera, but she'd sold that, too.

Leaning back again, she remembered working on a little lap quilt as a young teen while her sister played video games with their brother and neighborhood friends. *I was passionate about simple things while everyone else was into high tech.*

She thought of various fancy things she could have brought along—makeup, for one. And toiletries. But those weren't for a dedicated Amishwoman, as she intended to be. She'd walked out on her lipstick, her jewelry, most of her clothes, even her books.

It's time to live. Forget the stuff.

Just that quick, it occurred to her that Marnie might have forgotten to set things in place. Her emotions imploded. Surely not! Arranging things with the Lapps was vital—there was no backup plan. Oh, why was she thinking this way? If she couldn't trust Marnie to follow through, whom could she trust? *And given Marnie's excitement . . .*

Despite that, corresponding by letter about the arrangement now seemed terribly risky. Why hadn't Jenny gotten confirmation before she jumped?

Her heart pounded as she considered again the major changes ahead—changes that she was willing to make. *For the rest of my life . . . if the People will have me.*

She forced her gaze toward the heavens. *Lord, if you've put this desire in my heart, then here I am.*

Besides Jenny's strong feeling about all this, Marnie had nearly promised that her aunt Rebecca was the key to Jenny's pursuit. The Amish life lived under the watchful care of Samuel and Rebecca Lapp would lead Jenny aright, solve her lifelong desire. In every way, she was coming home.

Chapter 3

Rebecca Lapp lingered in Ella Mae Zook's snug kitchen longer than usual early that afternoon. During the past few days, she'd observed a perceptible change in her elderly friend, and Rebecca hadn't been the only one to notice. Indeed, Ella Mae still held her slight shoulders straight and smiled most readily, so there wasn't anything physical that Rebecca could credit this feeling to. But there *was* something.

Standing near the back door, Rebecca knew she should head across the field in case her niece's English friend arrived early. "I'd be happy to bring supper over later," Rebecca offered, resting both hands on the back of the wooden kitchen chair. "You just say the word."

Ella Mae smiled. Her middle part appeared wider and her hair whiter in the streaming light from the window. "*Ach*, ya musn't baby me, hear? Ain't nothin' wrong that some hot peppermint tea can't cure."

"You sure, now?"

"Go on, Rebecca dear. Time to greet the young seeker-woman. She'll need all the encouragement you can give her."

Ella Mae pressed her crinkled hand to her high forehead. "What's her name again?"

"Jennifer Burns, but I'm told she goes by Jenny."

"A nice enough name." Ella Mae looked out the window, her cane hooked on her scrawny arm.

"Well, the name's not the point," Rebecca added good-naturedly. "What matters is what she's made of."

"Mm-hmm," Ella Mae agreed. "Ain't many fancy folk who fit in with us, ya know."

Ella Mae had always been one to cling to her own strong opinions, even when most folk would have stood down—Samuel had once said as much years ago, when Ella Mae was causing a stink with the deacon at the time. But Ella Mae had never suppressed her view on things when it came to speaking up for what was right. At least what was right and good in *her* eyes, which meant she didn't always line up with the *Ordnung* or the bishop, either. Yet the usually stern Bishop Beiler let her be—she was too old to be put off church.

Rebecca looked away and spotted a drawing of a carved pumpkin on the refrigerator, doubtless the work of one of Ella Mae's many great-great-grandchildren. The pumpkin's smile had one tooth showing on top and two on the bottom, all staggered perfectly. She was a bit surprised Ella Mae kept it up, knowing how the older woman felt about anything to do with Halloween.

"It's not what ya think," Ella Mae said, breaking the quiet.

Rebecca blinked. "The jack-o'-lantern?" She returned her gaze to the fragile woman sitting at the table.

"Ach, no, for pity's sake."

"What, then?"

"The reason I'm so tetchy." Ella Mae pointed to the chair

across from her, and Rebecca pulled it out and sat down. "I hate to say anything, but when I heard what Marnie was up to, getting you and Samuel involved, well . . ."

"Marnie talked to you?"

"Twice already."

"Ah . . . you must be worried 'bout us opening our home to a stranger."

Ella Mae fixed her eyes on Rebecca. "That ain't the half of it."

Things always went more smoothly when Ella Mae's side of the conversation was permitted to trickle out without interruption. So Rebecca waited, quite aware of her friend's crumpled brow. Deep concern was embedded there.

"Think of it, Rebecca. The woman's a worldly outsider. Have ya thought of getting some instruction on this from the ministers? A seeker sure ain't something we hear of every day."

"Samuel and Bishop John put their heads together a couple days ago, so that's taken care of, I daresay."

Ella Mae stared at her fingers. "I'm surprised that Samuel agreed."

Rebecca cleared her throat.

"*Did* he, Rebecca?"

"Not at first, *nee.*"

"And now?"

"He's warming up to it; that's all I best say."

"Well, then, 'tis better . . . I s'pose."

"We'll just have to rest in that."

Ella Mae nodded slowly, her frown still evident. "I think ya could be askin' for trouble."

"Are you wondering 'bout her Proving? All the time it might take?"

"For certain." Ella Mae paused, shifting her weight in the chair. "And she's unmarried, ain't?"

"Far as I know." Rebecca looked right at her. "So then, you must think she's comin' here out of curiosity."

"Maybe. Or could be she wants to find herself a Plain husband."

Rebecca sighed. "Well, yes, I'd assume so if she wants to be Amish herself. But I really don't think marriage is her first priority."

"Well, aren't most seekers *married* couples with young children searching for a different lifestyle, lookin' to be set apart from the modern world?" Ella Mae leaned hard on the table, her face suddenly all washed out.

Rebecca nodded, mindful of her friend's serious expression. "*Jah.* Sometimes they're a-hankerin' for a church that meets their standards. Or they want their children to experience working the soil, raising their own crops—like the Englischer pioneers did, ya know." Rebecca smoothed out the placemat. "And some single men come seeking, too . . . wantin' wives to cook and keep house. Something, I guess, that's not very common anymore in the English world."

"But a single woman arranging to come here on her own? It's mighty suspect, I'll say," Ella Mae said. "I wonder what her family thinks of it."

"Well, just maybe her motives are untainted. After all, Marnie would surely know, since they've been exchanging letters for a number of years."

Ella Mae gave an odd little half smile and shook her head. "You'll be the first to know where her heart is, Rebecca. Just think on that."

Rebecca felt the weight of it. "You want me to watch for certain signs, is that it?"

"All I'm sayin' is keep your eyes and ears open." Ella Mae reached across to tap Rebecca's hand with her own. "The Good Lord may indeed have entrusted this seeker to you and Samuel. That's where it all starts—in the soul of a person."

"I can only guide her as far as she is teachable . . . or pliable."

"And I can tell ya one thing: She won't be as tender-hearted toward the church as our own young ones, growin' up in the ways of the Lord God." Ella Mae paused, her small blue eyes seeking out Rebecca's. "Any idea 'bout this Jenny's upbringing?"

"Only what Marnie says. Evidently she was taken to church as a child by her aunt and uncle for a few years, but her parents stepped in and decided she'd had enough religion."

"Might be, then, that she'll have a lot of catchin' up to do."

"I'd guess she will, although Marnie indicated she'd found a small church she enjoyed attending on her own after leavin' home."

"Regardless of how it turns out, you've got your work cut out for ya, Rebecca. I wouldn't want to be in your shoes. I 'spect she'll last a month, maybe two."

The Wise Woman was probably right. It wouldn't do to get too fond of the young woman, the way Marnie had.

Ella Mae insisted on serving more peppermint tea with raw honey before Rebecca was free to go. And all the while, Rebecca mulled the Old Wise Woman's words. Had God truly handpicked her and Samuel to look after young Jenny Burns's heart?

Rebecca inhaled and raised her shoulders, not sure she was up to such a task. That was a parent's calling, as she knew quite well. And she'd failed dreadfully with Katie, her only daughter.

Why'd the Good Lord choose me?

"Looks like it's one of the next big farmhouses on this side of the road," the cabbie announced, looking over his shoulder at Jenny. "Wait a minute. You're not coming here to *stay* with the Amish, are you?"

"As a matter of fact, I am."

He scratched the side of his head. "Well, I'll be!"

She inhaled slowly. "I plan to join the church if they'll have me."

He spun around to crane his neck at her. "You *cannot* be serious."

"Actually, I am."

He looked back to the road and reached up to rub the round circle of pink flesh on top of his head. "But why?"

She felt no obligation to share her reasons. "I just am."

"Well, you're in for some mighty hard labor. From sunup to sundown is what I heard."

She looked out the window. *I'm not afraid of hard work.*

Just then, they turned into Samuel Lapp's lane. She spotted the name on the large mailbox out front.

"Welcome to your new life."

"Thanks," she said, opening her purse to pay him.

He took the money and counted it carefully. "I wish you the best—you're going to need it."

She disregarded his comment and gave him a smile. "Have a pleasant afternoon."

He nodded quickly and got out to open the trunk and set

the oversized suitcase on the ground. He pulled out a card from his trousers and pointed to the phone number. "In case things don't work out, here's your ticket out of Plainville . . . back to the real world. Of course, there aren't any phones, so you'll have to find a neighbor to—"

"Thanks again," Jenny interrupted, relieved to have arrived at the Lapps'. She waved away his business card. *Why would I possibly need it?*

Chapter 4

Rebecca observed the Englischer's hefty suitcase as the slender young woman pulled it behind her, coming up the lane toward the house. She looked like she was planning to stay a good long time, just as Marnie had said. The seeker's abundantly thick hair was a lovely auburn hue, similar to Katie's—radiant as the sun's golden beams caught it.

Dear Gott *in heaven* . . . It took her breath away.

Rebecca remembered walking up this long driveway to the house as a young bride. Now it was as if a part of her were walking it again. *Ever so starry-eyed . . . like this dear girl,* she thought.

Rebecca hurried around the side of the house toward the attractive young woman even as Ella Mae's earlier call for prudence crossed her mind.

"*Willkumm,*" Rebecca called, finding her voice. "You must be Jenny Burns."

"Yes, and you're Rebecca Lapp, aren't you?" The girl's sweet face lit up, and she let go of the suitcase and stuck out her hand to shake Rebecca's.

"I surely am," Rebecca said, then looked up the road. "I 'spect Marnie will stop by any minute."

"Oh, I hope so." Jenny's light brown eyes shone as she took in the adjacent countryside. With a great sigh, she said, "It's perfectly gorgeous here, Rebecca."

"Samuel and I think so. The Lord's beauty everywhere ya look, ain't?"

Jenny nodded enthusiastically.

Rebecca asked, "Can I help you with one of your bags?"

"Thanks, but I packed as light as possible, knowing I'll be sewing some Amish clothes." The girl frowned at her own large suitcase. "It really doesn't look like it, though."

Smiling, Rebecca said, "That's quite all right. You'll have plenty of room upstairs for all your things."

"I can't express my gratitude to you enough, Rebecca—and to your husband. I am truly thankful."

Jenny Burns looked as modest, even as Plain, as many of the Mennonite ladies Rebecca encountered at the Bird-in-Hand Farmers Market. She didn't ask but assumed Jenny meant she wanted to start dressing Amish right away. "Well, *kumme mit*, and I'll show you where you're goin' to stay."

Jenny beamed as she said, "You'll have to overlook my enthusiasm. I've been living for this day for a long time."

Never before had Rebecca encountered anyone so thoroughly taken with the notion of Amish life. Already she liked Jenny very much. She just hoped the young woman wouldn't be disappointed. Had she set the People up on a pedestal, like so many Englischers did? And, as pretty as Jenny was, why on earth wasn't she already hitched up? Guessing such information might be forthcoming, she led Jenny into their hundred-and-fifty-year-old farmhouse, built by Samuel's forebear Joseph Lapp and his stonemason friend.

It'd be right nice, Rebecca decided, if she had a manual to follow. She wondered, for instance, how long she was expected to converse in English with Jenny. And was it her place to start teaching Deitsch? After all, if Jenny was serious about becoming a convert, she'd have to learn the language.

For now, though, Rebecca simply led the way upstairs to the room Katie had occupied for twenty years, prior to leaving Hickory Hollow. Her heart sank to her toes as she remembered those happy, happy days, raising her darling girl there on the farm.

Ach, she thought. Why hadn't she considered this situation more carefully, consenting to having a stranger stay in this very special room? All of a sudden, she felt downright disloyal to her adopted daughter.

What have I done?

Jenny tiptoed as if walking on holy ground. How could she not stare as she passed through the surprisingly modern-looking kitchen, into the large sitting room, toward the steep stairway? She assumed the appliances were gas powered, yet they looked like something one might buy at a regular kitchen store. *Interesting!*

The hallway walls were the delicate gray color she'd expected—not drab at all in person—and the wide-plank floorboards had a quaint hammered look, possibly original to the old farmhouse. Jenny shivered with pleasure. She was here, settling into an Old Order Amish house and making it her home for the foreseeable future.

Inside the airy bedroom, she admired the rich wood molding on the doorjamb and took note of the dark green shades neatly rolled up on both windows. The hand-stitched navy, green, maroon, and yellow bed quilt was definitely the Double

Nine Patch pattern—she recognized it thanks to a similar quilt that once hung in the antique shop back in Essex, where she'd lovingly eyed it for weeks until it was sold.

There was something tangibly beautiful in the atmosphere. Was it just her? Or was there truly something special about finally being here? She could not keep from smiling.

Jenny could hardly wait to join the ranks of Amishwomen. She envisioned the many canning bees and quilting frolics. The cordial gossip and close friendships to come. She felt her burdens lifting and sighed gratefully.

All is well, at last!

Marnie Lapp assumed it was best in every respect to give Jenny time to settle in with Aunt Rebecca. But it was all she could manage, making herself stay put at home with *Mamm* with her friend so near.

"I do hope someone's alerted Bishop John 'bout all this," Marnie's mother said while they crimped peanut butter cookies with forks. Mamm's tone suggested she was skeptical. "Don't ya think it's unusual, really? I mean, just think of it."

Marnie repeated what Aunt Rebecca had said about Bishop John and Uncle Samuel talking things over recently. "Why not trust the Lord God and the ministerial brethren, too?"

"So then, Bishop John's all right with this?"

"From what I've heard. He says it's up to Jenny Burns to live Amish and learn our ways for the time being. When she finishes her Proving time, we'll know better where things stand."

"Well, someone's got a lot to teach her—how to dress, how to speak our language, and the rules of the Ordnung. Why, she probably doesn't even know how to hitch a horse to a carriage!" Mamm's blue eyes widened. "Has anyone even considered that?"

Marnie nodded.

"So are you thinkin' of teaching her, then, Marnie?"

"Me?" She laughed, knowing full well she was not the best choice, at least for the hitching up. Not with her own clumsiness when it came to horses, buggies, and other moving things. "Maybe Uncle Samuel can help out—with the hitchin', anyways."

"Well, I'd be careful 'bout assuming that." Her mother looked too pink in the face. "Your uncle is awful busy running his big dairy farm."

"Maybe Cousin Andrew's a better choice, then."

"Oh, ya want *Andrew* to show her, do ya?" Mamm's eyes narrowed to slits. "*Puh*, he's got enough to worry 'bout, much less a wannabe convert—a single one at that! An Englischer's the *last* thing he needs."

"I'm not sayin' anything 'bout courtin', Mamm."

Marnie sighed. She certainly couldn't argue the point. And she *had* been straight with Jenny that finding a husband, if she was so inclined, would be very difficult considering just about everything. After all, most young Amishwomen were married in their early twenties, if not earlier. Jenny was already past the normal marrying age, and it would be some time before she could be baptized. Marnie wondered how Jenny Burns would be accepted by any of the older single fellows, as well as by Marnie's own family. *Especially Dat.*

Marnie's father was particularly apprehensive where the English were concerned. He disliked having much to do with them, even though more and more Amish were interacting with the world nowadays, working alongside them out of necessity, due to dwindling farmland.

"Have you told Dat 'bout Jenny's comin'?" Marnie ventured.

"Just yesterday," Mamm said, wiping her hands on her work apron. "Waited till the last minute, I guess."

Marnie understood. "Maybe Jenny will change Dat's mind about fancy folk."

Mamm waved her hand. "Not likely."

"You don't know her like I do. She's serious 'bout all this," Marnie said. "Jenny even discussed with me how she oughta dress today, when she first arrived."

"Did she, now?"

"She wanted to start off on the right foot. She even sold her car."

Her mother's head turned quickly. "Well, it sounds like she's mighty sure of herself."

"Oh, she is, believe me. This is everything she wants."

Mamm went to the oven, opened it, and removed a pumpkin pie.

"Smells awful *gut*."

"You always say that, Marnie." Mamm smiled. "Never fails."

"What could be better than pumpkin goodies in autumn?" Marnie loved October more than all the other eleven months wrapped up together. She'd felt that way since she was a wee girl, watching the trees, anxious to see the green turn to red, orange, and gold. So she marked this wonderful-good fall day and excused herself to head down Hickory Lane. "I'm itchin' to see my English-turned-Amish friend."

"I assumed so," Mamm replied, a glint of curiosity in her eyes. "But you'll return to help with supper, ain't?"

Marnie promised to.

"And just in case you get any ideas 'bout bringing her back here today, I think Rebecca's the best one to help Jenny get situated. All right?"

"I want to check on her, is all."

"Like I said, Rebecca can acclimate her just fine."

Goodness, but her mother sounded adamant. Marnie almost wished she'd told her mother more about the letters she and Jenny had written over the years. But, no, it was all right to have a few secrets.

"I won't be gone long," she told Mamm and went out the back door.

Jenny must be having the time of her life, thought Marnie, wondering if it was smart to pave the way too smoothly for a seeker. Any seeker, really. Jenny's struggle to adjust to the Plain life and insight would ultimately make her *niedrich*—humble—and stronger spiritually. *She'll have to look to God each and every day*, Marnie mused, hastening her step. *Just as we all do.*

Chapter 5

While unpacking, Jenny added several more things to her mental checklist. High on the list was asking Rebecca about the requirements for the Proving. That, and what things would be asked of Jenny at her baptism, some time from now. The day could not come soon enough.

Jenny went to the oak dresser and slid open a drawer. There was plenty of space for her undergarments there, as well as room beneath the wooden wall pegs for her plain black shoes. And her sneakers, which were appropriate for daily wear, since she knew that Marnie wore them, too. While Jenny hadn't brought along any makeup, she couldn't resist packing some light perfume, which she presently placed on a small tray on the dresser.

Enjoying this time to herself after the hectic day of travel, she opened her daily journal and turned to a fresh new page.

From this day forward, I, Jennifer Burns, will faithfully attempt to mimic Rebecca Lapp and the other Amishwomen here in Hickory Hollow for my Proving. My clothes, hair, and manner must reflect Gelassenheit—a compliant and submissive spirit. In short, I will give up my own wants and desires and yield to the ways of the People. And to God.

*I promise to abandon the English world and its modern
conveniences, including driving a car, using electricity, and
anything related to the World Wide Web, among other things.
All in favor of the Anabaptist life and the Old Ways.*

*With the help of my heavenly Father, I write this with a
reverent heart.*

—*Jennifer Burns*

Jenny reviewed the entry. It was rather formal, much like
her own mother. Even the navy blue journal, hardback and
with thick, high-quality pages, seemed to lend an air of so-
phistication not in keeping with simplicity.

She sighed, realizing the challenges that lay ahead, especially when it came to romance and the prospect of marriage.
Marnie had made it clear that finding an Amish husband
would prove difficult, if not impossible. Unless Jenny was
willing to marry one of the widowers with children, most
eligible men were already taken.

To think I'm nearly an old maid!

But Jenny could readily admit, if only to herself, that she
hoped to be the exception to the rule. If not, and she was
to live a Plain and single life till the end of her days, then
so be it. Becoming an Amish convert had never been about
finding a husband, but she certainly *desired* to share her life
with someone. And she sincerely believed that with God, all
things were possible.

Jenny admired matronly Rebecca in her blue dress and full
black cape apron as they sat happily in the adorable little

sewing room on the upper floor. The afternoon light sifted in through the west-facing windows, making the room even more pleasant. Their conversation about homemade dress patterns might have been anything but fascinating to someone outside Hickory Hollow, but for Jenny, this was what she'd dreamed of doing here—and so much more.

Creating her own pattern was something she hadn't really considered, although she fully intended to make her own clothes. She'd taken quite a few sewing classes and believed she was up to the task. *Using a treadle sewing machine will be interesting!*

Rebecca raised her own well-worn pattern for Jenny to inspect. It was obviously much too large for Jenny's slender figure. *The only thing missing in this sweet, homey moment is a cup of espresso,* Jenny thought as the afternoon slump began to set in. Her day, after all, had started very early when she'd caught a cab to Old Saybrook, where she had boarded the train at a little past eight o'clock. Then, close to noon, she'd transferred to the Philadelphia train and traveled on to Lancaster, arriving in just five hours total. Without a car, it was the most direct route.

After they'd discussed dress patterns and appropriate colors, Jenny asked, "What requirements must I meet to be baptized, after the Proving time?"

"Well, Samuel met with our bishop 'bout this. He says there are a number of expectations—and spiritual qualities—to fulfill."

Jenny was anxious to know.

"The church ordinance, what we call our Ordnung, must be followed at all times," explained Rebecca. "These are the unwritten rules determined by the membership and the bishop himself. That includes everything from how we dress and work to the order of the Preachin' service every other Sunday."

Jenny was familiar with this from her previous study. "What else?"

"You must learn to speak Deitsch, our German dialect; hitch up a driving horse to a carriage and be able to handle the horse well on the road; and attend work frolics and canning bees—in other words, fit in with our womenfolk. And like all of us, you must live in a way that exemplifies the teachings of our Lord Jesus Christ in the Sermon on the Mount."

Jenny listened carefully.

"You prob'ly know there's no jewelry, including rings and fancy wristwatches, although some wear plainer-looking watches."

The list was growing as Rebecca continued. Flying in planes was prohibited, as was joining secular organizations, filing a lawsuit, riding in a car on Sunday, and worldly pleasures such as TV, radios, and going to movies. Yet none of this was a surprise to Jenny.

"In all you do, keep yourself separated from the world and adhere to the collective wisdom of the People . . . and the Lord God," Rebecca said. "We teach our little ones to bend their will—give it up in complete submission."

Gelassenheit, Jenny thought, remembering what she'd written in her journal soon after arriving. She'd read about this, but hearing it directly from one who lived by that principle brought it home loud and clear.

Can I lay down all of my own wants and wishes for the sake of the People? she wondered.

"You'll be under the covering of Samuel and me," Rebecca added. "At least for the time of your Proving."

"Like a daughter?"

Rebecca's face flushed. "Well, not exactly, but looked after, for sure. Bishop John believes his wife, Mary, will be a *gut* mentor for you, as well." Rebecca paused. "She's in need of a mother's helper every so often, so as I understand it, you'll be over there occasionally. Marnie said you're trustworthy, so that's why you got the job."

"I'll do whatever the bishop thinks is best." Jenny recalled what Marnie had shared by letter about the Hickory Hollow bishop. The man was younger than most bishops, but John Beiler was apparently as strict as any bishop in the region. *If you look guilty, you are guilty,* Marnie had written. Jenny thought it was a strange stance on things, and sincerely hoped she would meet with his approval.

"Your Proving can be as short as six months and as long as two years. It'll depend on how quickly you consistently demonstrate the attitudes and skills I mentioned," Rebecca said.

Then, as if a light had gone off in her brain, Rebecca leaped from her chair. "Ach, how could I have forgotten? Our Katie's dresses and aprons might just fit ya, Jenny. *Kumme mit!*" She waved her into the hallway and toward the master bedroom.

Following closely, Jenny was perplexed. Why would Rebecca offer her daughter's clothes? Had Katie outgrown them? But Jenny was sure Marnie hadn't mentioned any children still living at home.

Not wanting to be meddlesome, Jenny was quiet as she waited in Rebecca's spacious room, where the older woman leaned down to open the large cedar chest at the foot of the bed.

"Ah, just lookee here." Rebecca pulled out a royal blue dress, holding it up momentarily before setting it aside almost reverently, draping it over the polished footboard. Then another long dress appeared, this one a deep green, and soon another—a fairly dull gray, and finally, a plum-colored dress. Had this Katie passed away, by chance? Why else were the dresses tucked away so lovingly in the beautiful chest?

"Why don't ya try these on?" Rebecca said. "It'll save ya from sewin' up some right quick."

"Are you sure?" Jenny was stunned yet pleased. Then again, she wasn't all that certain, second-guessing how she should react. Could she actually bring herself to wear a deceased woman's clothing? A strange lump nearly choked her as she struggled with the thought.

Rebecca handed her the dresses. "They'll need pressing, of course. You won't want to be seen in them publicly till ya do."

"Thank you, Rebecca." She looked at the dresses, limp on her arm. *I guess . . .*

"They're yours to wear, if they fit."

After trying on the blue dress, she returned to Rebecca's bedroom, still feeling a little queasy. She was very anxious to know about the former owner of these dresses but didn't want to offend her helpful hostess. Rebecca began to show her how to position and pin twenty-seven straight pins—no more, no less—to attach the top half of the apron to the waistline of the bottom half.

"Have you ever stuck yourself?" she asked, unable to erase the thought of Rebecca's daughter.

"Oh, rarely." Rebecca smiled. "And once you pin on your apron dozens of times, you prob'ly won't, either."

When they finished, Rebecca removed all the pins and had Jenny try to replicate what she'd done, handing her the pins in a plastic box. But it wasn't as easy as it looked.

Rebecca grinned when Jenny asked if there was a tall mirror around. "Just some hand mirrors," she told her with a tilt of her head, hazel eyes sparkling with mischief. "But if ya must see yourself fully, you could go out to the springhouse pond and see what ya look like Amish."

Jenny blushed and hoped she didn't sound vain. "Oh, that's all right."

"Next, would it be too pushy to talk about your bangs?" Rebecca asked kindly.

Jenny blew her bangs off her forehead. "You've probably never had such a dilemma, right?" There were no bangs on Amishwomen in the pictures or movies she'd seen, nor on the cable channel reality shows.

"Jah, that's so," Rebecca answered. "We train our wee girls' hair to part from early on—without bangs, of course. Then as it grows, it's twisted off to the side and into the hair bun." She went on to explain that the more conservative Amishwomen wore their hair bun low on their neck. "And the more progressive put them up a bit higher." Here, Rebecca's eyes twinkled a smile. "We don't have much to do with them, though."

Jenny knew from Marnie that the Hickory Hollow Amish were stricter than some conservative groups—it was interesting to realize how that affected even the smallest things. Yet she was eager to do up her own hair like Rebecca's. She doubted this aspect of her venture into Plain life would be difficult or even sacrificial, since she'd always loved wearing long homemade skirts and modest blouses. But her wispy bangs were definitely a problem.

"I s'pose we can wet them down till they grow out," Rebecca suggested, dimples in her plump cheeks.

"Or plaster them with hairspray." Jenny laughed.

At the mention of hairspray, Rebecca let out a chortle. "I really doubt there's any round here."

"Oh, sorry. Of course not." She felt silly. "Guess I forgot myself for a moment."

"You could try pinning them down, I s'pose."

"Are you permitted to wear bobby pins?"

"For our hair, sure. But we use straight pins to secure our *Kapps*."

"The prayer bonnets?"

"We don't call them that," Rebecca said gently. "They're actually prayer veilings, but we just refer to them as a cap." She paused. "Once you're baptized, you'll begin wearing yours."

Jenny nodded, glad she knew a few things.

"Would ya like to have a tour of the farm, then?" asked Rebecca.

"I'd love to! It's my first time visiting an Amish farm." Jenny wanted to go exploring immediately, eager to take it all in—the hen house, the large two-story barn, and the most appealing stone springhouse, not far from the Lapps' big house.

Yet where was Marnie—wasn't she coming?

I'll ask her about the clothes I'm wearing. She'll know about Katie.

Jenny wanted to do everything at once—take the farm tour with Rebecca, talk with Marnie, and go and sit on the quiet front porch to soak in what she'd already heard and encountered. Though the surroundings were peaceful, she suddenly felt as if she were on sensory overload and needed time to process.

What a completely different world!

Glancing toward the barn, she realized she hadn't met Rebecca's husband yet. *Samuel Lapp—an ideal name for a strong, loving Amish father.* Yet she knew so little about him. When she inquired, Rebecca nodded cheerfully. "Oh, you'll meet him soon enough—and our eldest son, Elam, along with several of our young nephews, too. Our younger sons, Eli and Benjamin, drop by with their families often, sometimes to pitch in and help." She waved her hand. "It takes a *gut* many to fulfill the many requirements of running a dairy farm."

"I've read some articles about it."

"Sounds like you've done your homework." Rebecca's round face spread wide with her smile. "If not before, you'll see Samuel when it's time for supper, after milkin'," she said. "We have an assigned spot for each meal. You'll sit on the opposite side of me, right where our Katie always used to sit."

Jenny glanced at the sawbuck table. "Katie? Your . . . daughter, you mean?"

Rebecca bowed her head. "Sorry, guess ya don't know 'bout her."

Know what?

Just that quickly, Rebecca raised her chin. "Come. I'll show you the rest of the house."

And with that, Jenny decided she had better start walking on eggshells where Rebecca's daughter was concerned. Despite the books she'd read, she was evidently still ignorant of some Old Order social dynamics, though she was ready to learn.

I've staked my whole life on it!

Chapter 6

Marnie Lapp held her breath and managed to avert a sneeze as she walked along the road to Uncle Samuel Lapp's place. She wondered how Jenny was managing so far. She liked the idea of having another friend around who was still single. Talking in person with Jenny Burns during a few days each of the past summers had been a treat after trading letters. Even so, Jenny hadn't shared much at all about her love life, or lack of it, and Marnie had kept quiet that she was nearly engaged to a handsome Amish beau—Roy Flaud—who lived and worked over in Bird-in-Hand. Even so, the two girls had clicked from Jenny's first stroll past Marnie's roadside vegetable stand.

The young Englischer was downright interesting, but despite her fondness for simple things, she wasn't much different from other English folk Marnie had met. She had a streak of pride, which must eventually be suppressed. Just like Marnie's own sneeze.

Most Englischers didn't realize that being Amish wasn't just about dressing Plain, riding in carriages, and living simply. No indeed. The Amish way primarily involved obedience to the community and to God. If Jenny wanted to join church, she would soon have to learn to deal with her strong will and submit to the rules of the Ordnung and the bishop.

Marnie let herself enjoy the fall breeze and clear skies. The start of Amish wedding season was just days away, and she already knew of several weddings she wanted to attend—all for first cousins. As for herself, she didn't dare think too far ahead, considering her own beau had indicated they'd most likely wait till next year to marry.

Returning her thoughts to Jenny, she whispered, "If I weren't Amish by birth, would I want to join from the outside?"

It was hard to imagine Jenny's gumption in quitting her job to come here. And Marnie wasn't sure how she'd chosen to tell her family. Jenny had been mum on all that, and Marnie figured it wasn't her place to probe, anyway.

With the exception of Jenny, there was only one other person Marnie had known to leave home and family. And in that moment, it dawned on her how odd it was that Katie Lapp and Jenny Burns had seemingly exchanged places, unbeknownst to each other. Jenny was, no doubt, staying in Katie's former room . . . left empty when Katie, excommunicated and shunned by the People, had turned to the Mennonite church.

One out; one in.

"Who would've thought?" Marnie said aloud. It wasn't that she'd consciously planned any of this, picking the Lapps' place for Jenny's temporary residence. It was her mother who'd insisted that Rebecca was the best choice for Jenny's mentor. And the bishop had agreed.

Marnie froze suddenly at a horrid thought. What if Jenny didn't make it through the Proving? She certainly hadn't given it much consideration till this moment. But no! She must dismiss the very possibility, because there should never be another time of deep sorrow for poor Rebecca, not after losing Katie. Still, the painful thought persisted, and Marnie had to shoo it away like a wasp.

Surely that won't happen. Surely not.

Marnie took hope in the fact that Jenny was utterly determined to succeed as a seeker. After all, she hadn't moved here on impulse. No, she'd formulated the move for some time, saving money and planning the smallest details, looking to the heavenly Father for guidance. So surely there was no worry that Jenny might fail to become one with the People. *None at all.*

Marnie waved and hurried her step when she saw Jenny running down Lapps' long lane toward the road, in full Amish attire, minus the Kapp.

"Well, look at that," she whispered. Marnie waved again and felt her heart soar. Where on earth had Jenny gotten a dress and apron so quickly?

"Hi, Marnie!" Jenny called to her, a big smile on her face.

"Hullo! Looks like ya made it."

"Still can't believe I'm actually here. Better pinch me fast!"

Marnie opened her arms and hugged her friend. "I'm ever so glad." She looked her over but good. "Ach, we're nearly twins, 'cept for your bangs."

"I've been letting them grow, but obviously they aren't there yet." Jenny laughed. "Rebecca helped me pin them down, as you can see."

"Did ya really need thirty bobby pins?"

Their laughter blended like apple cider and ginger ale as they headed back toward the house.

"Are you already unpacked?" Marnie asked.

"Almost."

Asking what things she'd brought, Marnie was still amazed that courageous Jenny had actually made the move. To think she'd willingly abandoned electricity and her car!

Jenny recited the various items she couldn't part with: two poetry books, her Bible and a devotional book, and a thick white bathrobe with matching slippers. "That's why I brought a large suitcase." She lowered her voice. "I think Rebecca was startled at its size."

"Did you bring any pictures of your family?"

"A few, yes."

Marnie smiled and suggested they sit on the front porch chairs Rebecca still had out, despite the chillier days. "I'm very curious to see."

"Well, I'm equally curious, Marnie. Is it okay for you to look at pictures of my family when you can't have any of yours?"

"I can understand why you might think that," Marnie said as two bobby pins slid from Jenny's bangs.

"Oh dear." Jenny picked them up and tried to put them back again. "I can hardly wait until my hair looks like yours."

"I can tell ya one thing for certain: Patience will become your closest friend during the Proving."

Jenny laughed. "Oh, I'm sure of that."

"So how are ya getting along with Aunt Rebecca?"

"She's very thoughtful." Jenny paused and cast her gaze toward the sky. "I do think she wonders what I'm doing here, however."

"Well, I can't imagine switchin' places with ya."

Jenny's smile spread across her pretty face. "Here I am! But I can't help wondering . . . do I really look Amish?"

Marnie laughed. "You look as Plain as I do. And you're goin' to fit in just fine here."

"I appreciate the vote of confidence."

Marnie frowned. "Did you ever doubt it?"

Jenny shook her head.

"Honestly, not many seekers stick around, from what I've heard—at least in other areas where this sort of thing is more common."

"I'll take it a day at a time."

"*Gut* idea."

"Jah, really *gut*."

Marnie laughed out loud. "Ach, you've picked up some Deitsch, then."

"I recognize a few of the simpler words and phrases already, thanks to two years of high school German."

"Remember, understanding and speaking are different things." Marnie reached to give her a hug. "You'll catch on eventually."

"I certainly hope so."

"Oh, you will." Marnie tried not to smile too big. "But first . . . I know exactly the place to take ya for a peek at yourself."

Jenny brightened. "Really?"

"Just you follow me."

Chapter 7

An autumn breeze trembled the treetops, creating a leafy shower below as Jenny followed tall, lean Marnie around the Lapps' old sandstone house. "I'd really like to see the springhouse up close," she said, intrigued by her earlier glimpse of it. "Rebecca says it's the closest thing to a full-length mirror."

"The springhouse pond?" Marnie turned and gave her a surprised look. "Why, that's precisely where we're headed."

"Perfect, then," Jenny replied happily.

Marnie stopped walking abruptly as they made their way down the lane. Grinning, she said, "Lookee there." She pointed in the direction of the large double-decker barn. A striking young Amishman with blond hair and wearing a straw hat was walking toward the main door. "My cousin Andrew Lapp is here, helping with milking this afternoon. He does occasionally, when he's caught up on his own work." She shielded her eyes from the sun. "You'll like Andrew . . . everyone does."

"If he's your cousin, he must be nice."

"Oh, believe me, Andrew left *nice* in the dust."

"He lives here in Hickory Hollow?"

"Rents a room from his parents." Marnie nodded. "Andrew says he baches it."

Jenny shook her head. "What's that mean?"

"Well, just that he's still a bachelor at twenty-nine. Guess he never found the right girl, but he keeps real busy with his welding business and helping Uncle Samuel, too."

"I thought Amish were *expected* to marry young."

Marnie laughed. "Jah, but every now and then a persnickety one comes along. Like Cousin Andrew."

Jenny watched him for a moment and then noticed Marnie looking at *her*. Marnie's eyes sparkled knowingly. "He's a real catch, but a lot of girls have tried to get his attention, believe me. Even so, he claims to be holdin' out for the right one. We tell him he's gonna hold out till his dyin' breath!"

As they continued down the hill, Jenny observed Marnie—her gentle mannerisms, her soft way of speaking—glad to be getting to know her even better, here on her own turf.

"Be careful on these steps," Marnie said, motioning toward the steep stone walkway leading down to the pond. "They're often slick."

Jenny loved how the site was set apart from the rest of the farm in a haven of sorts. The treed area provided exactly the right amount of shade, and the rock-walled springhouse and small spring-fed pond looked like the ideal place to relax or even pray.

"There." Marnie waved a hand gracefully toward the clear, placid water. "See for yourself what ya look like . . . in nature's mirror."

Jenny peered down at herself, feeling a little shy. *Amazing!* she thought. *I could actually pass myself off as Amish.*

"Well, what do ya think?" Marnie had moved closer.

"Like the saying goes—the clothes make the man. Well, the woman."

"'Tis the truth!"

They had a laugh, although it was Jenny who laughed longer. "I almost forgot the old me."

"You'll have plenty of time for that, Jenny."

Jenny stared into the pond, suddenly thinking that Pamela and Dorie would never believe what she was up to, despite knowing how keen she was on old-fashioned things. A lump sprang into her throat, surprising her. *I'll miss them.*

Ultimately, her friends would find other friends and fill the gap. And perhaps they'd understand something of her passion once she wrote and explained herself. *Maybe . . .*

Jenny stepped back from her reflection in the pond. "I'm curious to know about Katie, the Lapps' daughter. What happened to her?"

"Ach, she was shunned—and a mighty harsh shunning it was, too. All this happened almost seven years ago now, when Katie refused to destroy her guitar . . . and her music. She was even so brazen as to stand up our bishop, John Beiler, on their wedding day. Many think it enraged him when she jilted him, literally running away." Tears sprang to Marnie's eyes. "It was a very sad time for everyone."

"So she lives elsewhere?"

"Just on the edge of Hickory Hollow, with her husband, Daniel Fisher, who's also under the *Bann*. We're not s'posed to visit them in their home, exchange money, or take anything from their hand to ours."

"Wow—that's serious." Jenny looked down at her dress. "Does it matter, then, that I'm wearing Katie's former clothes?"

Marnie stared. "They're Katie's?"

Nodding, Jenny admitted they were.

"No, that won't hurt a thing," Marnie assured her. "Ain't like Katie's rebellion can affect you."

Jenny wondered how strict the same bishop would be with her. And knowing all this put her on edge. Would there be much grace for even the most innocent of mistakes? She sighed. "Is shunning very common?"

"It depends on the severity of the transgression. Of course, if you don't get baptized, you can't be shunned." Marnie leaned closer and whispered, "Katie Lapp was considered practically dead to the People for nearly a year during her initial shunning."

Jenny shivered at the thought. "That's horrible."

"Things loosened up slightly after that, but we never see her around here."

"So what happens if I fail my Proving?" Jenny had to know. "Could I be kicked out . . . like Katie?"

"Fail?" Marnie frowned, then grinned quickly. "Don't ya worry . . . there's no way that'll happen!" Marnie waved her toward the little rock building beside the pond. "Have ya ever seen the inside of a springhouse?"

"No."

"Come, then, I'll show ya."

They went to the small door and Marnie opened it. Stooping, they entered the damp room. Off to the right side, there was a long rectangular section on the ground, where spring water was rimmed by a cement ledge.

"Aunt Rebecca sometimes refrigerates milk cans and crocks of food in the cold water there," Marnie said, showing her the areas of deep and shallow water.

"It's charming." Jenny loved the quiet, private little space. She touched her face to make sure she wasn't dreaming.

Marnie folded her arms, all smiles. "I thought you might

like to see it. My mother wishes we had one on our property. Anyone who has a spring has a blessed thing, she says."

"Must be wonderful for keeping things nice and cold."

"Jah, that's just what we used them for," Marnie agreed. "'Course now we have other ways of doing that," she explained. "We rent space in our English neighbors' big freezer just west of here."

"Really? It's not an inconvenience?"

Marnie shrugged. "Oh, we're used to taking food elsewhere. It's not so bad, really."

"Do you also use the phone at your English neighbors' sometimes?"

"Not as often as you might think." Marnie explained there was a phone shanty positioned in a field, camouflaged by trees and tall bushes. "Our bishop doesn't like to flaunt it, he says." She opened the door to exit the springhouse. "You'll meet him on Sunday, at Preachin' service."

"I'll look forward to that."

"Oh, wait—on second thought, you might not meet him then, after all. He's visiting another church district this weekend."

Jenny fell into step with her Amish friend. "I love everything about Hickory Hollow. There's no crazy rushing here, like in the English world."

"Oh, trust me, you should see some of us early on market days, or hurryin' off to church . . . 'specially those with big families, who have to hitch up two horses to two carriages and pile all the little ones inside, if they don't take an open spring wagon." Marnie chuckled.

Jenny wondered if she would be expected to talk the way Marnie did when she spoke English, with '*tis* and *lest* and such. "I expect I've got a lot to learn. Speaking of which, are you up for teaching me to speak Pennsylvania Dutch?"

"Oh, I doubt you'll need to be taught it formally. You'll just pick it up over time."

Jenny wasn't so sure. "Well, about that. Is there a bookstore where I can purchase a Pennsylvania German dictionary?"

"Gordonville Book Store, not far from here. We'll go over there sometime soon if ya want."

"Great, thanks."

"*Denki,*" Marnie said with a smile. "Say *Denki.*"

"Jah, sorry," Jenny said, which made them both smile.

Chapter 8

After coming up the springhouse steps, Jenny followed Marnie back to the house, where Rebecca was waiting for them, sitting barefoot on the back step.

"Would ya like to meet my husband, Samuel?" Rebecca asked, observing both girls.

"Sure she would," Marnie replied. "And don't forget to introduce her to the others working in the barn—including my boy cousins."

Jenny noticed the furtive looks exchanged between Marnie and Rebecca. "If it's no trouble," she hastened to add.

"If the herd's calm, maybe you could start helpin' with the four o'clock milking," Marnie suggested.

"Now, dear," Rebecca said, hazel eyes widening, "no need to scare Jenny off her first day here, is there?"

Marnie shrugged, mischief on her face.

What's to be afraid of? Jenny wondered.

"Marnie." Rebecca shook her head. "Jenny won't need to help with milkin'. She'll work with me in the house—where we womenfolk belong." She gave Jenny a reassuring smile, yet Jenny felt somewhat disappointed.

"I'll fit in wherever you need me," Jenny remarked with a glance at Marnie. "So put me to work wherever you wish."

Rebecca nodded. "Even so, the men do most of the milkin'."

"Ah, you've been spared." Marnie laughed as she motioned for Rebecca and Jenny to follow her to the barn.

Rebecca nodded sweetly. "Has anyone thought to let the bishop and his wife know Jenny's arrived?" She asked this in a way that made Jenny think the good woman wanted Marnie to hurry off to the bishop's at that very moment.

"Well, *I* haven't," Marnie said. "And I doubt Mamm has yet, either."

Rebecca brushed her hands against her long black apron. "Might be nice if Jenny got acquainted with them real soon."

Marnie agreed and reached for the barn door, then heaved it open. She looked back at Jenny. "If he doesn't drop by in the next few days, it's not because he doesn't want to welcome you. Just remember that."

"Sure, there's plenty of time," Jenny replied.

With that, they stepped into the muggy barn, and Jenny got her first strong whiff of the smells of livestock, hay, and manure. And at that moment, she was quite glad Rebecca had spared her, as Marnie had so aptly put it.

———

Marnie found Uncle Samuel with his bushy brown beard pitching hay over in the stable, along with clean-shaven Cousin Andrew. Both men were wearing their oldest, rattiest straw work hats, though in a few weeks they would don their black felt hats for winter. Secretly, she preferred the looks of those over the straw hats.

Aunt Rebecca stepped forward and introduced Jenny to Uncle Samuel, who'd propped up his pitchfork against the wall, wiped his hand on his black work trousers, and offered it to the seeker. He smiled only briefly before his lips returned to a flat, hard line.

Jenny was the first to speak. "I'm pleased to meet you."

"Same to you."

Marnie was satisfied by her uncle's initial reception, though she wasn't sure how her cousin would handle things. Jenny was awfully pretty, but Andrew had been around lots of attractive Amishwomen. Of course, no Amishman in his right mind had any business taking a shine to Jenny unless she was entirely committed to joining church.

"Cousin Andrew," said Marnie gently, "this is my English friend, Jenny Burns."

His blue-eyed gaze honed in on her auburn bangs. "Fancy, then, ya say?"

"Well, she'd rather *not* be," Marnie said. "'Least not anymore."

"Is that right?" Andrew's face was sober. "Are ya here to join us as a people separated from the world, then?"

Jenny nodded enthusiastically. "I certainly am."

"Well, let me be the first to congratulate you." Andrew stuck out his hand, and Jenny shook it. "I'm sure my uncle and aunt will see to it that you get along well here as ya learn the ways of the Lord God . . . and the church."

Marnie felt much lighter, relieved that her friend was being received so hospitably. She gave her cousin an approving nod. "Let's show you round the stable," she said to Jenny. "You'll want to meet the driving horses—learn their names and let them get used to ya."

"It's nice to meet you both," Jenny said to the men, and Marnie noted that Aunt Rebecca was struggling not to smile too broadly as she fell in step with the seeker.

··· ➤ ➤ ···

Jenny drank in each new vista—the old corncrib, the wood-shed, and the glassy pond behind the two-story barn. The first hours here had flown like mere moments.

She followed Rebecca's example, washing her hands thoroughly at the well pump before going into the kitchen and scrubbing her hands there, as well. The whole chicken the women had prepared earlier was roasting, filling the kitchen with a delicious aroma as they set to work on the remaining supper items. Rebecca also recited a recipe for homemade lemonade so Jenny could write it down.

"Tomorrow I'll show you how to make bread," Rebecca told her. "We'll make egg noodles from scratch, too, here before long."

"This is so wonderful. Denki."

"*Wunnerbaar,*" Rebecca said with a small smile.

Jenny dipped her head with gratitude. "My mom didn't want me underfoot in her kitchen, so I never learned to bake at all. She loves to cook, but she's more focused on gourmet dinners than typical home cooking."

"I daresay you might not have been so willing to cook and bake with me had you come a few years sooner," Rebecca tittered, explaining how, at that time, Samuel had removed the old woodstove and remodeled the entire kitchen. "It was the talk of the hollow for a while. 'Specially when we put in a full bathroom off the back of the house."

"Marnie mentioned that in one of her letters. It wasn't long before others jumped on the idea, too, right?"

"Marnie told ya?"

"I doubt I'd be here if it weren't for your niece. She really helped make it possible." Jenny paused. "I'm sure she never shared anything you'd be uncomfortable with . . . or that wasn't common knowledge."

"Well, I should hope not." A shadow flitted across Rebecca's face.

"You can rest assured of that." Jenny gave her a smile.

"There's plenty of tittle-tattle round here, I'm afraid. Be forewarned."

It was human nature to want to share gossip, especially at social gatherings, Jenny thought. But to hear Rebecca admit this so freely made her a little sad.

"You look surprised," Rebecca said as she tossed a dish towel over her ample shoulder. "Remember, we certainly ain't perfect."

Jenny caught her breath.

"Did ya think otherwise?"

The People were God-fearing—Jenny believed that with all of her heart, no matter what Rebecca might say. For now, though, Jenny would leave things be.

"Hope you're not lookin' for the ideal church, Jenny. Please say you ain't."

Jenny considered that. "Well, the Amish church has to be better than some I've visited."

Rebecca looked away, then back at Jenny. "Keep in mind, once a person steps into a church fellowship, ach, it's no longer perfect. None of us is without fault, ya know. There was only one who was sinless—God's Son, the Lord Jesus Christ."

Jenny knew this. Still, didn't she have every right to believe in the worth of the Amish church? What was so wrong with that?

Chapter 9

J enny had expected paper plates and plastic spoons and
forks. Instead, she and Rebecca laid the table with a green-
and-white-checkered oilcloth and pretty flatware, along with
simple yet lovely white dishes. There were white paper napkins beneath each gleaming fork, and glass tumblers filled
with the delicious lemonade, made by Jenny herself.

Samuel came inside for supper with a quick smile for Rebecca,
then removed his straw hat, placing it on the peg inside the
door before heading directly to the washbasin. Soon, he
took his place at the head of the table and waited silently for
Rebecca and Jenny to bring over the chicken and potatoes.

Before he bowed his head and folded his hands, he said,
"Let's give thanks," which they all did. Jenny held back tears
during the long silent prayer, grateful to just be sitting here
tonight.

When the prayer was over, Samuel gave a little cough and
then reached for the large serving fork to choose his piece of
chicken. Rebecca asked Jenny to pass the large oval dishes of
potatoes and buttered peas once she'd served herself.

Jenny was surprised at how few words were spoken during

the meal; she wondered if Samuel might ask about her family, or something about her English life. But no such questions came, and she slowly began to relax and enjoy the meal. The truth of the matter was that Samuel was a busy man—he did mention to Rebecca that he and a few others would be cleaning the milking equipment right after supper. "Andrew's comin' back to help me scrub out the bulk tank tonight, too."

"Is the vet still due tomorrow?" Rebecca asked quietly.

"Well, it's scheduled, so he'd better. I don't have time to fool around waitin' for him this time." Samuel reached for his lemonade and took a long drink. When he was done, he wiped his mouth on his sleeve.

"We have a guest, dear," Rebecca said, reaching for his napkin and fluttering it at him.

Then, and only then, did Samuel cast a look Jenny's way. She didn't know if she ought to smile or not, given the man's disposition.

"It's been quite a day," Rebecca said.

"Lots to do yet tonight, so I'll be goin' back out to the barn, soon as dessert's served."

Will he compliment Rebecca—or me—on the meal? Jenny wondered.

Then, as if Rebecca had thought the same thing, she told her husband that both she and Jenny had prepared the food. "Jenny's a right *gut* help, she is."

Samuel kept chewing, his eyes cast down. He muttered something in Deitsch.

Rebecca looked at Jenny and shrugged. "Soon enough you'll pick up what's bein' said."

"What's that?" Samuel raised his head suddenly.

Jenny considered his response as Rebecca spoke to him in Deitsch. It would be very interesting to understand some of the asides the Lapps shared. In fact, she was sure that's what Rebecca meant.

"What 'bout church?" Samuel asked.

"Well, she'll come along with us, ain't so?" Rebecca offered a warm smile to Jenny.

Samuel smacked his lips and leaned back in his chair. "I didn't mean that. Shouldn't ya tell her what to expect?"

"Well, why not explain things now?"

"You go right ahead, Rebecca."

Jenny heard her sigh. "There must be a lot on your mind, Samuel."

He didn't say there was or there wasn't. But the awkwardness continued even after he asked for another serving of chicken.

Jenny was beginning to think Samuel viewed her as an intruder. Or was it just his way? *I don't have to be liked immediately*, she decided, glad for women like Rebecca and Marnie.

"We have leftover bread pudding, dear." Rebecca broke the stillness. "Would ya care for some, Samuel?"

He gave a bob of his head, and Rebecca rose quickly to get it from the stove, where she'd had it reheating.

Jenny's first meal with Marnie's relatives certainly had been eye-opening, but she was not faint of heart. She was here for the long haul—and nothing whatsoever was going to change her mind!

Rebecca gritted her teeth and served Samuel his black coffee. She offered some to Jenny, who politely refused. It kept her awake if she drank coffee too late in the day, Jenny said.

Smiling sympathetically, Rebecca hoped the seeker wouldn't be put off by Samuel's unfriendly manner. Heaven knew his temper could rise, and she found herself thinking again of

Katie and the precious grandchildren she'd managed to see a handful of times in the past months. Samuel would pitch a fit, for sure, if he got word of it. *I best be more careful.*

"I'm goin' to show Jenny how to hitch up the driving horse to the family carriage after supper, if ya don't mind," said Rebecca.

Samuel shook his head. "Just remember you'll have to unhitch, too." He finished his bread pudding, then downed the rest of his coffee. "Why not wait till daylight, Rebecca?"

She had her reasons.

Samuel didn't press further, and he leaned forward for the second silent prayer. As he again bowed his head, Rebecca and Jenny did the same.

Chapter 10

Jenny felt as tight as a fiddle string and wasn't ready yet to fall asleep. The palpable strain at the supper table between Samuel and Rebecca still troubled her. Besides that, Rebecca had become flustered while teaching the names of the various parts of the equipment for hitching up—the harness, bridle, back hold straps, shafts, and the like. In the end, Jenny had merely watched and tried to comprehend. Last she'd looked, the horse and carriage were still parked in the driveway.

Presently, she sat in bed, writing in her journal, three full pages. When she was finished, she shuffled out of bed to the hallway. *What if I went out and sat on the front porch? Would it bother the Lapps?*

The present tranquility was the kind she'd longed for back home. That, and nearly everything else Hickory Hollow had to offer. Turning again to her room, she realized she could see herself in one of the bedroom windows; the gas lamp glowed on the table beside her. She stared at the silky canary yellow nightgown in the reflection and sighed. "I don't look like I belong here," she whispered. Sooner or later, she'd have to sew a long cotton nightgown to sleep in.

What does Marnie wear to bed?

She admired herself again. It was the only pretty nightie she'd brought along. *Just for tonight—I'll wear it one last time.* The truth was Jenny adored beautiful sleepwear and wondered who would ever know.

But she also wanted to be wholly Plain, from the inside out—from her inner heart and ideals to her external attire. "I'll discard this little number tomorrow," she promised herself.

She thought then of her mother, who would be aghast if she knew Jenny was living here at all. As would Kiersten, whose opinion as the older sister always prevailed. What she said was to be respected . . . never questioned. *She'll be wondering a great deal now,* Jenny thought, a little sad. *Since I'm missing . . .*

As for Cameron, his response would be the worst. "*Out-and-out ridicule,*" as Rebecca Lapp or Marnie might say. Jenny groaned. If the Lapps knew the behind-the-curtains Burns family dynamics—well, lucky for them they didn't.

Jenny's father was the only one who might not mind her running off to the Amish. But how would anyone ever know for sure? When it came to anything other than his work, he had little time to spare. He took not noticing to new levels.

But she didn't need to imagine what her friends might think. Dorie, especially, would think she'd flipped out. "*You're crazy, Jen,*" she would laughingly say, but she'd mean it if she knew. *So it's best I kept it to myself.*

She did plan to write letters to them eventually—they deserved as much. Cameron was the only one Jenny wasn't sure about contacting. After all, her mother would inform the rest of the family without delay.

Jenny regretted the way she'd left things with them unfinished, but there was no room for second-guessing. She thought of all the resourceful gleanings she'd received from Rebecca in her shining kitchen. She'd even learned how to trim a kerosene lantern wick, light it, and put it out. To top things off, there was even more in store after Samuel's evening Bible reading. Rebecca had Jenny sit next to her at the table and taught her some basic needlepoint, something she'd seen her aunt do years before. Jenny had taken to it tonight like a child to her first taste of chocolate.

I've missed so much by being born English.

Tomorrow was Halloween, but Amish people wouldn't think of celebrating the day. Regardless, Rebecca said they had pumpkins to deliver for pies and invited Jenny to help distribute them in the neighborhood.

Fondly, she looked around the room. So this was not a *deceased* daughter's former bedroom, although Marnie had whispered before she left that Katie had been considered practically dead to the People. The idea of such a severe shunning made Jenny clench her teeth. Poor Katie!

She extinguished the lantern and moved back to the window, inching closer to see the moon-drenched grazing land and the pasture beyond. It was hard to stop thinking about Samuel and Rebecca's daughter.

Suddenly, Jenny spotted someone dash outside and get into the waiting carriage. She peered closer and saw that it was Rebecca.

Lowering herself, Jenny crouched and watched, wondering where the woman of the house was hurrying off to at this late hour. It struck Jenny as not only strange but rather eerie.

Incredibly curious, Jenny considered waiting up until Rebecca returned. But she felt so exhausted, it was difficult not to return to bed and stretch out beneath the sheet and quilt. She gently traced the quilt's pattern and its stitching, not forgetting to thank God for this remarkable dream come true.

Then, with a deliberate sigh, Jenny relaxed and gave in to blessed sleep against the embroidered pillowcase.

··· ➤ ➤ ···

The matching white ceramic lamps on either side of the burgundy-and-white-checked sofa cast such brightness upon the front room, Rebecca had to squint as she sat there with darling brown-eyed Katie. The light gleamed in the otherwise darkened house until, ever so slowly, her eyes became accustomed to it.

Electric, Rebecca thought with regret, although she must not let her concern overtake her. She was altogether pleased her daughter had stayed up to see her, as they'd planned two weeks ago.

"You look tired, Mamma." Katie was curled at one end of the sofa in her soft blue bathrobe, holding tiny, sleeping Kate Marie. The toddler's blond hair fell in lovely ringlets.

"Never too tired to see you." Unable to resist, she scooted over and touched her granddaughter's smooth cheek with her finger. "Just look at the little sweetie—she's growin' so fast, jah?"

"You must see the changes more than we do." Katie stroked her little one's locks.

"Well, no doubt." *Ain't like I wouldn't visit every day if I could*, Rebecca thought.

"Does Dat know you've started coming to see us?" asked Katie.

"I've managed to keep it from him."

"What will happen if . . . "

Rebecca's dream came to mind. "That's why my visits must be after dark."

"Oh, Mamma. This sneaking around seems so unnecessary."

"Well, the Bann's to be upheld." Rebecca felt suddenly guilty again. "By most of us, that is."

Katie shook her head and pushed her hands through her own auburn hair. "It's just been—"

"Too long since you saw your father . . . your brothers?" Rebecca asked. "That could all change, if only—"

"Mamma, *please*. We're happy in our new church. We're doing God's bidding. We believe that." Katie placed her sleeping daughter onto the sofa and leaned back. "And we've started a Bible study."

"Ach, really?"

"Daniel felt the Lord nudging him to invite anyone seeking to delve into Christ's teachings."

"Is that so?"

"You're welcome to come, too, Mamma. We'd love to have you."

"Well, I . . ."

"Just think about it, all right?"

Rebecca thought two seconds and knew there was no way she'd be permitted to attend, even if she wanted to. Yet she was torn.

They sat there quietly, Rebecca's thoughts churning. Thoughts she could not voice.

"When's Benjamin planning to take over the farm for Dat?" asked Katie out of the blue. "I thought he was nearly ready to do that several years ago."

Rebecca explained that Katie's youngest brother helped Samuel daily to run the dairy farm, along with a few of his cousins. "Keep in mind that when Benjamin married, his father-in-law helped them buy their own place."

"So you and Dat will continue to live where you are, then?"

"For the time bein', jah." Rebecca wondered when Katie had last seen her three brothers, especially Benjamin, whom she was always closest to. "Do the boys keep in touch with you at all?" she asked.

"Just Eli—mostly a note now and then from his wife." Katie looked away, biting her lips and squinting her eyes. "Elam's written me off. . . ." she whispered.

All the People did, Rebecca thought miserably, thankful for the bishop's lifting the Bann slightly so they could correspond by mail, though only a few did so.

Then, looking down at tiny Kate Marie, Katie smiled. "I think she's starting to resemble Daniel a little, don't you, Mamma?"

She finds her joy wherever she can. . . .

Rebecca agreed and leaned forward a bit. "Her looks are changing, that's for sure."

"Here lately, people have been saying so, though I've thought it, too."

"Sammy's always looked more like you, with his auburn hair," Rebecca said, a lump still in her throat. "To think he's never met his *Dawdi* Samuel."

"No, sad but true."

They pushed past their grief over the Bann and talked about the children, mostly everyday things—how little Kate was beginning to put more and more sentences together. Rebecca didn't say it but wondered if any of those were Deitsch.

Katie's face beamed suddenly and she lowered her voice. "Mamma, I'm expecting a baby again. We found out just this week."

"Such happy news. Any chance of twins?"

Laughing softly, Katie said, "You must really want doubles, Mamma."

"Why do ya say that?"

"Well, this isn't the first time you've mentioned it."

Rebecca had to chortle. "Is that right?" She knew it was true.

Katie nodded and looked again at her precious girl, whose pudgy arm twitched as she rolled to face the sofa. "Whatever the Lord sees fit to give us, Daniel and I'll be ever so happy."

"You look real *gut*, dear one. Healthy as always."

"The doctor says so," replied Katie, going on to say the baby was due the first week in May. Katie smiled. "Little Kate will likely still be in diapers."

"And you'll have your hands full for sure."

"I don't mind one bit. I love being a wife and mother," Katie said, yawning.

Just not an Amish one, thought Rebecca.

"Oh, and not to change the subject, but I heard you and Dat were keeping an Englischer over at the house."

"That's right. She arrived just today."

"Someone from the outside who wants to join the Amish church?"

Rebecca said it was so. "How'd ya hear?"

"Daniel's sister Annie."

Elam's wife. Nodding, Rebecca replied, "Jenny Burns is awful nice, I'll say that. And she seems sincere, too."

Katie was still.

"This is so rare, ya know, we hardly know how to go 'bout it," Rebecca volunteered.

"Surely Bishop John has a plan, jah?"

Rebecca loved it when Katie slipped back into her old ways

of expression. "That he does. John Beiler's told your father it's a matter of letting Jenny learn our ways at her own pace."

"So Dat's all right with it?"

"Well, he's cautious."

"No wonder."

"Can't be too careful," Rebecca said. "But I don't mean there's anything to worry 'bout. Just that Jenny must fit in with the membership before she'll be given the chance to become one of us."

"Does she speak any Deitsch?"

"Only a word or two. But from what I can tell, she's determined to do what's necessary."

"Where'd you put her—which room?"

Rebecca paused. "Does it matter to ya, daughter?"

"Not really."

"Well, since your old room's the largest besides ours, I offered her that." A shadow crossed Katie's face, and for that instant, Rebecca worried she'd made a blunder in doing so. "Is that all right, dear?"

"Of course. Why would I mind?"

Rebecca was mighty sure she did. "It's too late to change things," she said, wishing she'd brought it up with Katie before now. "She's nicely settled."

"Really, Mamma, it's all right." Katie drew a long breath. "I just hope she finds whatever she's looking for."

"Jah, and who's to know what that might be."

"It's hard to think of an Englischer wanting to be Amish," Katie said in a near whisper.

Hard indeed, Rebecca thought sadly.

Chapter 11

J enny dreamed she was scrambling eggs and frying German sausage, and she awakened to the same delectable aromas. She guessed Rebecca Lapp was up already and making breakfast for Samuel.

And I'm still in bed!

She peered at her watch on the bedside table. *Six o'clock!*

There had been no discussion about what her morning chores were to be, or how early she should rise. She was told yesterday that Samuel would have a bite before going out for the early morning milking at four o'clock, which meant this must be a more substantial breakfast that Rebecca was preparing.

"Remember, we're not here by accident," Rebecca had said yesterday while they worked together in the sewing room. *"Just like these dress patterns have a purpose, so do we. . . ."*

Jenny pushed back the bed quilt and rose to go to the window. Lifting the green shade, she stared out at the beauty dawning before her eyes.

"I'm here for a purpose," she said softly.

Today she wanted to help Rebecca in any way she could.

Her first priority was here at home, learning the ways of an Amishwoman. Speaking and comprehending their language was an essential part of that. *If I can just get my hands on a Pennsylvania German dictionary.*

She went to the dresser to get her brush and tried to remember how to put her hair back the way Rebecca had done it up yesterday. But she kept failing, and her bangs were a nuisance. *I need a larger mirror!*

She decided to try again to pull her bangs back to accommodate a full middle part, perhaps downstairs in the bathroom. Except that the cabinet mirror there might not be much help, either, considering it was rather small. Despite that, it was better than nothing, so she would just slip down there in her modest bathrobe, hopefully unnoticed, and shower or wash up before dressing. Swiftly, she gathered her things.

Rebecca greeted her as she hurried through the kitchen to the bathroom, and Jenny noticed the dark circles under her eyes. "No need to rush, Jenny. The men will be outdoors for a while yet." She explained that she sometimes liked to offer a nice hot breakfast to Elam and her nephews. "It's not always the same young men each day, since most of them have other part-time jobs."

Jenny couldn't help wondering how late Rebecca had stayed out last night . . . and where she'd gone at that hour. But it wasn't her place to inquire, and she made her way into the bathroom for her shower and hung her silky nightgown over her bathrobe on the door hook.

When she'd finished, she wrapped her hair in a towel and dried off, then stepped into one of Katie's discarded dresses, recalling the small spring-fed pond by the springhouse. She couldn't run off to look at herself in its reflection each morning. She'd have to trust Marnie's assessment that doing her hair the Amish way would become second nature in time.

··· ➤ ➤ ···

Marnie could hardly wait to finish cooking breakfast in her sick mother's stead. Mamm was resting this morning, nursing a bad headache. Marnie assumed it was another migraine, so it was also up to her to get the lunches packed for her three school-age siblings, and in a big hurry, too.

Once the kitchen was redded up and her younger siblings were out the door, she washed the floors by hand in the utility room, kitchen, and the small sitting room near the front room. Then, while they were drying, she went upstairs and sat down to write a letter to her beau, Roy Flaud, who had invited her to attend an area Bible study next Tuesday evening. He'd written that he would pick her up, if she wanted to go.

Not wanting to turn him down, she'd thought about it overnight, unable to sleep. It was odd, really, because naught but a week or so ago she had heard Cousin Emmalyn—Andrew's nineteen-year-old sister—talking about a couple holding such meetings, somewhere on the outskirts of Hickory Hollow. The concern was that some of the unbaptized Amish young folk might head over there out of curiosity. *And eventually wander out of the Amish church.*

"If Emmalyn got wind that I attended that meeting, I'd be all but cooked," she whispered. "And that would be the end of Roy and me." The thought of anything tearing them apart made her head hurt. *Like poor Mamm's!*

Quickly, Marnie took a pen from her desk drawer and began to write to her darling.

Dear Roy,

I was glad to receive your letter yesterday afternoon. Right away, I wanted to write you back to thank you for the invitation. But honestly, it's not a good idea for me to go to the Bible study. I don't want to have trouble brewing with my parents. Or worse, with the ministers here. I hope you understand.

As you know, my father is not progressive in any manner, shape, or form—we've discussed this, you and I. Besides, if word got out to Bishop John, well, I'd have some fast explaining to do, even though I'm in my Rumschpringe like you.

It would break my heart for anything to divide us, Roy. I look forward to seeing you again. I'll wait to hear from you to find out when that might be.

I'm really sorry about not joining you.

Yours always,
Marnie Lapp

She folded the letter and slipped it into an envelope, glad she'd kept her romance secret for all this time. Oh, goodness, she hoped this problematic invitation wasn't just the tip of the haystack!

··· ➤ ➤ ···

Jenny offered to wash the big black griddle for Rebecca as the smell of baking bread permeated the kitchen. The breakfast they'd served to Samuel, Elam, and three of the Lapps' teenage nephews was heartier than any Jenny had eaten in recent memory. Along with fried potatoes, scrambled eggs, and sausage, there was also orange juice, black coffee, and a snitz pie Rebecca had made yesterday.

The young men hardly made eye contact as they dug into their food. And just as he had last night, Samuel still seemed tentative about talking to Jenny, which didn't surprise her. *I'm still a stranger.*

She was finishing up the dishes while Rebecca dried when suddenly a frustrated stream of Deitsch came pouring from within the bathroom.

"Ach no!" Rebecca said, turning crimson and darting toward the bathroom door.

What's happening? Jenny wondered.

Rebecca talked through the door in their language. *Another private conversation,* Jenny mused.

At last the door opened narrowly, and Rebecca squeezed inside, disappearing behind it. More muffled talking ensued. Jenny hoped Samuel hadn't become ill.

Then Samuel emerged from the room, his head bowed as he scurried away like a terrified mouse toward the utility room and out the back door.

What's going on? Jenny thought as she returned to scouring the sink.

After a few moments, Rebecca called to her. "Will you come in here, please, Jenny?"

"Coming." She stepped into the bathroom. There, she found Rebecca gingerly holding up the silky yellow nightie by the straps. "Is this . . . uh, little item yours, dear?"

Jenny gasped and felt her face flush. "Oh, I forgot to—"

Rebecca's eyes were beyond serious. "We have but one

bathroom in this house, as ya know." The woman looked absolutely appalled. "That's all I'll be sayin' about this."

"Really, I'm so terribly sorry. It won't happen again," Jenny assured Rebecca—and herself.

During the bumpy ride in the spring wagon to haul the plump and beautiful pumpkins, Jenny's embarrassment followed her like a stalking dog. But just as Rebecca had stated, she did not mention the incident further.

"What does your family think of your decision to come here?" asked Rebecca after a while. "They must be shocked." Her hands were tight on the reins.

Jenny drew a long breath and slowly let it out. "Actually, they don't know."

Rebecca turned toward her, frowning. "Whatever do ya mean? You didn't tell them?"

She shook her head. "I knew they'd try to talk me out of coming."

Rebecca sighed loudly. "So they *could've?*"

"I worried they'd pressure me to change my mind, yes."

The older woman raised her eyebrows. "And why's that?"

"It's not that I'm easily talked out of something, if that's what you think." Even to Jenny's ears, the words sounded defensive.

"Nee?" Rebecca gave her a doubtful look. "Are ya sure?"

Jenny nodded. "This kind of life is all I've wanted since I was a girl."

"But you can't just disappear from your family and not tell them what's in your heart."

"You don't know my family, Rebecca."

"True. But even so."

The conversation made Jenny feel even worse than she'd felt earlier, when Samuel had found her nightgown.

"I did tell my mother I was leaving town for a while."

Rebecca's pretty eyes became even more sober. "So you really don't know if you're goin' to stay put, then."

"I *do* know."

"I'm confused, dear. And I wonder if you're not equally so."

Jenny's frustration was mounting. "I told my mother I'd contact her in a few weeks."

"Yet you didn't tell her where you are or what you're doing." Rebecca's face drooped as though with sadness. "This is so peculiar to me."

Jenny sat up taller in the wagon. "You don't understand."

"You're certainly right."

A lengthy and embarrassing pause followed. Then quietly, slowly, Jenny tried to explain. "My family is nothing like yours, Rebecca. I've never felt like I fit in with my parents or sister and brother."

"Never felt like it, or just never did?"

"Both, I guess."

Rebecca reached over and patted her knee like Jenny was a child. "I don't mean to question. I just wonder if your Mamm wouldn't rather know where you are."

Jenny stared at the road, seeing the grooves on the other side, where carriage wheels had worn down the pavement. Rebecca had no idea how aloof her family was. She sighed. "Do you think I can make it through the Proving?"

"Considering what you've told me, I'd be hesitant to say."

"You mean because I haven't been forthcoming with my family?"

Rebecca smiled faintly. "The truth is always best, no matter what a stir it might cause."

"I believe that, too. I even meant to tell them, but . . ." Jenny mentally kicked herself. She'd known all along what she should have done.

I just didn't do it.

Chapter 12

Rebecca and Jenny stopped first at the home of Preacher Ephraim Yoder and his wife, Lovina, where Rebecca introduced Jenny to the reserved older couple before dropping off two pumpkins. Jenny was astonished at the length of the minister's tapered brown beard, speckled with gray. But despite his bristly brows, his deep-set eyes smiled a convincing welcome, and she believed he was a kind and gentle man. Lovina only eyed her at first, warming up more slowly before eventually offering chocolate chip cookies and hot coffee. Jenny was happy to sit at their table and nibble on the snack and sip the black coffee. But she wondered if they viewed her as a distraction since they were required to speak English in her presence. *I won't take it personally,* she thought as she noticed the Scripture wall calendar nearby. *They'll grow to trust me . . . to know me.*

The Lapps' driving horse, a black mare named Star, reared her beautiful head as they got back into the wagon. And when Rebecca reached for the reins and the horse began to move forward, Jenny noticed how very taut the reins were.

This horse is raring to go! Would she ever be able to control such a spirited animal?

Soon, they were coming up on Nate and Rhoda Kurtz's

farmhouse, the Lapps' neighbors to the south of their cornfield. Rhoda Kurtz was nearly as welcoming as Lovina had been, but still somewhat guarded, with only an occasional forced smile. Nate Kurtz, on the other hand, scarcely acknowledged Jenny, saying nothing at all.

When they returned to the wagon, Rebecca explained that was Nate's reticent way. "Don't feel bad. Some folk are nearly tongue-tied around Englischers, 'specially here in our little neck of the woods."

"Who can blame them?"

"And there are a number of farmers who basically speak with their eyes and hands. Guess they don't feel it necessary to talk much."

"My father's a little like that," Jenny said. "When he does speak, it's mostly about things no one else really comprehends or cares to discuss."

"Well, I feel for ya, then." Rebecca went on to say her husband was nothing like that—"quite the opposite. But there's no guessin' where Samuel stands on any issue."

"He was real quiet at supper yesterday."

"Oh, you just wait till he gets to know ya. He'll nearly talk your ear off."

Jenny wondered how long it would be before that might happen. Samuel Lapp wasn't just cautious; he was opposed to her being there. Of that, Jenny was almost certain.

In a few minutes, they made another delivery, this time to Samuel's brother's farmhouse, where they were met at the door by a young blond woman. "We've got more pumpkins than we know what to do with," the girl said as she stood in the doorway, obviously blocking their entry. "Dat suggested we just put them on the English neighbors' front porches." She frowned at Jenny, and Rebecca intervened.

"Jenny, this is my niece Emmalyn Lapp, Andrew's younger sister—you met Andrew at our place yesterday."

Jenny nodded and smiled. "Another of Marnie's many cousins."

Emmalyn stared back. "You must be the fancy friend."

"Well, I *was* fancy. And I am Marnie's friend, jah."

Emmalyn shrugged. "Dressin' the part doesn't make it so."

Jenny wholeheartedly agreed. "I would love to have been born Amish, like you." She'd put it right out there, wondering how Andrew's sassy sister might respond.

But Emmalyn merely folded her arms and turned to her aunt Rebecca. "I'll let Mamm know you dropped by."

"Are ya sure your mother doesn't want this pumpkin?" Rebecca was still holding it. "'Cause she ordered it from me."

Emmalyn shook her head. "Why not give it to her yourself, then? See if she takes it."

"Just tell your mother I was here." Rebecca put the pumpkin down, and that was that.

Her jaw set, Rebecca made no excuses for Emmalyn, like she had for Nate Kurtz. She simply got into the wagon, picked up the reins, and clicked her cheek.

Jenny felt chagrined at Emmalyn's rudeness and barbed remarks. *Some people are just a nuisance!*

She wondered if Rebecca was all right but didn't know her well enough to ask. So she looked the other way, watching the world of Hickory Hollow pass at a snail's pace.

The final stop was Bishop John Beiler's spacious farmhouse. His young wife, a rather plump but pretty woman named Mary, was giving her three youngest children a morning snack of juice and crackers when they arrived. Rebecca had mentioned the girls on the way into the house: chubby Mary Mae, just turned five—Mary's first child with the formerly widowed bishop; petite Emily, who was three; and little Anna, eighteen months. There were five other children with the bishop's first wife, Rebecca had said, most of them school age now. However, Hickory John and Nancy, the two oldest, both worked for other Amish families—Nancy in Sugarcreek, Ohio, where she assisted the bishop's elderly aunt.

It was quite an effort for Rebecca to talk over little Anna's cries. Nevertheless, she did her best, stating that Jenny was the seeker her niece Marnie had helped bring to Hickory Hollow. "I wanted you to meet her."

"Ach, you'll have to excuse my little one today," Mary said, her blond hair falling out of the bun in several places. "She had a fitful night and is a little out of sorts today."

"I well remember such times with my own youngsters, so don't fret," Rebecca said, leaning over to stroke the older girl's fair hair.

Jenny smiled at tiny Anna, whose golden hair was pulled back into braids fastened into a thin knot on the back of her head. Jenny pulled a silly face, which made the tot cease her crying at once.

"Well, that's much better," Mary said, kissing her daughter's wet cheeks.

The women talked further, and later Rebecca offered to carry in the pumpkin. "Is the back porch all right?"

Mary agreed as she switched Anna to her other hip. "It's awful nice of you to drop by, Rebecca."

"You'll be able to make several big pies, ain't?" Rebecca said before heading out to the spring wagon for the pumpkin, leaving Jenny alone with Mary and the children.

"We've all been so curious 'bout you, Jenny Burns. I hope you're finding a *gut* willkumm here," Mary said, her angelic smile filling her round face. "Are ya?"

The pleasant woman's comments made Jenny feel warm all over. "Thanks, er . . . Denki. So far I've only met a few neighbors, but Rebecca's been just wonderful."

"There's no one quite as kind—or long-suffering—as Rebecca Lapp, I agree." Mary set Anna down on the floor to play with Emily. "We've got quite a few folk asking 'bout you," she mentioned. "Everyone's very interested. In a *gut* way, of course."

Jenny knew what she meant. And when she saw Rebecca coming up the back steps with the large pumpkin, she scurried to the door. "Here, let me help," she said, thankful to have this distraction.

"I've got it," Rebecca said, gently placing the pumpkin on the floor. "There ya be, Mary."

"I'll get some money right quick," Mary said as she searched her dress pockets.

"Ach, there's no charge for the bishop's family." Rebecca wiped her hands on her black apron. "'Tis an offering of thanksgiving."

"Well, aren't you nice!" Mary lightly touched Rebecca's arm. "Denki to you and to Samuel, too." Mary's girls were quiet now as they stared up at Jenny with three sets of blue eyes.

"Your girls are precious," Jenny said, wishing they might stay longer.

"I think they must like you." Mary punctuated her words with a nod and a smile.

"Maybe they've never seen such unruly bangs." Jenny reached up and felt for the bobby pins.

Mary shook her head. "Oh, I didn't mean that. . . ."

"The bangs *are* a problem. But it's just a matter of time." Jenny smiled at Rebecca.

"Time is the key to many things, don't forget," Mary said with the sweetest smile.

"I'm real happy to meet you, Mary." Jenny offered to shake her hand.

"We'll get better acquainted soon," Mary replied, receiving the handshake. "Has Rebecca talked with you 'bout coming to help me now and then with the little girls?"

"She has, and I'd love to." Jenny smiled and waved.

After she and Rebecca had made the loop at the top of the driveway and headed back out to the road, Rebecca remarked, "I've never heard young Anna carry on like that before, just so ya know."

"Oh, that didn't bother me."

"Workin' as a mother's helper might be a *gut* way to learn Deitsch quicker," added Rebecca. "Since the children are learning to speak it, too."

"It's going to take some time, like Mary said. Jah?" Jenny enjoyed using the word.

"I daresay you're right."

Hesitantly, Jenny forged ahead. "What about your husband—is he really okay with me staying at the house?"

Rebecca paused for a moment. "Oh, never ya mind Samuel. He'll come around . . . in time."

So I was right. Her being here *had* created conflict between them. *Heaven knows there's enough of that.*

Then, recalling the earlier incident at the Lapps', she cringed again at the blunder with the yellow nightie. Here it was her first full day in Amish country, and she'd already made a fool of herself. And to think it was her reluctant host who'd discovered the gaffe!

Chapter 13

J enny sighed and stretched and dragged out of bed when the
alarm sounded at five o'clock Friday morning. Her third
full day here, and already she felt fatigued from the dawn-to-
dusk routine of cooking from scratch—three big meals a day.
In her entire life she'd never minced so many onions. Nor
had she boiled and then chopped so many eggs. There were
numerous recipes to master, all of which Rebecca had stored
in her head. Not a single recipe written down! The woman
was a living, walking miracle, the way she managed all that
was expected of her.

*And there's no chance, even at my young age, I can even dream
of keeping up with her!*

Rebecca had taught Jenny how to beat rugs, iron with a
gas iron, gather eggs, and scrub wood floors on all fours. And,
oh, the mountain of mending! She'd also shown Jenny how
to make bread, but thus far Jenny's bread looked nothing like
Rebecca's: plumped up on top, done to perfection.

Jenny sat up in bed with a start. Just yesterday, she'd darned
one of Samuel's socks completely shut. Rebecca hadn't seemed
to mind and had a good laugh over it. She'd simply handed

Jenny a seam ripper and, with a smile, requested she reopen the closure. And Jenny had started all over again.

Along with indoor chores, Jenny had also assisted Rebecca with the daily customers who knocked on the back door, coming to purchase a variety of jams and jellies. She quickly learned that Rebecca Lapp's preserves were known all over Lancaster County.

But the temptation to beat herself up with her own yardstick of perfection persisted. *I'm not a wimp . . . I'll get used to all of this. I have to!*

Eventually, she pulled herself out of bed and dressed, glad to have showered the night before. When her hair was brushed and swept back into a thick bun, she hurried downstairs to help Rebecca make the hot breakfast for Samuel and whoever happened to stay around. They never knew how many of the Lapps' nephews would appear for any given meal, but Rebecca had warned that this was the norm. Anyone was welcome, and Samuel was grateful for the help.

Plenty of room at the table, too, Jenny thought.

After the breakfast dishes were washed and dried and placed back in the cupboard, Jenny was pleased to see a blue van pull into the driveway. Marnie jumped out, wearing a big smile, and came around to the back door.

"Are we going to the bookstore?" Jenny asked when she met her there.

"Jah, but I can't be gone for long. Need to get back to help Mamm cook for the weekend," Marnie told her.

"Same here." Still, Jenny jumped at the chance to go. She found Rebecca in the sewing room upstairs, cutting out fabric for Samuel's new work pants. "Do ya mind if I go with Marnie to Gordonville to the bookstore?"

"Just right quick, jah? We have lots of pies to bake this afternoon." Then Rebecca waved her off.

"Denki," Jenny said and hurried to her room to grab her purse. She dashed back downstairs, where she followed Marnie outdoors and into the nearly empty van. It was hard to imagine how Rebecca had juggled all the indoor duties prior to Jenny's coming. The thought of it boggled her mind.

Too bad Katie isn't allowed to drop by and help, she thought, still puzzled by the day-to-day consequences of the shunning.

··· ➤ ➤ ···

At the bookstore, Jenny found a veritable storehouse of reading material—everything from Amish school curriculum to realistic fiction for children, such as *The Pineapple Quilt* and *The Only Sister*.

Marnie tugged at her arm playfully, reminding her of the urgency to return home, and led her to the stack of paperback dictionaries. With a grin of assurance, she placed one firmly in Jenny's hands. "Here 'tis. Your road map to speaking fluent Deitsch. This will help ya make more sense of what you're already soaking up."

Pleased, Jenny could hardly wait to look up various words she'd heard repeatedly since her arrival, words like *ferhoodled* and *Nachtmohl*.

The chatter in the van en route to Hickory Hollow increased greatly when two Amishwomen climbed aboard after waving down the driver outside the nearby Amish shoe store. Despite her fatigue and their talking, Jenny would not be deterred from her hunt through the dictionary. She quickly learned that *Nachtmohl* was Holy Communion, which she hoped, even prayed, to be eligible for as a bona fide church member.

Will I endure the Proving? she wondered, the test stretching out before her like a grueling path. And to think she'd only lived Amish for a few days!

———

Marnie could see how captivated Jenny was by the dictionary, so she let her browse through it while she talked with the womenfolk in the van. "Jah, she's here to stay," Marnie told them in Deitsch when they inquired. "There's no question in my mind."

"Honestly, it's hard to think of goin' from the fancy English world to ours," Ella Mae Zook's married granddaughter Rachel Glick said, casting furtive looks Jenny's way.

"Oh, I agree," Marnie replied. "Just think of all you'd have to give up: cars, phones, television . . . pretty clothes."

"Honestly, what would make someone from the outside want to join our church?" Rachel's aunt asked.

Marnie wasn't free to divulge Jenny's confidences. That was for her friend to share later, once she had steady footing amongst the People. "Maybe someday she'll tell you."

This caused Rachel to roll her eyes, then shake her head. "Makes not a whit of sense, if ya ask me."

"She's not askin' you." Marnie smiled.

"Well, aren't you something?" Rachel teased.

"Sorry," Marnie offered. "Hope I didn't sound mouthy."

The other women exchanged glances.

"She's learnin' our language, so very soon we'll be including Jenny in all our conversations," Marnie added hastily, not wanting to exclude a friend.

Rachel was quick to nod her head.

"What lengths would you go . . . to make a dream come true?" Marnie asked in an attempt to change the tone of the conversation.

"Not sure." Rachel frowned. "Why?"

Marnie went on to say she thought Jenny Burns had done nearly the impossible, moving heaven and earth to get here. "It's remarkable, really."

The women nodded, now staring at the back of Jenny's head as she read her dictionary.

Jenny chose that moment to enter their chatter. "Why's the spelling for *ferhoodled* different?" she asked, turning to face Marnie. "I was paging through and stumbled upon a spelling I've never seen before in books."

"Show me." Marnie leaned over to look at the book.

"It's spelled *v–e–r–h–u–d–d–e–l–t*," Jenny said, showing her the word and the meaning—confused, entangled, mixed-up.

"Oh, that's not surprising, really."

Jenny looked at her, puzzled.

"Some of my circle letter friends in Ohio, for instance, spell our words completely different," Marnie explained. "It's not like German, where there's a set standard for spelling."

Jenny grimaced. "Uniformity would be helpful."

Marnie could see that she was struggling—and not just with words in a dictionary. No, Jenny looked sleep deprived.

"You all right?" Marnie whispered.

"Sure, why?"

"Just checkin'."

A few minutes later, the driver took an unexpected turn, and they headed down the road where her shunned cousin, Katie, and her husband, Dan, had now lived for more than five years. "Look over there," Marnie said softly, pointing. "That's Katie's house."

Jenny turned quickly to look.

There was the familiar meadow, with the creek running through it in the background. Although she'd never darkened the door of the place, Marnie found the clapboard house rather appealing. "Perty, ain't?"

Jenny nodded, still staring as they passed. "And no one's allowed to visit her?"

She shook her head. "It's all part of the Bann." Marnie felt sad just saying it.

"Can't anything be done to alter it?" asked Jenny. She certainly was one to nose out the facts.

"Aside from Katie offering a kneeling confession in front of the membership, what's done is done." Marnie wished she hadn't brought it up. She'd been little more than a schoolgirl when Katie left, yet the pain of separation still tore at her own heart.

Chapter 14

The driver dropped Marnie and Jenny off at Uncle Samuel's, and they strolled up the lane toward the house. "Let me know if there's anything you need, all right?" Marnie said.

Jenny tapped the dictionary. "I think this is going to help."

"Remember, you'll pick up our language faster by listening and attempting to speak it."

Jenny nodded, but her face looked downcast.

"What is it?"

"This has nothing to do with speaking Deitsch." Jenny seemed hesitant.

"Go on."

"I'm wondering. How do you think Rebecca's daughter would feel about my wearing her Amish clothes?"

"Goodness, I doubt she'd care."

"You're sure?"

Marnie nodded. "Katie's moved on. I guarantee it. Maybe you'll run into her at market or somewhere. She's a spunky sort."

"Does she stay in touch with any of her family?"

Marnie paused. "Bishop John allows written correspondence, as I understand it."

"The Bann seems cruel."

"I'm sure ya think so. But the shunning's for the purpose of bringing a wayward church member back into the fold. And it works, at least for some folk." She could see that Jenny was unconvinced. "Of course, Katie ran off for different reasons than most—wanted to search for her birth mother, of all things."

"She wasn't born Amish?" Jenny's face was suddenly ashen.

"No."

"This must be so hard for everyone who loved her."

"*Loves,*" Marnie insisted. "Ach, my heart breaks for Aunt Rebecca, the Mamma who raised her. I can't abide the thought of losing a grown daughter to the world."

Jenny glanced away, and if Marnie wasn't mistaken, there was a tear in her eye. In this awkward moment, was Jenny thinking of her own family back in Connecticut? Here she'd left everything behind for the Amish life, and Katie had done just the opposite.

A heavy sorrow settled in the pit of Marnie's stomach. Was this another common strand attaching Jenny to Katie, like stitches in a quilt?

Dancing splotches of light scattered over the road as Samuel Lapp drove the enclosed family carriage to the Preaching service on Sunday morning. The smell of tilled black earth and a predawn rain fused in the atmosphere as Jenny sat on the back bench of the buggy, peering out at the road behind them. She felt like a modern-day pilgrim watching at least a half dozen other such carriages form a gray caravan. Along the way, she noticed signs posted near mailboxes or at the end of lanes: *Bunnies for Sale, Rubber Stamp Supplies,* and *Firewood for Sale—No Sunday Sales!*

Jenny spotted a young Amish boy on in-line skates who held on to a long rope, attached to the back of one buggy. He couldn't have been more than eight years old as he skated his way to church. She was tempted to ask Rebecca, sitting up front to the left of her husband, if this was even safe. It certainly looked like fun, and the boy held on tightly as he swung way out and around when the horse and carriage made the turn left.

"Oh, stink!" Jenny heard Rebecca say.

"What is it?" Samuel replied.

"I left my best hankie at home."

"Well, is that any reason to be upset?"

Rebecca went silent.

"You want me to turn the horse round and go back, is that it?" Samuel said in the irritated tone Jenny had heard before.

"Nee, go on," Rebecca replied. "It's my fault for rushin' around so."

"You're sure, now?"

"We'll be late for church otherwise." Rebecca sighed. "No, I'll make do."

Samuel was quiet for a few moments; then Jenny heard his breathy "Haw," as he directed the horse to turn left into the deacon's lane.

This close now, she realized that the carriage pulling the skater was crowded in the back with young children. *One way to accommodate an extra passenger!* she thought, grinning.

The sun shone through the oak trees along one side of the deacon's driveway. Jenny squinted at the sky and felt hesitant yet joyful at the thought of attending her first-ever Amish church service. She'd gone to bed *"with the chickens"* last night, as Rebecca had strongly urged. Jenny had been staying up much too late, unable to rise and shine by five o'clock each morning. *"There are no shortcuts to becoming Amish,"* Rebecca had gently pointed out to her. Consequently, there had been no late-night session with her journal yesterday, either.

Still, anything worth doing is worth doing right, Jenny decided, embracing Rebecca's philosophy as she fell in step with her mentor. Jenny felt a little unsettled knowing the blue dress and white cape apron she wore today was the one Katie had worn for her botched wedding to Bishop John Beiler. Jenny wished Rebecca hadn't spilled the beans earlier, while they cooked breakfast together. *Why tell me?* Jenny wondered and decided she would sew her own Sunday clothes as soon as possible.

She followed Rebecca to the line of women and children, which included a number of small boys. Jenny enjoyed the cool air and the overall feeling of anticipation. She expected the church meeting to be a reverent one. Since much of the service would be in German, Rebecca had informed her of the order and explained what would transpire. Even though Jenny was dressed like the rest of the women, she was still considered a visitor. An English one, at that. She would be thought of this way until she was a full-fledged member of the Hickory Hollow Amish church. *After my Proving,* she thought, standing with Rebecca until the long line began to shift toward the back door of the farmhouse. Rebecca whispered that it was time for her to take her place with the unbaptized teenaged girls, at the back of the line.

On her way there, Jenny couldn't help noticing Andrew Lapp in the procession of men. Besides Samuel and several of Samuel's nephews, Andrew was one of the few men she recognized. *Besides Preacher Yoder.* That man had offered a kind smile and a dip of his head earlier when he had arrived with Lovina.

Near the tail end of the line, a young woman motioned for her to step ahead of her, making Jenny the fifth from the last. "Denki," she whispered, and the girl nodded but did not smile.

Marnie held her breath as she observed Jenny Burns. Goodness, she'd failed to tell Jenny not to look over at the menfolk. You just didn't do that on Sunday mornings, when everyone's mind—and heart—was supposed to be fixed on worship. She didn't think Jenny was actually eyeing the young men, of course. There was so much the seeker would have to learn in order to be thought of as humble and submissive! Glancing over at the men lined up for church wasn't going to make the best first impression.

Ach, but Jenny has a good heart. All the letters Marnie had saved surely pointed to that. Marnie glimpsed her again and noted that Jenny looked better rested than on Friday, which was wonderful-*gut.* There was not much worse than being dog tired on a Preaching Sunday!

Prior to leaving to stand with the unbaptized girls, she said softly to her mother, "Mamm. I want you to meet my friend Jenny today."

"Ach, must I?"

"She's my *friend,* Mamm."

Her mother was quiet for a moment, then looked away.

"Isn't it about time?" Marnie whispered. "She's been here five days already."

"Well, might make better sense to see if she stays around."

It bothered her that Mamm wasn't interested in welcoming

Jenny with open arms. *She just doesn't want to meet her*, Marnie thought glumly, glancing back at her English friend again. *I must talk to Jenny before the common meal*, Marnie decided, lest the seeker make a serious misstep.

Jenny quickly decided, once the hymns were finished, that the back of the large front room of the deacon's house was a perfect spot for a newcomer to fight sleep. Which Jenny certainly did, though less because she was tired and more because she was discouraged. Thanks to Mr. Zimmerman's high school German class, she had an idea what the first and the second sermons were about, but her head was hurting with the effort required to comprehend even that. And she didn't think she could sit for another minute, let alone the next full hour. Her seat was numb and her back ached from the hard wooden bench. If it wasn't so difficult, it would have been comical, especially since she'd read this very thing about Englishers who'd visited Amish church meetings.

She noticed Rebecca and her married sisters, as well as Marnie and her mother and younger siblings, all sitting straight as pins. She hoped to meet Marnie's family today, as well as a myriad of others. Yet she knew she would need to wait for them to make the first move—pushing into this cloistered community was not the best way to be accepted.

When eventually everyone turned to kneel at their bench, she did the same thing, surprised her legs actually worked, as anesthetized as they'd become. She thought of all the times she and Kyle Jackson had gone to college football games, taking along flat bleacher pillows to sit on. She liked the idea of having one for the Preaching service in two weeks.

Will I even last that long, Lord? she mused, aware of her stomach's rumbling while everyone else prayed silently. *Will I manage to abandon my selfish upbringing and cushy modern lifestyle to bow my knee in contrition and meekness as a baptized Amishwoman?*

Chapter 15

After the service, Jenny was told there was to be a meeting for only church members. Those who were not baptized headed to the screened-in back porch behind the kitchen. A few teen girls in identical blue dresses to Jenny's looked shyly at her in passing before wandering down the steps and over to the barn in a cluster. The boys, matching in black trousers and coats with white shirts buttoned to the neck, sauntered in the opposite direction, toward the woodshed.

Jenny pulled on the black shawl Rebecca had loaned her for the day and waited on the porch with a handful of small children who sat along the wall on a padded bench. Several eyed her while talking softly among themselves in Deitsch. In time, two of the older little girls popped up and began a quiet clapping game, spinning around in between claps, their organdy aprons fluttering about. Jenny wished she could speak their language—she longed to interact, feeling again like the outsider she was. But she continued to watch the well-behaved, even demure youngsters from her corner.

Sighing, Jenny wished again that she'd grown up here. She wouldn't have so much catching up to do. *And I'd be able to handle the long Preaching service, too!* Her previously easy life had spoiled her, making this entry into the Amish world more challenging than she'd ever imagined.

She looked off toward the distant hills, the landscape shining with the freshness of the day. Birds tweeted and horses neighed in the stable, the sounds of nature blending with the intermittent laughter coming from the nearby woodshed. In the background was the steady drone of the preacher's voice as he spoke to those still in the house.

It was some time later, when the private meeting adjourned, that Jenny was greeted by Emmalyn Lapp, who wore a maroon-colored dress with her white apron and Kapp. Her golden blond hair was perfectly parted in the middle and neatly slicked back on either side.

"Hi, Emmalyn," said Jenny, hoping she might be more pleasant this encounter.

"*Wie geht's?*" Emmalyn asked, her pale blue eyes wide.

"I'm fine—how are you?"

"Ah, so you *do* know." The teenager smirked. "Wunnerbaar-gut."

"I'm slow but sure."

"But are you as hungry as I am?" Emmalyn moved her head gracefully in the direction of the kitchen.

"I'm starving. How do you say that in Deitsch?" Jenny laughed softly.

"Did ya understand anything the preachers said?" Emmalyn asked, seemingly ignoring Jenny's question.

"Not much."

Emmalyn pulled her shawl closer, a slow smile on her face. "If you want to ward off your hunger, just go in and help yourself to some slices of lunchmeat or cheese and whatnot."

"Really?"

"Just to hold you over, ya know."

Jenny didn't have to be told twice. She moved past Emmalyn and went inside, caving in to her hunger pangs. She reached for two slices of bologna and one of Swiss cheese, rolled them up, and took a bite. Then, seeing a pile of bread, she took a slice of that, as well.

On the way back to the porch, she noticed the bishop's wife staring at her. Not only Mary Beiler, but also Andrew was looking her way—and grimacing.

She kept going, her head down a little, and made her way back outside, taking another bite of her delicious snack as she went.

Emmalyn was no longer in sight when Jenny returned to the porch, so she stood over in the corner, pushing the meat and cheese into the bread and folding it over to make a half sandwich. She was thankful for Emmalyn's suggestion as she nibbled away but could hardly remember a worse Sunday worship experience. Was she just impatient . . . in need of humility? *I want to be one of them*, she thought. *If I have the fortitude.*

She thought again of the backbreaking service.

"Uh, Jenny Burns, isn't it?"

She whirled around as Andrew Lapp stepped onto the porch.

She wiped her mouth on the back of her hand and refrained from eating the last delectable bite.

He moved toward her, eyes narrowing. "You're partaking of food before the brethren?"

She nodded, not sure she ought to say it was Emmalyn who'd given her the go-ahead. "Is it all right? I mean—"

"Well, now, the first seating for the shared meal is always for the ministers and folk up in years," he informed her.

"But I thought it was all right to . . ." But, no, she wasn't going to throw his sister under the bus, even though it seemed evident Emmalyn had deliberately misled her.

"The second seating is for younger marrieds and single young people. You'll likely sit with my aunt Rebecca and her sisters." His direct words did not match his mannerly tone. He had a thoughtful way about him, Jenny noticed, and it comforted her, especially now.

"Denki, Andrew. I really appreciate knowing."

At that moment, Lovina Yoder appeared in the doorway, blinking and twisting the front of her apron into a knot. "Ach, I . . ." the preacher's wife murmured, then hurried back inside.

Jenny had no clue what was wrong. "I'm terribly confused." She looked up at Andrew, who still offered his calming presence.

His blue eyes held her gaze. "Ask me anything at all."

"I've obviously made a mistake by preempting the meal with a snack."

His eyes twinkled suddenly. "And did ya pray a blessing over this nibble?"

"Actually, I did not." She paused and noticed a couple of young women looking out the window. One of them was the bishop's wife. She cringed. "Are we not supposed to be . . . talking?"

Andrew drew in a long breath and folded his arms. "The age-old rule is that women are to congregate with like women on Preachin' Sundays—married women together, and single women with others who are single."

"So the men and women mustn't mingle on Sunday?"

He was nodding slowly, still gazing intently at her. "Not before or after the Preachin' service, nee."

"Gotcha," she said, forgetting momentarily that she was supposed to be a quaint, soft-spoken Amishwoman.

He smiled, his lips parting. "You'll catch on soon enough, Jenny."

"That's encouraging, thanks."

"Do ya mean Denki?"

"Jah, and that, too."

"*Da Herr sei mit du.*" Andrew turned to head down the back steps, toward the woodshed.

I'll have to look that up, Jenny told herself. Did he mean *God be with you*, perhaps? She ate the last of the unsanctified snack and watched Andrew go, hoping he would keep walking and not look back and see her still staring.

Chapter 16

Jenny hoped neither Andrew Lapp nor anyone else was observing her later that afternoon as she watched Marnie's father, Chester Lapp, hitch up the driving horse and carriage. Chester eyed her warily while he and Marnie slowly backed the driving horse between the shafts as, all the while, Marnie described the process in English. Jenny tried hard to remember the various steps, aware of the hollow feeling in the pit of her stomach. How many times would she have to be shown this before she could do it herself?

Once the horse and carriage were successfully hitched, Chester Lapp called for his family to get settled inside for the ride home. Marnie quickly introduced Jenny to her mother, Peggy, who seemed reluctant to shake her hand and greet her. Then, that quickly, Marnie was waving as she climbed into the back with her younger siblings. "I'll see ya sometime this week, all right?" Marnie said.

Jenny nodded. "It was nice to meet your parents today."

Marnie smiled apologetically. "Keep your chin up, Jenny!"

"Denki," Jenny replied and trudged over to the deacon's house, where Rebecca stood waiting patiently, a compassionate smile on her face. "Would it be possible to write down the steps for hitching up?" Jenny asked her. "Might be a good idea."

"Of course, but I think you'll learn better just by doin'," Rebecca said.

Sure doesn't seem that way.

"I daresay you're fretting yourself, ain't so?"

Jenny couldn't verbalize the truth—that she was afraid she'd never get it right.

"You have plenty of time, remember?" Rebecca motioned her inside. "Come now, I'd like you to meet some of my friends before they leave for home."

Not in the best frame of mind to socialize, she followed Rebecca into the house, where an elderly woman sat in an oak pressed-back chair near the window, holding her cane just so. Her small blue eyes shone as Jenny approached her.

Rebecca leaned down near the older woman. "Ella Mae, this is our seeker, Jenny Burns," she said. Then, turning to Jenny, she said, "And, Jenny, I'd like you to meet my lifelong friend, Ella Mae Zook."

The white-haired woman stretched out her gnarled hand. "Hullo, Jenny Burns. It's *gut* to meet ya."

"Jenny's from Connecticut," Rebecca added, straightening to her full height.

"Well, dearie, you're a long ways from home," Ella Mae said. "Ain't so?"

Jenny hadn't thought of it quite like that. "It would take a very long time by horse and buggy, absolutely." She smiled down at the petite woman.

"Did ya have a nice trip here?" asked Ella Mae.

Jenny told how excited she'd been last Tuesday. "That day is a complete blur to me."

Ella Mae cocked her head. "You have a little accent, don't you?"

"No one's ever mentioned it." Jenny was actually charmed by the diminutive lady, who had a smile that was a fascinating blend of reassurance and mischief. *"She's never met a seeker,"* Jenny recalled Marnie telling her. *Not in her lifetime. I'm a rarity.*

"You'll have to drop by and have a cup of my peppermint tea sometime," Ella Mae said in her delicate voice. "I'd like to hear your story."

Jenny was taken aback, but seeing her lovely smile reappear, she assumed the woman was only being friendly.

"I'm quite serious," Ella Mae added. "Do come visit me anytime."

"Thanks, um . . . Denki. How nice of you!"

"It's time we got acquainted."

Jenny nodded, feeling better suddenly, though she didn't know exactly why. Ella Mae's demeanor was as much of an encouragement to her as Andrew's had been earlier.

"Why not go 'n' see her on Tuesday, after Monday wash-day?" Rebecca suggested.

"Tuesday it shall be," Ella Mae piped up even before Jenny could agree.

And Jenny did so with a cautious smile. *Is this Rebecca's idea?* she wondered.

··· ➤ ◀ ···

During the ride to the Lapp farm, Jenny again sat in the back of the buggy. It wasn't long before she noticed the same carriage with the boy skater attached by rope, coming fast upon them, about to pass them on the narrow stretch of road.

The driver was a middle-aged man with a bushy dark brown beard that protruded out over his chest. And if she wasn't mistaken, he was looking over at her, grinning. Instantly uncomfortable, she looked away. *Who is that?*

When they pulled into the Lapps' lane, Jenny offered to help unhitch the horse, but Rebecca intervened and suggested Jenny'd had enough for one day. She urged her to spend some quiet time alone in her room, which Jenny welcomed. She had been so busy the past two days, she'd failed to write in her journal, so she sat on the bed and began to jot down her thoughts.

It's amazing what a person can absorb in a few days' time. I never gave butchering chickens much thought, but now I can pluck feathers and prepare the bird for cooking. Rebecca knows how to break a chicken's neck humanely, with the least amount of pain for the bird. She is a stronger woman than she appears and can do this chore without help . . . whereas I could hardly watch the first time. I tried to think of having nothing to eat but that poor full-grown chicken. Guess I'll need to think like a homesteader if I want to fit in here.

Rebecca told me that sometimes the weakest chicken will get pecked to death by the others, and I've wondered if I'll end up like that, too. I don't mean that anyone's really picking on me . . . well, except Emmalyn Lapp, who obviously set me up today before the common meal. Thankfully, her brother Andrew didn't think poorly of me for eating ahead of time. Or then again, he may have concealed what he truly thinks. Who knows what any of them are whispering about now.

At times like this, I can't help thinking about my former home. I'm even starting to miss my family—I wish I hadn't kept them in the dark about coming here.

There are moments I don't even know what I think anymore, other than the fact that Andrew Lapp has to be the best-looking Amish—or English—guy anywhere!

··· ⊱ ⊰ ···

"Our young seeker is discouraged," Rebecca told Samuel as they rested in their room that afternoon. "I can see it on her face."

Samuel was still for a while, his eyes closed. Then he drew a slow breath. "Jenny Burns is not solely your responsibility, Rebecca."

She knew as much and was glad Jenny would ultimately be overseen by the bishop. Even so, she wanted to see the young woman succeed more than anything. Well, almost. Her thoughts flew to Katie, as they often did on the Lord's Day. Pity's sake, they'd lost one girl from the Amish church. Oh, she hoped she could manage to keep concealing the visits. It was imperative, though she never thought of going to see dearest Katie as actually sinning. *But the ministerial brethren would certainly think so. As would Samuel . . .*

"Have ya thought of lettin' things run their course?" Samuel said drowsily. "Have ya?"

She looked at him in surprise, her mind still on Katie. "What?" Her throat was terribly dry.

"Jenny must find her own way," he said.

Goodness, she was relieved. Although she hadn't thought that way at all since the young woman had walked through the back door and into her life. *Their lives.*

"Are ya napping now, Rebecca?" her husband asked, rolling over to peep at her before he shut his eyes again.

"Not just yet."

"Well, what do you think 'bout what I said? Are ya deaf, or just playin' like it?"

"I don't know what to say."

He smiled, his eyes still closed. "I think ya do." Sighing, he adjusted the pillow. "You're getting too attached to her, I daresay."

Rebecca shrugged. He was probably right.

"If she fails, you'll be terribly troubled, jah?"

"Well, she won't."

"You don't know that for sure." His eyes flicked open. "Mark my words, Rebecca. You'll get your heart all bound up in Jenny . . . won't be *gut* for ya. You hear?"

She'd heard but she also had high hopes. "The girl needs help if she's goin' to get through to her baptism."

"That's what I'm talking 'bout."

Rebecca turned and stared at the dresser and the gas lantern. Then and there, she remembered her dream from a couple of weeks ago and trembled. She was thankful when Samuel slipped his burly arm around her and held her that way till she fell fast asleep at last.

Marnie left the house soon after they arrived home, as she often did on a Sunday afternoon. Even on a fairly chilly afternoon such as this, she liked to get out and walk. It was easiest to sort through her thoughts when she was alone beneath the sky and sun. Sometimes, too, Roy came by in his open buggy, soaring down Hickory Lane. *Just maybe.*

She hoped with all of her heart he'd understood what she'd written in her letter, which he would have received by now. There was enough time for him to have replied, as well, but she knew he was busy helping his father these days, baling corn fodder for stable bedding.

Still, it nagged at her that he and his family seemed to be moving in the opposite direction of the Old Order. She couldn't help but wonder if Roy's parents were as interested in the Bible studies as Roy was.

She couldn't fret her afternoon away, but she hoped to know the answers, and surely she would, soon enough. "If Roy drops by," she whispered, nearly holding her breath every time a courting buggy made the bend in the road and headed this way. Oh, what she'd give to feel her hand in his on this beautiful November Lord's Day!

Chapter 17

The following Tuesday morning, Jenny was reminded of her visit with Ella Mae Zook. Rebecca brought it up right after she said *Guder Mariye* when Jenny appeared in the kitchen to help with cooking.

Jenny repeated the words, which meant good morning. She smiled as she recalled how Rebecca had been spending more time teaching her Deitsch since just Sunday evening, when they'd sat down together following supper. Jenny had noticed an almost maternal change in Rebecca's demeanor and was delighted for the extra help. Samuel, on the other hand, seemed quieter than ever, but Jenny assumed the reverence of the Lord's Day had something to do with it. *Except his reticence has continued into the week,* she thought.

"There's a bit of ironing and mending to do after breakfast," Rebecca said. "Then we'll clean the main level of the house before making the noon meal. And, while we work, why don't we practice speaking Deitsch?"

Jenny was heartened. "I'd like that. Denki."

"We'll start with a review of the more common expressions, then go over some household words."

It was great how Rebecca was jumping on board with Jenny's goal. She hurried to get the flour out of the pantry, and on the way noticed Andrew Lapp through the window, walking across the yard toward the barn. He was waving his straw hat at something, and she caught herself smiling. For the life of her, she couldn't understand why such a handsome guy was still single, especially in Amish country. She remembered what Marnie had said—something about a number of young women trying to catch his eye but failing. Andrew's being unattached was a mystery, indeed.

When Samuel and two of his nephews came in for breakfast, Jenny wondered if Andrew might also join them. But when she glanced out the window again, she saw his spring wagon heading up the road. Not once had he shared a meal there since her arrival. But then again, he came to help sporadically; undoubtedly he had to return to his own work.

Besides, it was silly to set her eyes on a man, no matter how appealing he seemed to be. *I don't need any distractions!*

"Eli needs my help repairing his horse fence this afternoon," Samuel stated to Rebecca during breakfast. "I'd like ya to groom Ol' Molasses for me." She nodded quickly, then glanced at Jenny. "We did have plans already to go 'n' see Ella Mae."

"You'll just have to postpone" came Samuel's swift reply. "You can't be takin' the oldest horse out on the road anyways. He will have his fill of miles by then."

Rebecca was torn between wanting to say something privately to Samuel and demonstrating her willingness to submit in all matters. *Especially now*, with Jenny observing. How else was the young woman going to learn to be a good wife someday?

"Maybe I'll send Jenny over there on foot by herself," she replied mildly. She didn't want to spoil Jenny's plans, and Ella Mae would be expecting her, even looking forward to the visit.

"Maybe she could stay home and work on hitchin' up instead," Samuel shot back. "Or spend time helping you with groomin'. 'Tis the best way to bond with a horse, ya know."

Rebecca stiffened, resenting his tone but refusing to let it get the best of her. *Why is he so blunt?*

She simply nodded again and cut into the sausage and scrambled eggs on her plate. Oh, she hoped Jenny understood that Samuel was a kind man and good husband, not as demanding as he seemed here lately. Sadly, his benevolent side had all but disappeared.

Jenny realized Rebecca was doing her husband's bidding and sacrificing the time for her own chores by grooming the aging horse. She accompanied Rebecca out to the stable, offering to help. Thus far, Jenny had seen no sign of any delayed resistance to Samuel's earlier demands, which surprised her. Hearing Samuel bark his orders at the table had given her a headache. In fact, she wanted to mention something to Rebecca but knew she'd better not. Observing the woman's meek behavior with her husband reinforced what Marnie had written in her letters about the importance of submission in marriage and in the community. *Surrendering her will,* thought Jenny. *Resigning selfish wishes and desires in the silence of the soul.*

After Rebecca shooed her back to the house to clean up the kitchen, Jenny wished she could hurry down to the little springhouse to collect her thoughts . . . and pray for humility.

And to reside quietly in Christ. Because if a future husband ever spoke that way to her, she *knew* she would stand up to him. The core of her heart was anything but obedient. *Far from it.* "Mom talks right over Dad," she whispered. *Yet she's devoted to him.* But everyone interrupted and talked over everyone. She considered the twenty-four-hour news shows on TV and talk radio . . . even conversations with co-workers or friends.

At that moment, Jenny could see a marked difference between her father and Samuel Lapp. One was well satisfied to let a woman have her say, and the other had to have the upper hand.

She recalled Samuel's remark that she ought to stay home to practice hitching up. Actually, it was the last thing Jenny wanted to do this afternoon. Would discounting his wishes be stubborn and haughty?

I'll ask Ella Mae about submission, Jenny decided, wishing she had the right to wander at will today. A brisk walk might help her get past the frustration over Samuel's insistence. But could she find her way around Hickory Hollow without Rebecca's help?

The air was chilly and a light wind had come up as Jenny set out to follow Rebecca's directions down Hickory Lane and beyond. Rebecca had said Ella Mae was known for her specially brewed peppermint tea, which would be waiting for Jenny upon her arrival, *"to warm you up."*

The way Rebecca had rebounded from the earlier conversation with Samuel still surprised Jenny, even though nothing more had been said at the noon meal. She was beginning to think her own skin must be too thin. As good-natured and compliant as Rebecca was, she must have already forgotten or even overlooked Samuel's words.

Jenny planned to note in her journal the times when Rebecca acquiesced to Samuel. She'd never known such a humble spirit. It just wasn't human nature to be that way. She heard a horse *clip-clop*ping behind her but didn't want to glance over her shoulder, in case it was a man driving this way. She was still finding her way through the labyrinth of social expectations. *I don't want to make another misstep!*

Next thing she knew, the horse was slowing to keep pace with her as she walked quickly along the roadside. Uncomfortable as it was, she did not dare turn to look.

"Hullo there." The voice was surprisingly familiar.

She spied Andrew Lapp there, riding in his spring wagon. He held the reins taut, his muscular arms parallel to his knees. "*Wie bischt?*"

"*Yuscht* fine, and you?" she replied, wondering why she felt so lighthearted around a man she hardly knew.

"Say, I believe you're comin' along with your Amish."

"*Denki*, but it's pretty jumbled."

"We all begin somewhere, ain't?"

She wondered if he was going to offer her a ride and almost hoped so. Was it written on her face?

"Are ya headin' anywhere in particular?" he asked, and there was that twinkle again. Was he really just a flirt?

"Out for a long walk."

"But not aimlessly walkin', jah?" He chuckled. "You remind me of someone." He slowed the horse even more. "Spunky . . . and with the same color of hair."

"Anyone I might know?"

"Well, now, I'm tryin' to think who 'tis."

She laughed softly. Was he fishing to see what she knew

about Katie Lapp Fisher? Marnie had said on Sunday that Jenny could be mistaken for Katie's sister.

She kept walking, picking up her speed a little now and wondering if he'd make his horse follow suit.

"How're things goin' so far?"

"Wunnerbaar-*gut*," she replied.

"Glad to hear it."

"By the way, I'm headed to Ella Mae Zook's—am I going the right way?"

"You certainly are. Not much farther now before you turn to the north." Andrew grinned and cued his horse to trot, giving her a big wave before he moved along. "*Hatyee*—so long, Jenny!"

She fought a smile of her own, unable to get a read on his peculiar actions. What made this man tick?

Chapter 18

J enny passed by Marnie's house on the way to Ella Mae's but didn't see her friend anywhere outdoors. *Probably busy helping her mother prepare food for one of the first of many Thursday weddings*, she thought, remembering what Marnie had said last time.

A row of potted orange mums on the front porch steps caught her eye with its colorful display. Marnie had written more than a month ago about going to a nearby greenhouse to purchase autumn plants from their Amish neighbor, Maryanna, whose young children helped her prepare orders for customers.

The wind rose even more by the time Jenny made the right-hand turn at the far end of Nate Kurtz's massive cornfield, where she could finally see the farmhouse Rebecca had so perfectly described.

Ella Mae Zook, minus her cane, greeted Jenny on the small white porch off her side of the complex of houses attached to the main one. She ushered Jenny inside out of the cold, into a pleasantly snug kitchen that smelled appealingly of peppermint. A yellow ceramic teapot adorned with a yellow-and-green tea cozy awaited on the counter.

Jenny took off her black shawl and outer bonnet, both of which belonged to Rebecca. "Where would you like me to hang them?" she asked politely.

"There's an empty hook over yonder." Ella Mae pointed toward the back door, her expression serious.

Is she scrutinizing me, too? The older woman seemed guarded, similar to almost everyone else Jenny had encountered in the past week.

"How was the walk over?" asked Ella Mae, going to the counter and opening a cupboard above her white head. She reached for two teacups and set them on the counter.

Jenny said she'd enjoyed it very much, then quickly explained that Rebecca Lapp had stayed home to help her husband groom a horse.

"That's all right. Rebecca comes here quite often." She pulled out the chair and seated Jenny as if she were an honored guest. The gesture was sweet and reminded Jenny of something her mother might do. "Would ya care for some homemade pastries with your tea, Jenny?"

"I'd love some. Denki."

Ella Mae's eyes brightened. "Well, you sound nearly Amish."

"I have a feeling I'll speak Deitsch long before I'm able to embody the spirit of submission. Like Rebecca . . . and the other women in the community."

Ella Mae nodded. "That quality comes more easily for some, I'll admit." She carried the teacups to the small table, each one perched on its matching saucer, and set one in front of Jenny on a place mat embroidered with yellow roses. Her wrinkled hand trembled, which caused the other cup and saucer to jingle as she situated it on her own place mat directly across from Jenny. "Our mothers here begin training their wee tots in obedience from the time a child is two. You won't see many *rutschich* little ones at the table, for example. They're taught to sit still and be patient."

"Do you mean submission can be taught?"

Ella Mae smiled. "To a clean slate—a young child—jah. Although some youngsters have stronger wills than others, of course. They're taught to recite this old school verse and take it to heart: 'I must be a Christian child, gentle, patient, meek and mild; must be honest, simple, true, in my words and actions, too. I must cheerfully obey, giving up my will and way. . . . Must remember God can view all I think and all I do.'"

Jenny considered Ella Mae's remarks and the traditional poem.

"Are ya havin' some trouble with this?" Ella Mae gently asked.

"It's just that I know myself too well." Jenny was reluctant to say more.

"Chust remember the Lord God knows your heart better than you know it yourself."

It was hard not to like this woman. "And He still loves us, in spite of ourselves," Jenny added.

"Jah, despite our shortcomings."

They sipped their tea; several cups' worth, it was so tasty. A large plate of treats graced the middle of the table, including two Jenny didn't recognize. Her generous hostess seemed happy to name them off: pineapple cookies and walnut drops. There were sand tarts, as well.

"You're spoiling me," Jenny said.

"Well, now, you've been through a rough week, I s'pose. So why not sit back and enjoy?"

Jenny agreed. "You're very kind, thank you."

Ella Mae dipped her head and demurely peeked up at her.

"I'm awful glad you came, or I would've been takin' tea alone this afternoon."

"Do you have tea at different times of day like the Brits do?"

"I honestly don't know what they do over there, dearie. I've been known to drink tea three times in a day, sometimes with my noon meal, which is considered dinnertime amongst the Amish."

Jenny smiled. "Marnie filled me in on that and many other things before I made the decision to come here."

"Marnie's a *gut* and faithful friend."

"Jah, and it's almost as if we've grown up together."

"Did you see each other a few times before you started writing letters?"

"Actually, it was after we first met that we began exchanging letters. Each summer after that, we've visited at the Bird-in-Hand Farmers Market, taking several walks together."

"But you never stayed in an Amish home till now?"

"No." She didn't say that Marnie's mother had been nervous about her daughter being friends with an Englisher.

"It must be quite the experience, livin' in an Amish house."

"It's different than I thought."

"In what ways?"

Jenny mentioned the nearly nonstop work, as well as the specific duties required of women versus men. "There's so much cooking. No matter how much food Rebecca and I prepare, there are rarely leftovers."

Ella Mae tittered. "There aren't many shy folk at the table round here. Second and third helpings are mighty common."

They talked about the current wedding season, and Ella Mae mentioned she had three great-granddaughters getting married between this Thursday and the middle of December. "Thankfully, they all didn't choose the same day!"

"Could you possibly attend more than one wedding in a day?" Jenny asked.

"Well, that's just the thing . . . ya can, but not the whole day, ya know." Ella Mae reached for another sand tart she'd been eyeing. "It's all right to eat a few of these, ya know. They're ever so thin."

Jenny smiled. "I noticed that, too. Trust me, these cookies are an art form. You should see mine—well, maybe not. They're at least five times thicker."

Ella Mae gave a wave of her hand. "Ach, I have little else to do nowadays. My eyes are wearin' out, so I don't do tatting or embroidery anymore." She looked about the kitchen and the small sitting room adjoining. "I much prefer to bake, and the more I do, the thinner my sand tarts get, I daresay."

Jenny wondered if, at times, even baking posed a challenge for the frail-looking woman.

"Growing old has its moments." Ella Mae's voice grew weary. "Times of reckoning, for sure and for certain."

"Do you have any regrets?" Jenny asked, hoping she wasn't being too prying.

"Honestly, if I think on it, I'm embarrassed by some of my youthful decisions." Ella Mae paused to touch one of the strings of her Kapp. "And, if I may be so bold to say, some of the church's, too."

Jenny was so surprised, she didn't know what to make of this.

"Ach, but you're startin' out . . . chust comin' into the Old Ways." Ella Mae turned her face to the window. "I'd never want to discourage you on your journey. Never."

"Rebecca tells me the People aren't perfect—no church is," Jenny said.

"And she's right." Ella Mae reached over and took hold

of her hand. Her eyes welled up as she searched Jenny's face and gently squeezed her fingers. "Never forget that, dearie. Keep your eyes fixed on the Lord Jesus, and you'll never be disappointed."

The words of the Wise Woman, as Rebecca said she was called, settled in as Jenny thanked Ella Mae for inviting her to the lovely tea, then reached for the shawl and bonnet before heading out the door into the cold air. Even colder now that the sun was concealed by a long, flimsy cloud, like a windblown bridal veil.

She's embarrassed by some of the church's decisions. Jenny stood silently on the porch, letting Ella Mae's poignant words linger. At the very least, she hoped she might return for another visit. Perhaps she might become a helpful friend to the elderly woman who had affected her so deeply, moving her in ways Jenny did not fully comprehend.

Was she giving me a warning? Jenny wondered as she walked down the narrow sidewalk. Then again, Ella Mae had stated that she didn't want to discourage Jenny.

She turned to look back at the little dwelling built onto the larger house, which belonged to Ella Mae's daughter Mattie Beiler. And as she did, she noticed a man with a very bushy brown beard walking out of the main farmhouse across the small yard. When he spotted her there, his ruddy face broke into a broad smile.

"Aren't you Jenny Burns, the seeker from Connecticut?" he asked, coming her way.

"Yes, uh . . . jah." She'd seen him before—the middle-aged man in the buggy that had passed them on Sunday after church. This was the father of the boy who had skated to and from Preaching.

"Well, I'm mighty pleased to meet ya." He stuck out his

big callused hand. "Hezekiah Stoltzfus is my name. Just call me Hezzy, if you don't mind."

"Denki." She quickly let go of his hand.

"I'm Mary Beiler's uncle, just over pickin' up some mending." He nodded in what Jenny assumed was the direction of the bishop's place. "I go over there to help the minister out some with the livestock and whatnot all." He glanced back toward Mattie Beiler's house. "Ya might not know the bishop and Ella Mae's son-in-law, David, are brothers." He laughed heartily. "Goodness knows, nearly all of us are related here in the hollow."

She gave him what she hoped was a polite smile, noticing how dark his beard was compared to his peppered, graying hair. It crossed her mind that he might be using hair dye on his beard, assuming an Amishman would do such a thing. "Well, I'd better get going."

"I'm headin' out, too . . . why don't I give you a lift, Jenny?"

Yikes, she thought, wondering how to get out of this gracefully. No way was she getting into his carriage. Next thing, all of Hickory Hollow would have her linked to this older man!

She was thinking of what to say so as not to offend him when she heard the squeak of Ella Mae's screen door, followed by her thin voice. "Jenny, dear?"

"Excuse me, please," she said, grateful for this unexpected yet convenient distraction. She ran back to Ella Mae's house. "What is it?" Jenny asked.

"Won't ya come inside for a moment?" Ella Mae pushed the door open wider and eyed Hezekiah, who appeared to be waiting for Jenny's answer.

"Thank you," Jenny whispered, trying to keep a straight face, even though Ella Mae did not. She remembered her manners and turned to offer a polite wave to the man, who nodded, seemingly disappointed, but there was a hopeful glint in his eyes.

"*Gut* to meet ya. Maybe another time?"

"Have a nice day!" Jennie practically blurted. And then, when the door was closed, Jenny breathed a sigh of relief. "You saved me!"

Ella Mae's grin was mischievous. "You stay right here till he's *gut* and gone, if ya'd like."

"Believe me, you don't have to ask twice." And Jenny thanked the Wise Woman once again.

Chapter 19

J enny followed Ella Mae through the connecting door to her married daughter's farmhouse. There, she was introduced to Mattie Beiler, who'd only just returned from visiting a sick relative. The woman looked as though she was in her sixties—evidently her husband, David, was the bishop's much older brother.

"Mattie's helped deliver many a baby here locally," the Wise Woman said.

"Your mother certainly is a lovely person," Jenny said as she shook Mattie's hand and smiled back at Ella Mae.

"I agree," replied Mattie. "And her peppermint tea's not bad, either."

They laughed, exchanging glances.

Like every other Amishwoman Jenny had visited, Mattie offered a treat, along with something to drink. Almost without waiting for their response, Mattie began to pour some hot coffee. "I heard from my sister-in-law Mary—the bishop's wife—that she'd like you to stay with her three youngest children tomorrow morning, Jenny. She needs to run some errands for a couple of hours."

Jenny asked what time she should be over there.

"Right after breakfast is fine. The bishop's place is real close to Samuel and Rebecca's—right across the field, in fact," Mattie said.

"Yes, I've been there." Jenny glanced at Ella Mae. "And anyway, I managed to find *this* house, didn't I?"

That brought a chuckle from both women, and the three of them sat down and sipped black coffee and had some fresh-baked oatmeal-and-raisin cookies. A few minutes later, Mattie brought out little cakes topped with coconut, and some tempting butterscotch cookies, too. Jenny was starting to think the women who lived in this house were always either baking or eating!

"I noticed Hezzy out there talkin' to ya," Mattie said, looking right at Jenny. "He's Mary's widowed uncle—has a whole passel of children. But he's just friendly."

"He means well," Ella Mae added, looking tired.

Jenny wondered if she might have overstayed her welcome. "I should get back to help Rebecca," she said, smiling her thanks again to Ella Mae. "The goodies were delicious," she told Mattie. "I'm going to get fat if I keep snacking like this."

"Well, have yourself a nice walk back," Mattie said. "And if Hezzy swings round to catch ya on the road, don't be timid 'bout talkin' to him."

"Oh, for pity's sake, Mattie," said Ella Mae. "Leave the girl be! She's just begun her Proving, remember?"

Mattie was grinning. "Puh! I have my opinion and you have yours, ain't?"

"Isn't that the truth?" replied Ella Mae.

Jenny laughed, but she wasn't keen on the idea of going back to the Lapps' without the covering of a carriage—a place to hide from Hezzy's very wide grin. If only she'd hurry and learn how to hitch up a horse!

All the way up Hickory Lane, she was vividly aware of the many carriages and wagons coming and going. She even held her breath as they passed—and was quite relieved when they did.

Marnie was more than pleased when a letter arrived in the afternoon mail from Roy Flaud. Her heart fluttered to beat the band. *Glory be!* He'd kindly offered to meet her at her cousin's wedding on Thursday morning. Marnie could hardly wait to see him again, she missed him so.

I'd like to talk to you further about the house meeting I mentioned in my earlier note, he'd written toward the middle of the page. Roy went on about how it was something he'd contemplated a lot. *I feel we ought to go as an engaged couple . . . making our own choices.*

She read further, realizing that it was just as clear from the rest of the letter that Roy wanted her to reconsider her stance. *Maybe he'd best talk to Dat about this,* she thought. *Dare I even suggest that?*

Roy was so very important to her; she knew without a doubt he loved her. But it was peculiar that he was pushing her this way. She'd pondered more than a few times that he hadn't been baptized into his Bird-in-Hand church district yet. But then, neither had she joined church in Hickory Hollow, waiting to follow her beau's lead. Still, being solidly Amish was as serious a matter for Marnie as it was to her parents.

A shiver ran down her back at the thought of upsetting

her father over such a thing. *Never!* she promised herself, recalling his rage over her older brother's brief flirtation with the fancy world.

··· ➤ ◄ ···

Rebecca had long since finished grooming Ol' Molasses. Presently, she made preparations for supper without Jenny's help, wondering what was keeping her. She continued chopping the onions, celery, and carrots for her thick stew, aware of the vacant spot at the counter where Jenny usually worked. Rebecca pursed her lips to keep them from quivering. What was wrong with her, checking the wall clock every five minutes? Was she already that wrapped up in the seeker?

She brushed such thoughts aside and tried to focus more on understanding why Jenny had kept her family in the dark about coming here. *Was it really because they hold enough sway over her to change her mind? Or is there something else, something she hasn't yet revealed?*

Rebecca stopped her work to wipe her forehead with a hankie. Goodness, maybe she ought to take to heart Ella Mae's initial concerns about Jenny's motives—whatever they might be. Even so, if the young woman was staying in Hickory Hollow only to search for an Amish husband, her demeanor and attitude did not lend itself to those leanings.

Truth be told, Jenny's auburn hair and personality were a constant reminder of Katie, who had also left her family to follow her heart. Rebecca's breath caught in her throat.

Dearest Katie, living out her days as a Mennonite. Sighing deeply, Rebecca couldn't help but wonder if her adopted daughter ever missed her former Amish life, the heritage of her childhood. *The life Samuel and I gave her.*

Rebecca gathered up the chopped vegetables from the wooden cutting board and placed them in a large bowl, then added some cubed beef for the stew. Silently, she offered up a plea for Dan and Katie's return to the church of their families.

How much longer, O Lord?

... ➤ ➤ ...

I managed to catch up with my chores as soon as I arrived back from the interesting visit with Ella Mae Zook—and her daughter Mattie Beiler. Dived right into baking some pumpkin walnut bread and twelve dozen chocolate macaroons, which Rebecca plans to take to market tomorrow while I help the bishop's wife with her youngest children.

Also, after supper, I helped mend Samuel's shirts with Rebecca, who didn't talk as much as she usually does while we worked. I caught her looking at me rather suspiciously once or twice. Is something bothering her?

And, because I really want my own clothing, instead of wearing Katie's old dresses, I cut out two—one blue, one green. It was strange, having the house so quiet while I worked in Rebecca's small sewing room down the hall, but both Samuel and Rebecca seemed extra tired today. Maybe grooming the horse wore Rebecca out, and now, in retrospect, I wish I would have stayed to help her. Such a hardworking woman! Yet I so enjoyed spending time with Ella Mae. I can see why everyone refers to her as the Old Wise Woman.

As for tomorrow, I'm nervous about taking care of the bishop's kids, wanting to do everything exactly as Mary wishes. I've never cared for the children of someone "anointed by God," as I've heard the People describe the bishop. To think I've yet to even meet this revered man!

As often as she committed tomorrow to the Lord, Jenny had difficulty shaking off her apprehension of the man who'd put Katie and her husband under the dreaded veil of the shunning.

Chapter 20

Rebecca hardly made eye contact with Jenny during breakfast preparations the next morning, though she was cordial enough. Perhaps she was only tired—Rebecca looked worn out, despite the fact she was typically a whirlwind of energy. Considering this, Jenny felt reluctant to leave the house to help Mary Beiler today, even though Mattie Beiler had said Jenny was expected over at the bishop's. It seemed strange that Jenny hadn't heard directly from Mary about this. Was it the Amish way for one person to tell another until the information found its way to the correct set of ears?

No need for cell phones here!

Rebecca quietly handed Jenny a platter of pancakes to carry to the table. Her hostess's rather sudden detachment weighed on Jenny. What had changed between them?

When Jenny arrived at the Beilers' farmhouse, the back door was standing open, but the storm door was closed. So she knocked softly, her pulse fluttering like a hummingbird in her throat.

I'll be working for the man who holds my very future in his hands! No one came, and she knocked harder, hoping Mattie hadn't gotten her wires crossed about Jenny's being needed this morning.

Should she keep knocking?

Unsure of herself, Jenny raised her hand again, and at that second Mary appeared, coming this way through the utility room. She beamed when she spotted Jenny and appeared dressed for errands in a pretty maroon dress and matching apron. Her black outer bonnet was already perched on her blond head, its black strings hanging down the front.

"Oh, *gut*, you did get the message from my sister-in-law. Mattie said you'd be visiting Ella Mae yesterday." Mary smiled. "The girls are lookin' forward to seeing you again. Emily and Anna are playing with their dollies in the playpen." She continued, saying Jenny didn't have to entertain them. "Just be close by if they need anything." Mary waved at Mary Mae, who sat at the table coloring.

Jenny wondered why the two younger girls were confined so, but she didn't ask.

"You'll find fresh-baked cookies in the cookie jar," Mary said, pointing to the counter on the left side of the sink. "John's out in the barn, feeding the livestock. He won't be inside till I return to cook the noon meal. But if ya need anything, just holler."

Jenny nodded, careful to pay close attention.

"If you wouldn't mind peeling those potatoes for me, that'd be a mighty big help." She indicated the mound on the counter in a large plastic mixing bowl. "Mary Mae likes to scrub 'em, so she'll be a *gut* little helper."

"Sure, that's fine," Jenny replied, glancing at the three darling girls sitting so quietly.

Mary reached down and touched the baby's head. "You children behave yourselves for Jenny, won't ya now?" The girls looked up at her solemnly as Mary repeated her instructions for them in Deitsch.

"I love their names," Jenny said.

Mary smiled and blushed a bit as she reached for her black woolen shawl and tied her black bonnet under her round chin. She picked up a wicker basket with a blue-and-white-checked cloth covering over it. "Like I said, I'll be back shortly. Denki ever so much, Jenny."

"Take your time." Jenny followed her to the back door, wondering if she should secure it behind her. Not knowing for sure, she locked it anyway.

Mary dashed out to the waiting horse and family carriage, her heavy wrap swooshing against her calves.

Just knowing she would likely not encounter the bishop today put Jenny more at ease. Turning back to the two younger girls, she sat on the wood bench on one side of the long table and smiled down into the playpen at them.

"*Wu is Dat?*" three-year-old Emily asked, grinning at her coyly, then standing and leaning her little head against the playpen railing.

"Your daddy's outside," Jenny said in English. She hadn't brought along the Deitsch dictionary and couldn't piece together anything the child could understand.

"Dawdi?" the little girl said.

"Nee, not Dawdi . . . Dat."

Oh, was this ever frustrating! Mary Mae looked at her curiously, then said something softly to Emily, which seemed to satisfy the younger girl. *Maybe this will work out after all*, Jenny thought.

A half hour later, someone startled her with a knock at the back door. Jenny looked up in the midst of playing dolls with the girls. There stood Hezekiah Stoltzfus, peering in against the pane of glass, jiggling the door handle.

"Oh boy," she whispered, glancing back at the girls as she made her way through the kitchen.

"Yes, what is it?" she asked through the door, keeping it closed—she wanted to be known as a principled young woman in this place of conservative expectations.

"Is Bishop John around anywhere?" he asked, surprise evident on his face, as well.

"Mary said he's in the barn."

Hezekiah smiled and straightened up. "Well, all right, then." With that, he turned and hurried across the lawn.

She closed the inside door, which made the utility room less bright, but she felt better about it.

Remembering the potatoes, Jenny began to wash and set about peeling them, amazed at the happy sound of the unintelligible murmurings between the adorable little girls in the corner.

In a few minutes, Mary Mae slid off the bench, scooted a chair over to the sink, and crawled up on it to stand next to Jenny. Very soon the two of them had a system going as the heap of potatoes on the counter began to diminish in size. Mary Mae washed them and passed them on to the opposite sink for peeling by Jenny. The long strips piled up quickly in the second sink.

While she worked, Mary Mae chattered to Jenny in Deitsch, as though Jenny understood. It was so endearing. She loved having this opportunity to work alongside such a small Amish girl.

If my sister saw this, she'd be shocked speechless!

When Jenny finished peeling the potatoes, she washed her hands, dried them, and checked on little Anna, who'd fallen asleep on one of the cloth dolls in a corner of the playpen. Meanwhile, Emily continued playing in the opposite corner, talking quietly to her doll. Mary Mae went to a hutchlike buffet on the other side of the kitchen, opened the second drawer, and pulled out some construction paper and a blunt pair of scissors. Then, without being told, she slid onto the wood bench and sat at the table.

This job is a piece of cake. As Jenny wandered into what Rebecca called the front room, she wished Mary had assigned her more housework. A large German family Bible lay on top of a beautiful wooden writing desk, but she didn't touch it, only admired it.

In the near corner stood a tall oak cupboard, obviously custom made and quite old, though not an antique. She was especially drawn to the tea sets and decorative plates inside, all lined up in a colorful fashion in their respective grooves.

Seeing these items reminded her of the shop in Essex, where she'd enjoyed the parade of furnishings and trinkets from long ago. It had been fun to assist the customers who had come to purchase antiques. *Cherishing the past.*

Jenny wandered back toward the kitchen, through the small room just beyond the front room, and smiled to see a rocker made of beautiful bleached willow branches. It crossed her mind to sit in it to see how comfortable it was, but Mary hadn't actually said to make herself at home. Not like most of the women she'd baby-sat for as a teenager, who had shown her the soda in the fridge and offered stacks of movies to peruse.

Just then she noticed Hezekiah Stoltzfus walking outdoors with another man, presumably the bishop, who looked younger than she'd envisioned. Better looking, too—tall, blond, with the predictable full beard of a married Amishman.

The two men stood and talked for a short time before getting into Hezekiah's carriage and riding off.

"The bishop must trust me a lot," Jenny whispered.

Had Rebecca put a good word in for her? Why else would Bishop Beiler be comfortable with a near stranger in charge of his youngest children?

Mary Mae's head leaned close to her paper and scissors as she worked to cut out various shapes. Jenny strolled about the kitchen, intrigued by the unusual wall clock with fanciful black trim and the large pastoral calendar hanging on the back of the cellar door. If their cold cellar was anything like Rebecca Lapp's, there were rows and rows of canning jars lining the shelves down there. *"As many as eight hundred,"* Rebecca had said.

Jenny noticed a slip of paper in the center of the gaspowered fridge and tried to read the Deitsch: *Dan un Katie Fisher hawwe Gemee an die Haus.* The names startled her—it was something about Rebecca's son-in-law and daughter. And as Jenny read the Deitsch, she realized she understood it—even *Gemee,* which she'd heard Marnie say. The words were similar to their German counterparts. Evidently Dan and Katie Fisher were having meetings of some kind in their house. *Bible studies, perhaps?* Jenny wondered. She knew this wouldn't be acceptable in Hickory Hollow, but Dan and Katie were shunned.

What's the purpose of this note?

Jenny was so curious, she determined to find a way to ask Rebecca about it. *As if she'd know . . .* Then Jenny realized that was silly. Neither Samuel nor Rebecca would likely be aware of this.

Would Marnie know?

"*Gucke, Maidel.*" Mary Mae's voice broke into her thoughts. The little girl smiled and pointed to her cutout design.

"Oh, it's very pretty," Jenny said. Then, trying to communicate better, she went over and lightly touched the art before pointing to her own smile. She so wanted to talk to Mary Mae, but the language barrier was just that—an obstruction between herself and the sweet girl.

Jenny sat on the bench next to her and picked up a green crayon, drawing a smiley face in the upper right-hand corner of one of the sheets of paper. "Jah?"

Mary Mae's eyes sparkled. "Jah," she replied, bobbing her head up and down. She reached for the coloring book and pointed to the right side, babbling nonstop in Deitsch as she poked the page closest to Jenny.

"You want me to color with you," Jenny said, happy to indulge.

Some time later, Emily began to squirm and stood up waiting quietly for Jenny to give the nod that she could get out of the playpen. When Jenny got up to get her, Emily had already leaned over the railing and climbed out.

Unable to resist, Jenny offered her a hand and brought her over to look at Mary Mae's artwork. She sat down with Emily next to her, and was surprised when Mary Mae put a blue crayon in Emily's hand and turned the page, talking to her in Deitsch. "It's always nice to share with your sister," Jenny said, smiling again at the five-year-old, delighted at this gesture. The youngster obviously exemplified the training of her Amish mother. Sharing was precious, but it had to be taught.

Jenny heard a commotion outside and turned toward the kitchen window. Unbelievably, a cow ambled past, heading down the driveway. "Oh no!"

Another cow came along, right behind. Glancing at Anna, still asleep in the playpen, and the two older girls sitting at the table, Jenny hurried to the utility room to look out the windows there. A third Holstein bellowed after the first two. She unlocked the back door and stared out. It certainly appeared the barnyard fence was broken or someone had accidently left a gate open. What else could have happened?

Jenny's first inclination was to rush and secure the barnyard fence, but then she looked toward the road and saw the trio of cows lumbering down that way.

Oh, what should I do? She wrung her apron hem, distraught. *Dare I leave the girls alone and attempt to bring back the cows?*

Chapter 21

Rebecca Lapp gasped. She could see three black-and-white heifers rambling down the middle of Hickory Lane. "Samuel, *kumme schnell!*" she called out the back door, then reached for an old jacket and hurried for the steps.

In no time, Samuel flew out the barn door and came running across the yard, this way.

"Someone's cows got out," she hollered, not waiting for Samuel to catch up. But he quickly outran her, headed straight for the road. "Pity's sake, whose are they?"

Samuel kept going, taking off his straw hat and calling, "Coboss! Shoo . . . get on home now." He blocked their way, waving at the lead cow. "Coboss!"

"Oh, goodness. Ain't the bishop's, are they?"

Samuel nodded. "Certainly are."

Rebecca's heart sank. Surely this had nothing to do with Jenny Burns.

Ach, mercy no . . . surely not!

Jenny felt nervous about leaving the children unattended and went back to the kitchen to check on Anna, who remained sound asleep, her little head cushioned by a light blanket.

Smiling, Jenny reached for Emily and motioned for Mary Mae to come along with her, as well. She led them to the utility room, where she swiftly helped Emily put on her coat and a small black winter bonnet while Mary Mae dressed herself. Jenny then slipped on Rebecca's shawl and woolen scarf before hurrying outside with both girls.

"See there?" Jenny pointed to the barnyard and tried to explain what she assumed had happened. And she soon verified what she'd suspected—the barn gate was open just enough for the cows to wander out. Had more escaped than she'd seen?

Reaching up, she secured the gate and heard voices in the field behind her. She and the girls turned to see Samuel Lapp herding three cows across the harvested cornfield, Rebecca coming close behind, her cheeks bright pink from the cold.

"Oh, good, the cows are back," Jenny said, relieved. *I think we'd better open the gate again*, she thought as Mary Mae and Emily clapped their hands, all smiles.

Once the cows were safely corralled, Jenny invited Samuel and Rebecca indoors to warm up. She offered them the hot coffee already on the stove, and Rebecca suggested they ought to wait around for Bishop John and Mary to return. Jenny wasn't sure why they felt the need but was glad to see Rebecca acting more like her old self.

Samuel played with Emily, bouncing her on his knee till she could hardly stop giggling. Mary Mae showed off her coloring pictures and cutout designs first to Rebecca, then to Samuel before placing them on the refrigerator with magnets of pigs and cows.

Jenny was tempted to show Rebecca the refrigerator note about Dan and Katie's house meetings but decided against it, not knowing how Samuel might react to that sort of news. *I can only imagine. . . .*

Later, when Mary returned, Rebecca was quick to tell her what good care Jenny had given the girls. "She even managed to keep an eye on the cows—got the gate closed before more scurried off."

Mary nodded and looked pleased as she took it all in. But before long, Jenny noticed Mary glance at the fridge, frown, and rise promptly to remove the note. Without saying a word, Mary opened the cupboard and slipped the note inside.

So she didn't *want me to see it . . . let alone Samuel and Rebecca!*

The feast began shortly after Marnie's cousin Linda Ebersol's three-hour wedding service the next day. Marnie blushed when she caught Roy gazing fondly at her from across the room. Her heart did a little flutter, and she thought ahead to that evening's barn Singing for the courting-age youth. *Many of them are couples like Roy and me.*

But she didn't have to endure the long afternoon hours waiting for that particular gathering to bring them face-to-face, or for the feel of her small hand in his. After the delicious meal and a brief time of hymn singing, Roy gave her a sign with his brown eyes and a meaningful dip of his head. He slipped out the back door, intending for her to follow, which she did, after donning her warmest woolen coat and black outer bonnet and gloves.

"Oh, Marnie. I could hardly wait to be alone like this,"

Roy said as he led her around behind the big barn, where the sun shone against the white wood slats and made it more tolerable to be out in the cold.

She smiled, longing to say the same thing back but letting him do the talking instead. And just that quick, he was leaning closer, smiling down at her, blocking the sun from her eyes. She looked up at him, taking in the arch of his brow, the intensity of his gaze . . . and all the while her heart pounded nearly out of her ears.

"The Lord Gott is ever near, Marnie," Roy whispered. "As close to you—and to me—as we are now. Closer, really." He paused a second. "And I believe He wants us to understand how much He cares for us through the experiences we're havin'."

"What experiences?" She could hardly speak.

"The one I'm askin' you to share with me." He leaned ever near, his breath on her face. "Marnie, I want you to go with me to the house meeting I wrote you about. More than anything."

"But—"

Roy tilted his head and sweetly kissed her cheek. Then, moving slightly back, he looked deep into her eyes. "Will ya do this . . . for me? Just this once?"

"I'd do anything for ya, Roy . . . you know that."

"Then you'll go?"

Those pleading eyes of his . . . how he adored her. She simply could not refuse her darling beau. "Jah, I'll go along. But only once."

His face beamed as he leaned down to kiss her other cheek. "You've made me a very happy man today, my sweetheart-girl."

Oh, she wanted to wrap her arms around his neck and never let go. "When's the meeting?" she asked, folding her hands against her wrap.

"I'll pick you up next Tuesday evening, round six-thirty."
He reached for her right hand and began removing her glove.

"What're ya doin', Roy?"

"You'll see." He raised her smooth, bare hand to his lips and
kissed the back of it so tenderly she thought she might cry.

"I love you so," Roy said, pressing her hand to his chest.
"You know that, don't ya?"

Marnie smiled and nodded her head, locking eyes with
her future husband. "You sure know how to change my mind,
ain't so?"

And concerns of her father's displeasure flew fast away.

Chapter 22

The following Monday, Jenny helped Rebecca run the dirty laundry through the wringer washer. It was so tedious and time-consuming, she actually missed using an automatic washer and dryer. As the two women worked side by side, they talked about the remainder of the wedding season, as well as other upcoming church-related activities.

Finally, after considering it to death, Jenny got up the nerve to tell Rebecca about the strange note she'd seen on Mary Beiler's refrigerator. "I wondered if I should say anything," Jenny said quietly. "I don't want to be inappropriate."

"Well, I'm glad ya spoke up." Rebecca's naturally rosy cheeks drained of color.

"What do you think it means—or isn't it important now that they're . . . um, outside Amish jurisdiction?"

Rebecca nodded slowly. "S'posin' if I'd seen it, maybe I'd know who wrote it. That'd be a clue."

"I guess there's a lot I don't understand about being Amish."

"Never mind that, Jenny. Either the bishop was informing Mary, or vice versa, is my guess."

"A warning?" asked Jenny.

"Katie and her husband are adults," Rebecca said, frowning. "What they do is their business."

Jenny wasn't surprised at her response. On one hand, Rebecca had every right to be defensive. Yet on the other, shouldn't she reflect the mindset behind the shunning and in line with the church ordinance? *And the bishop*.

"Maybe I shouldn't have brought it up," Jenny said.

"Nee, I'm glad ya did." Rebecca took out another of Samuel's shirts before she said more. "It's just that I sometimes feel awful sorry for Katie. Same for Daniel."

Jenny heard the pain in her voice. "I'm sure you miss them terribly."

Rebecca pressed her lips together and said nothing for a moment. "More than I could ever say."

"I shouldn't ask this, but do you exchange letters sometimes?"

"Now and then," she replied, adding quickly, "'cause writing letters is allowed."

Jenny noticed an odd blink of Rebecca's eyes and a twitch of her head. Was the probing question out of order?

"Talking about this makes you sad, I can see that." Jenny sighed. "I'm sorry for that."

Rebecca remained silent. And Jenny decided to say no more regarding the agonizing topic.

··· ➤ ◀ ···

The afternoon was perfect for drying clothes on the line, thanks to a brilliant sun and a steady breeze. Jenny finished sewing the last of her new dresses while Rebecca worked on the final three pink roses on a pillowcase to be sold at market.

Rebecca set down her work at the kitchen table and

mentioned that the bishop had dropped by that morning to speak to Samuel. "He was mighty impressed with your '*gut* judgment' last week when his cows got out."

"I'm sure he was equally grateful for your help, and Samuel's, in bringing them back."

"Jah, that, too . . . but he's been tellin' everyone what you did, Jenny." Rebecca's eyes were serious. "You did well. Wasn't like it was a planned test."

But a test, all the same.

They worked silently for a time, and Jenny let Rebecca's words sink in. To think this had come from a man she still had not had the occasion to meet.

Seemingly out of the blue, Rebecca said, "We must always work to improve ourselves, ya know. It's one of the best goals."

"Where does grace come into play?"

"Ah, the age-old question of God's grace versus our obedience to His commandments. Many mistake obedience for tryin' to work one's way into the kingdom," Rebecca said solemnly.

Jenny wished she weren't so hung up on whether she was doing the right thing. "Do you think the Lord sometimes wants us to move out of our comfort zone?"

"Depends on what ya mean."

"I've been thinking," Jenny said hesitantly. "What would you say if I invited my parents to visit me here?"

Rebecca's needle stopped in midair, and she looked toward the window. Was it just Jenny's imagination, or was Rebecca trying to gather her wits? "Perfectly fine with me." Rebecca put down her sewing and looked right at her.

"I've been considering it for a while."

"Well, I'd say that's a wonderful-*gut* idea, Jenny. It may be time your family knows your plans, ain't?"

"I've gone back and forth—even had a dream about it. It feels right to me now. And I'm more confident about talking to them."

"'Tis *gut.*" Rebecca fixed her eyes on her.

Just then Jenny saw Marnie coming down the road. She excused herself and dashed out to grab the shawl off the wooden peg.

Marnie saw her waving and headed into the lane. "Hullo, Jenny. Wie geht's?"

"*Recht gut.*"

Marnie smiled at Jenny's reply, and they chattered happily, though mostly in English. Marnie noted how well Jenny was picking up common phrases in Deitsch.

"How was your cousin's wedding?" asked Jenny.

Marnie filled her in on the special day, her eyes alight when she revealed that her boyfriend from Bird-in-Hand had spent the whole day with her. "And . . . we've got some interesting plans. But that's all I best be sayin'."

"A boyfriend, you say?" Jenny smiled. "Sounds to me as though you have more than one secret!"

"Most definitely . . . and I hope I don't catch it later."

"You aren't going to run off and get married, are you?"

"Goodness, I wouldn't miss out on havin' a regular wedding. Not for anything." Marnie grinned.

"Great, since I'd like to attend."

Marnie asked if she had the pictures of her family. "Not to pester, but I'd like to see 'em."

"Oh, I'm happy to show you." Jenny invited her into the house, stopping for Marnie to greet Rebecca, who was still sewing at the table.

When they were upstairs, Jenny latched the bedroom door and went to the dresser to retrieve a small book of photos.

"It's the only album I brought," she said, going to sit with Marnie on the edge of the bed. "Funny, but I haven't looked at it even once since I arrived."

"Really?" Marnie cocked her head. "Do ya think it will make ya miss your family more?"

Jenny hadn't thought of that. "I guess we'll find out, jah?"

Marnie placed her hand on top of the album. "Seriously, I don't have to see it today."

"Don't be silly; I want you to." Jenny opened the book and displayed more than a dozen pictures of her parents, Kiersten and Robb, and Cameron. Slowly, she flipped through the snapshots, answering Marnie's questions about who was who and the events surrounding each photo. It was nice to see Marnie so interested.

Then, turning to the last page, Jenny was shocked to see a shot of Kyle Jackson and herself smiling, cheek to cheek. "What's this doing here?" she muttered. *I thought I destroyed all the pictures!*

"Who's *that?*" Marnie peered closer, her Kapp strings falling forward.

"Just a guy."

"Well, it looks like you're in love with him."

Jenny recalled the special evening and all the joy surrounding that day of her college graduation. Kyle had surprised her, flying in with her parents and brother. Jenny remembered the way he'd leaned close to her right as the picture was taken, how he had smelled of spicy cologne.

She felt overwhelmed at the clarity of the memory and the many emotions the picture evoked.

"Jenny . . . are you all right?"

"I *did* love him, Marnie," she whispered, tears welling up. "I loved him very much."

"And by the looks of you, maybe ya still do?" Marnie touched her arm.

"Actually, I don't know why I said that. It's ridiculous." She explained that the relationship had ended sadly—he couldn't understand her passion for the Plain life, the one thing she longed for. "But that was two years ago," she added. "He's apologized since for not handling our breakup with more tact. He's not a bad guy . . . just not the one."

"Your first love, then?"

Jenny nodded.

"Roy's mine." Marnie shook her head and looked at the ceiling. "Honestly, I don't know how I'd manage without him. Ach, I shouldn't have said that. Don't mean to make things hard—"

"Don't worry," Jenny assured her. "I'm happy for you."

Marnie opened her mouth to say something but stopped and shook her head.

"What is it?" asked Jenny.

"Just thinking, is all."

Jenny wondered how long Marnie had been dating Roy but didn't ask, thinking perhaps she and Marnie had shared enough for one visit. "Would you care for a snack?"

"Sure, I'm always ready for sweets."

Jenny put away the album, still shocked the photo of her and Kyle had managed to follow her here. *Our best picture together, too.*

Leading Marnie downstairs, Jenny felt embarrassed that she'd mentioned Kyle Jackson. Considering the reason for their breakup, he was the last person she ever wanted to talk about in the midst of her adjustment to Amish life.

Chapter 23

As was her custom following Bible reading and silent prayers, Jenny usually spent the rest of the evening prior to bedtime in her room reading her devotional book or writing in her journal.

Tonight, however, she decided to go ahead with the letter she had been formulating in her mind for days. *Time to tell all.*

Dear Mom and Dad,

Thanks for your patience. You're probably wondering what I've been up to. I hope you will try to understand what I've been doing for the past nearly two weeks. And where I'm living.

Do you remember when I pleaded for an Amish bonnet for my twelfth birthday, Mom? You somehow managed to purchase a handmade one, and I proudly displayed it on my dresser mirror.

Well, my goal is to own—and wear—a real head covering someday: the Old Order Amish kind. So I'm renting a room from Samuel and Rebecca Lapp, who live in a small area of Lancaster County called Hickory Hollow, just east of Bird-in-Hand, Pennsylvania. I'm surrounded by farmland,

and I love it. My hope is to live, dress, and work here as a baptized Amishwoman for the rest of my life.

This isn't an easy path, but it's my heart's desire . . . and perhaps you're not too surprised. Haven't I always loved the countryside and doing things the old-fashioned way?

I'd really love for you to visit me here and to meet the Lapps and the other wonderful people I've come to know. Samuel and Rebecca have encouraged me to invite you, so you'll be very welcome.

Please reply to me at the return address on the envelope.

With love from your daughter,
Jenny

She held her breath thinking how her mother, especially, might receive the news. Rereading her letter, Jenny felt it was a bit stiff, even unemotional. But not knowing any other way to relate to her parents, she folded it and placed it in the bedside table drawer.

What if Mom and Dad show up and want to take me home? she thought unexpectedly. She could almost hear her father expressing his concern about certain cults or brainwashing. *Will they try to interfere?*

Jenny felt restless. Once or twice before, she'd contemplated going down to the springhouse to pray, and tonight she needed the fresh, cold air. So, taking her flashlight downstairs, she slipped on her warm outer bonnet and Rebecca's shawl. She opened the back door, thankful it didn't squeak, and made her way over the walkway and toward the peaceful haven. How she looked forward to talking with God! She yearned for more humility and for divine help in caring less about how she appeared to others. *It's prideful to worry so,* she thought, still hung up on the possibility of future faux pas . . . even her hair, though she was slowly getting used to not peering into a mirror each morning. She seemed to be in a tug-of-war with submission. Could she ever be as meek and obedient as Rebecca?

Turning off her flashlight, she knelt near the pond adjacent to the entrance of the little springhouse. Jenny folded her hands and bowed her head. "Dear Lord," she began to pray quietly, "my heart is bursting with thanksgiving tonight. I'm so grateful for your constant help . . . your continual presence."

She raised her eyes to the dark sky and watched the stars appear, one by one. "Please soften my parents to my plans," she whispered. "Prepare them for my letter. I know it will be strange, but if it is your will, please help them understand my heart for the very first time. . . ."

She paused. Just then across the pond, she saw a flicker of white. Was someone there?

Peering into the murky darkness, she saw what looked like the figure of a man perched on the stone wall near the water. Concerned, she stood quickly and hurried toward the steps away from the springhouse.

"Jenny . . . is that you?"

The voice was deep and familiar.

She turned. "Andrew Lapp?" Her reply echoed against the pond's surface.

"I didn't mean to frighten you," he said, coming her way, his flashlight guiding his steps.

"What are you doing here?" she asked, rattled at the knowledge she hadn't been alone.

"I come here to pray, too. Have for years."

She nodded dumbly, still trying to get over her surprise at being discovered here . . . and by him.

His chuckle lifted into the night. "Did I disturb you?"

She opened her mouth to answer but smiled instead.

"No better place to be alone with the Lord God, in my opinion," he said. He stood there looking at her, and she remembered bumping into him on the porch at Preaching service that first Sunday. "It's a wonderful-*gut* spot."

"Jah," she said softly.

"When it's bitter cold, I sometimes sneak inside the spring-house to finish my prayin'."

A twig cracked loudly in the near distance, and Andrew turned to look.

Jenny thought she saw movement in the trees along Hickory Lane. "Is someone watching us?" she whispered, unnerved.

"Prob'ly just a small critter." He smiled down at her. "I hope you're not nervous."

She was surprised he'd noticed. "I guess I am," she replied. "I wrote to my parents tonight, and I'm a little worried what they'll do when they read the letter."

"Just a *little* worried?"

She laughed timidly. "Okay, a lot."

"And why's that?"

"I doubt they'll understand." *They never have. . . .*

He was still for a moment. "But Gott does, don't forget."

"Denki for the reminder."

He inhaled audibly. "And, Jenny . . . something else."

"Jah?"

"I'm prayin' for you, too."

She blushed and wondered whether he could tell in the glow of the flashlight. "That's so kind of you."

"Honestly, I doubt I could do what you're settin' out to do. I mean, if the tables were turned and I was tryin' to find my way in the English world . . ."

"Thank goodness you aren't," she blurted before thinking. "I mean—"

"Don't fret; I think I know what you meant."

"Denki."

"You're one very thankful woman, I daresay." Andrew stepped back slightly. "Well, I'd best be on my way now. *Gut Nacht*, Jenny."

She almost hated to see him go. Waiting for a moment, she knelt again on the cold cement. But try as she might, she could not recover her prayerful attitude, not when she could hear Andrew's footsteps heading up the rocky wall toward the plowed cornfield.

So the private little area was not exclusively hers. A *shared altar of sorts*, she thought, feeling not at all disappointed by the discovery, but surprisingly warm inside. Warm . . . yet tentative.

Jenny rose, turned on her flashlight, and made her way back to the farmhouse.

Before going to bed, Jenny composed a letter to her friends Pamela and Dorie—the two sisters were roommates. While she wrote, she prayed their reactions, especially Dorie's, wouldn't be as negative as she feared. *Though justly deserved.*

Jenny considered inviting them to Hickory Hollow, too. But she decided against it before sealing the envelope and placing it in the drawer with the letter to her parents.

Later, as she nestled beneath the bed quilts, it was neither her parents nor Pamela and Dorie who occupied her thoughts. Rather, the memory of Andrew Lapp's emergence from the darkness at the springhouse looped round and round in Jenny's head.

Chapter 24

The Bird-in-Hand Farmers Market parking lot was crammed with cars, SUVs, and minivans Wednesday morning. Jenny presumed the milder weather had coaxed people out of their homes this mid-November day. After the cold snap of the past two days, the sun felt wonderfully warm, and there was not a cloud in the alluring blue sky.

Jenny and Rebecca carried in the carefully ironed embroidered pillowcases and hand-quilted potholders and matching place mats from the carriage, hoping to sell them within the first few hours. Two teen girls, obviously tourists, looked Jenny over, staring at her Amish garb. It wasn't the first time—there had been glares and pointing, even smothered laughter. All the same, Jenny felt embarrassed for the many Englishers who'd ever made fun of anyone unlike themselves.

Rebecca stopped to introduce Jenny to a number of vendor friends, including Elizabeth Miller and her pretty strawberry-blond daughter Tessie at Country Crafters. She also stopped at Groff's Candies and Aunt Ruthie's Specialties. But it was Emmalyn Lapp who caught Jenny's notice as Jenny took care to place the handmade items in the correct piles on the display table. Jenny was pleased as she stepped back to take a better look, glad she'd come to help Rebecca today.

Jenny kept tabs on Emmalyn out of the corner of her eye as the young woman inched closer. So as not to postpone the inevitable meeting, Jenny told Rebecca she would be right back and wandered over to the booth where Emmalyn was selling wooden horses and other handmade toys. "How are you, Emmalyn? I thought I'd come say hi."

"I saw *you* the other night," Emmalyn said, not bothering with a greeting.

"When?"

"Just think about it. . . ." Emmalyn's voice held a strange tone.

"What are you talking about?"

"You've honestly forgotten?" Emmalyn glowered. "You were with Andrew at the springhouse pond."

So she was there, too, snooping around!

Jenny refused to honor her accusing tone with a response. She glanced back at Rebecca, whose hands were moving rapidly as she talked in Deitsch.

"Don't get too close to my brother" came the angry words.

Jenny shivered. What was wrong with this girl?

A young Amish mother with identical twin boys tucked into a double stroller rushed past them, apologizing as she went.

"Listen, Emmalyn, I don't understand what you want from me."

"I want nothin', and the same goes for my brother. You're not one of us, Jenny Burns. Just keep that in mind." And Emmalyn turned away.

Jenny took that as her cue to return to Rebecca, quite aware of her pounding heart.

··· ➤ ➤ ···

Despite the long day at market, Rebecca was determined that evening to make good on her latest note to Katie. She waited till Samuel was asleep to get out of bed and take her clothes downstairs. In the kitchen, she turned on the smallest gas lamp and tiptoed to the bathroom to change out of her nightgown.

She went to the utility room and reached for her warmest black coat and gray scarf, along with her waterproof mittens, which kept her hands cozier than the ones she'd knitted last winter.

Then, moving quietly out the back door, she was conscious of the shuffle of her shoes against the pavement. The air was brisk and a slight gust of wind made her shudder as she hurried down the lane, deciding to go on foot.

Oh, she ached for Katie and the little ones again. Her heart throbbed every single day, missing them. Allowing one or two weeks to pass between visits was becoming an unbearable situation, because each visit made her yearn for more, like someone with a sweet tooth needing more and more sugar.

She didn't dare talk about this terrible loneliness with Samuel. But without saying their names, she alluded to them now and then. She suspected that making reference to their daughter and her family by name would hurt Samuel, and she refused to let him know just how much their shunned daughter occupied her thoughts. Rebecca's elderly mother had once told her without blinking an eye that most folk will do what they believe is best for themselves, no matter what's expected. *"They just do what they think is right, when all's said and done."*

In the shadows, Rebecca looked about her, hoping she could manage yet another furtive visit up the road. She dared not pray to that end, though, not when she was being disobedient. Oh, such a tear down the middle of her soul!

She sometimes wondered what her own sisters or mother would do in a similar place. Die Meinding had broken her heart, for certain. But the dreadful experience had also served to remind her how much she loved Katie.

Rebecca would do whatever it took to stay in touch with her daughter. If only the bishop could understand the very heart of her and kindly look the other way!

Jenny quickly realized it was cooler again tonight as she made her way to pray near the springhouse once more. As before, she walked the path that snaked away from the house, down an incline toward the wide stone steps. She crept toward the spot and then knelt and prayed silently, in case Andrew was concealed from view, bringing his own petitions before God. *Praying for others . . . and for me.*

Tonight Jenny was pleading for wisdom in dealing with Andrew's own sister in addition to her usual plea for a humble heart. Despite Jenny's attempt to focus on God, Emmalyn's sharp words continued to resound in her mind. Nevertheless, Jenny asked the Lord to *"tender her heart,"* as Rebecca Lapp had once said.

The night was hushed and still, except for the sound of two hoot owls calling from the branches of distant trees, and the occasional tinkle of tack and traces as unseen courting buggies passed by. The sky was filled with sharp white stars. Embracing the tranquility, Jenny wished everyone might have the opportunity to know and absorb such peace, at least for a moment.

She eventually rose and headed toward the stone steps, noticing an amber light in the kitchen window as she stepped onto the driveway. Had someone gotten up and discovered she was missing from her room? She couldn't imagine it, since she kept her bedroom door closed even when she was gone.

Jenny heard quick footsteps on the driveway and turned to look. Was Emmalyn spying again?

Something rose up in her in spite of her prayers for a peaceful, gentle spirit. Irritated, Jenny followed the footsteps of the figure, a woman hurrying along the roadside without even a flashlight. When Jenny was within perhaps a quarter block of her, she realized the silhouette was too matronly to be Emmalyn.

This must be Rebecca, decided Jenny, although she couldn't know for sure. But why on earth would Rebecca Lapp get up after going to bed and rush off to parts unknown?

Jenny followed the mystery woman until she came to the crossroad that curved south, toward the house where Katie and her husband lived. She remembered Marnie's pointing it out the day they'd gone to the Gordonville Book Store.

The woman picked up her pace as she approached the familiar house. Hanging back, Jenny watched as the woman gently patted the mailbox. *What was that?* From this distance, Jenny couldn't be sure what she was seeing.

Then, suddenly, she felt a sneeze coming on and pinched her nose tightly shut. But try as she might, a wheeze slipped out, and the sound was magnified in the vacuum of night.

The woman stopped and turned in Jenny's direction. "Who's there?" she called.

Rebecca's voice.

Jenny stepped gingerly behind a tree trunk, trying to avoid uneven roots protruding from the ground.

"Hullo?" Rebecca said, moving away from the walkway, the welcoming porch light behind her. "Is someone there?" She was not giving up.

Heart thrumming, Jenny struggled, unsure what to do. Rebecca's gait was decisive as she approached the tree, not ten yards away. Rebecca would keep coming until she discovered Jenny's hiding place.

At last, stepping out of the shadows into the soft, pale light of the moon, Jenny said softly, "Rebecca, it's me—Jenny."

The older woman inhaled sharply and seemed to grow a few inches.

"Why are you followin' me?"

"I wasn't—I mean . . ." Jenny was surprised at her sharp tone.

"Go back now, and erase this from your mind."

Shaken, Jenny turned and began to walk toward Hickory Lane, confused by what she had just witnessed.

Chapter 25

J enny had never felt so perplexed as she showered and
washed her hair before bed. When she'd dried off, she
slipped on one of three cotton nightgowns she had sewn
with Rebecca's help since the incident with her fancy one.
Instead of discarding the problem nightie, however, she'd
placed it in a zipped pocket of her suitcase, which lay beneath the bed.

She replayed the uncomfortable encounter with Rebecca
in front of Katie's house. Annoying thoughts kept her from
sleeping, so she turned the gas lamp back on and sat up in
bed with her devotional book.

What was Rebecca doing?

Jenny reviewed all that Rebecca had taught her regarding
obedience and submission—the highest calling. Wasn't Katie
under the Bann, shunned for life? If so, wasn't it disobedient
for Rebecca to visit her daughter's home?

Much later, as Jenny was dozing off, the lamp still on, she
heard someone knock at her bedroom door. "Are you awake,
Jenny?"

Quickly, she opened the door to Rebecca, who hurried

inside and closed it behind her. "I'm glad you're still up." She sat on the edge of Jenny's bed, cheeks cherry red from the cold. "As you know, it took great trust when Samuel and I opened our home to you." Rebecca's hazel eyes looked dark in the dim light. She bit her lip and continued, "Ach, if anyone happened to get wind of this, I'd be persecuted right along with Katie. The bishop would put his foot down, and I would no longer be able to correspond with my daughter and family, let alone risk seeing them face-to-face." She sighed heavily. "Staying away from them is something I can't adhere to—not any longer. Of course, my family would never forgive me if I ended up shunned like Katie and Dan."

Jenny's heart broke for her. Yet Rebecca knew the rules. How could Jenny offer comfort?

"Other bishops might be more lenient to a parent in my position, but it's hard to be sure," Rebecca said. "Bishop John is mighty strict, so you must keep my secret. Will you, Jenny? Will you keep this to yourself?"

Jenny drew back, shocked. "What if the People were to find out, though, and discovered that I knew all along but didn't say anything? What then?" she managed to say. "I don't want you to be shunned, Rebecca. How could I live with myself, knowing I was party to that? But I—"

"You're wonderin' if *you're* at risk, being a seeker 'n' all."

Jenny nodded, disheartened at the thought. And this after her few strides forward these past weeks. "The bishop wouldn't give me much, or any, leeway."

"Nee—none at all." Rebecca lowered her head. "I won't lie to ya. Keepin' my secret and being found out will *verfalle*—put you to ruin."

The two women stared sadly at each other. Rebecca looked away first. "But I *have* been careful. Ain't been caught yet."

I caught you, Jenny thought. "Not by the ministers, no."

Rebecca nodded circumspectly. "I can't keep my distance from my Katie-girl." She went on to add in a whisper how she loved her grandchildren, Sammy and Kate Marie. "You just don't know." Her lower lip quivered as a single tear spilled down her cheek. "Please forget what you saw tonight. Promise me."

Jenny trembled. "You're asking me to defy the Ordnung."

"Still, you're not baptized yet, don't ya see? You're not under the ruling of the church."

"But I'm striving to be. It's everything I hope for."

Rebecca rose, her shoulders stooped as she trudged to the door. Silently, she turned to look down at Jenny. Her face was solemn. "I beg you not to say a word." Then she opened the door and left the room.

Jenny blew out the gas lamp and curled up in the warm bed. She made an effort to understand how a devout believer like Rebecca could justify violating the Bann. As honorable as the woman had appeared to be—and considering the attributes she'd repeatedly urged Jenny to follow as an Amish seeker—the thought was nearly profane.

Exhausted, Jenny prayed yet could find no peace. Everything she'd believed about Rebecca Lapp had come crashing to the ground.

The next morning, Rebecca awoke to the sound of Samuel whispering his prayers in Deitsch. When she opened her eyes, she saw him sitting next to her in bed, two pillows propped behind him. She listened, not letting on she was awake, and was shocked to hear that he knew of Dan and Katie's home Bible studies. *Of all things!*

Samuel sounded distraught as his voice cracked when speaking to the Almighty about his excommunicated daughter and her husband. Rebecca couldn't help wondering how on earth he'd heard about this.

She waited for his amen, then moved a bit, stretching. "You're awake early, dear," she said quietly.

He leaned down with a sigh and kissed her, then sat back up. "Lots to be in prayer 'bout this mornin'."

"Oh?"

"Bishop John stopped over yesterday and shared some mighty surprising news. Seems lately our son-in-law has been the instigator of a house gathering."

Now was not the time to share that she'd been invited to one of them by Katie herself.

"Bishop wants to find out if some of our young folk are goin' over there . . . hearin' Mennonite doctrine."

"What's that mean?"

"Declaring one's salvation, which is only the Lord God's to declare."

"Jah . . . on the Judgment Day," she agreed with him.

"We have the hope of salvation, sure, but it's wrong to go round sayin' you're saved like Daniel Fisher's teachin'."

Rebecca had heard all this before, back when Katie up and left the Amish church. Even six years later, she and Dan were quite outspoken about their beliefs. "What's the bishop plannin' to do?" she asked.

"Well, for one, Preacher Yoder's goin' over there next time they meet, to spy things out."

She bristled. "Makin' a list of our folk?"

"Sure sounds like it."

"Bishop must be desperate, then." *Not surprising,* she thought.

"Now, Rebecca, watch what ya say," Samuel reprimanded. "John Beiler's the anointed minister of God."

"Jah, Samuel. Ever so sorry." She felt like a hypocrite down to her very bones—knew it as sure as she ought to be getting up right now and dressing for the day.

Yet this coming on the heels of the events of last evening nearly paralyzed her—how could she not have known this might happen? She realized she ought to be very thankful it wasn't one of the People but rather Jenny Burns who had found her out. Rebecca yearned to cover up with the many quilts, burrowing down where she'd be safe from prying eyes.

Will Jenny keep mum? she wondered as Samuel rose and went to put on his old work trousers.

Rebecca hoped so, but she did not pray it. She knew better.

She also knew that if she was *schmaert*, she'd write her daughter a letter saying she must be more careful about her visits . . . or not go anymore at all.

The sun was concealed by a gray blanket of clouds as bleak as her spirit that morning. Jenny knelt on the cold wide-plank floor and poured out her heart. Even though the ministerial brethren were unaware, hadn't she already broken the rules of the Proving? Yet coming clean to alleviate the guilt of her knowledge would cause even more pain. Not just for herself, but for Rebecca and her family, who'd already been through the wringer.

Jenny remained in a contrite position, asking for forgiveness, knowing she must trust in divine wisdom and not *"unto her own understanding."*

Rebecca's pleas for confidentiality plagued her, and Jenny

prayed all the harder, filled with despair. What if she'd never heard any footsteps last evening . . . never followed them up Hickory Lane?

I must put it out of my mind like Rebecca urged. But can I live with myself?

Over the ensuing days, Jenny's relationship with Rebecca continued to decline. Although they worked side by side in the kitchen when Jenny wasn't helping the bishop's wife, the once warm and inviting camaraderie had all but disappeared. Meanwhile, Rebecca seemed more weary than ever. Was it the love burden or the deceit she carried?

However unwilling, Jenny felt like an accomplice, a seeker with merely a righteous face. Yet when she pictured herself revealing Rebecca's transgression to even Samuel, her knees locked and her back straightened. *I am not humble, nor am I obedient.*

Still, her silence was only part of the sin, and Jenny was stuck between an impenetrable wall and a boulder, with no breathing room.

Rebecca welcomed Jenny's help washday morning, but she was relieved when Jenny left early to go baby-sit the bishop's little girls. She needed a reprieve from the disappointed looks poor Jenny could no longer disguise. She felt just wretched, praying for forgiveness even as she willfully refused to comply with the Bann. She knew herself too well to change that, barring locking herself in the attic and crawling into the old wooden trunk. *Where Katie's pink satin baby gown was first discovered* . . .

Rebecca leaned over the big basin in the cellar and let the tears fall. There was simply no place to turn.

···➤ ◀···

Jenny was almost positive Rebecca was sobbing her eyes out somewhere in the house. She'd seemed despondent since their talk in Jenny's bedroom. *Katie's room,* thought Jenny, never quite able to forget.

When Jenny arrived at her neighbors', Mary Beiler greeted her at the back door, saying she wanted to introduce Jenny to the bishop. The timing was unnerving. And when the tall, rather attractive bishop appeared out of the kitchen, holding little Anna, Jenny felt out of sorts and didn't know how to address the man she'd wanted to meet all this time.

"Our little ones enjoy having you baby-sit," the man of God said as he extended his right hand. His eyes were discerning yet kind, and his voice did not thunder down the fiery brimstone she knew she deserved. "Denki, Jenny."

She tried to work her facial muscles into what she hoped was a convincing smile. "I love taking care of your little girls." She didn't have to say it, but the words flowed freely. It was the only aspect of this delayed meeting that felt natural.

"I commend you for wanting to be one of the People," the bishop surprised her by saying. "Not many succeed, you must know."

This wasn't exactly what she needed to hear, but Jenny found herself nodding. "The way of Gelassenheit is not easy."

"Nee," he whispered, bowing his head. "We must die daily to our wants and desires, as the Scriptures instruct."

She was dying all right, with nearly every breath.

"Before I forget, there were two young ladies—Englisch- ers in their twenties, I'd guess—lookin' for you earlier." The bishop shifted sweet Anna in his arms.

"This morning?"

"Jah. Said they'd gotten lost and needed the right address."

Could it be Pamela and Dorie? Jenny wondered, a surge of excitement rising after the bishop left for the barn and Mary headed for the waiting horse and buggy. Seeing her dear friends again might help Jenny get her mind off herself, if only for a while.

Rebecca told the dolled-up Englischer sisters at her front door that Jenny was indeed staying there. "But I'm sorry she's not home right now." To think they'd already been over to the bishop's place, and less than an hour ago, too. How on earth had they gotten lost in such a small area as Hickory Hollow?

"We drove to the end of West Cattail Road," the older and shorter of the two sisters explained, seemingly flustered. She wore a dizzying display of colors—a salmon-hued sweater and a lime-green scarf showed beneath her rust-colored leather jacket.

"Then we turned west onto the highway and circled all the way back to that town with the odd name." The younger woman dabbed at her very thin eyebrows.

"Ah, 'tis Intercourse Village," Rebecca prompted her. "Jenny's just over yonder, behind the plowed field, taking care of the bishop's children. You can go over there if you'd like."

"Thanks," they said in chorus, then returned to their bright red car in their pencil-thin blue jeans.

Why'd they come? As she hung up the cold, wet washing in the cellar, Rebecca couldn't help thinking the fancy girls' surprise appearance might be useful to her. Why, if Jenny Burns threw in the towel and abandoned her attempt to become Amish, it might just save Rebecca's skin.

Oh, but she felt guilty for thinking that way. Sighing, she shook her head, downright disgusted with herself.

Chapter 26

Jenny squealed with joy when she answered the knock at the back door and saw Pamela and Dorie Kennedy standing there. Quickly, she pushed the door open.

Pamela's jaw dropped as Dorie bent to better inspect Jenny's long dress and apron. For a moment, the three of them simply gawked at one another.

Dorie was the first to find her voice. "Whoa, Jen. You've turned . . . *Amish!*"

Pamela reached for Jenny, who returned the hug, followed by Dorie, who nearly squeezed the life out of her before they all shared in a group hug. Standing back again, Pamela's blue eyes shone. "You really, really look the part, Jen."

"Bravo!" Dorie was clapping.

Then, remembering the bishop's children, Jenny cringed and held her pointer finger over her lips. "I forgot," she whispered, "two of the kids are sleeping." She gestured to Dorie and Pamela to follow her into the utility room, closing the door behind them. "It's so good to see you two! You must have read my letter."

"Did we ever!" Dorie teased with a roll of her pretty green eyes.

Pamela smiled sweetly, apparently unable to stop staring at Jenny's clothes. Dorie touched the fabric of her dress. "What're we going to do with you, girl?"

"Hmm . . . you're not into vintage?" Jenny joked, feeling flushed.

"Your new look, it's just so, well . . ." Dorie paused.

"Plain?" Jenny said.

"I think you look pretty," Pamela spoke up. "In an Old World sort of way."

Jenny explained that she didn't know if it was a good idea to invite them in. "I'm not sure what the bishop's wife would say."

"That's okay," Pamela said. "We don't mean to barge in."

They stood and talked there in the outer room while Jenny glanced at the children in the kitchen from time to time.

"You look like you fit right in here," Dorie said.

"Except for my dreadful bangs." Jenny patted her head. "I'm still growing them out."

"Listen, if that's your one and only flaw, you're good." Pamela fluffed her own chin-length hair.

"Oh, there's far more to being an Amish seeker than meets the eye," Jenny said as they quickly caught up on one another's lives. This included Pamela's exciting new job as a publicist for a celebrity author, and Dorie's purchase of a townhome in Hartford, near Mark Twain's former house.

"I'm going to have a new roommate."

"You're parting ways?" Jenny asked, surprised.

"It's time," Dorie said with a smile.

"Any serious guys on the horizon?" asked Jenny.

"Career first," Pamela said. "Romance can wait."

"What about *your* life here?" Dorie probed. "Aren't you tired of getting up with the chickens?"

Jenny laughed. "Who could ever adjust to that?"

"Are you saying there's hope?" Pamela asked.

Jenny's gaze swept the narrow room. "I'm living the simple life, as you can see. There's nothing quite like it."

An awkward pause settled in, and Pamela's face darkened. "Seriously, Jenny . . . when are you coming home?"

"Dorie, honey . . ." Pamela eyed her sister. "Be nice."

"Um, that *was* nice."

They were both looking at her, waiting for an answer.

"I explained everything in my letter. You read it, right?"

Dorie nodded. "Sure, but now that you're here . . . I mean, *really?*"

Jenny's heart sank but she smiled anyway. "I'm very happy."

There was another pause.

Dorie sighed, followed by a subtle shake of the head. They must believe she'd lost it. "So . . . do you have to wear that funky black apron all the time?"

"This?" Jenny smoothed her apron. "All the women wear them. White on Sundays for single women, though, for Preaching service."

"There's probably a lot we don't get, Dorie," Pamela said. "Right, Jenny?"

She bobbed her head.

Dorie frowned. "Well, I'm worried about you."

Pamela touched Jenny's arm. "Your mom's worried, too."

"You've talked to her?"

Pamela nodded and exchanged glances with Dorie. "The truth?"

"Always."

"Your mom's flipped out." Pamela's eyes were serious again.

Dorie added, "She sent us on a reconnaissance mission."

"Sniffing out what I'm really up to?"

"In so many words," Dorie admitted.

"And was there a reward involved?" Jenny laughed but felt ill.

"Oh, Jen . . ." Pamela said, looking cheerless.

"She offered us cash," Dorie said, a humorous glint in her eyes. "But we refused."

"It's nice to have friends who can't be bought off." Jenny chuckled but felt she had to change the subject. "Would you like something to drink? I could bring something out here," she offered, but they shook their heads and politely declined.

"We'd better get going," said Pamela. "Any parting words?"

"In Deitsch or otherwise?" Jenny said, relieved the awkward reunion was coming to an end.

"English is good," Dorie replied.

"Just greet my parents for me." Jenny paused, thinking there was more she'd like to relay to her family.

"By the way, your brother has a new girlfriend," Pamela said. "He broke it off with Tracie."

Jenny was sorry to hear it. "Wow, I thought she was the one for Cameron."

"Oh, you know, things happen," Pamela said, looking as miserable as Jenny felt. "Hey, maybe you could visit for Christmas and get the whole scoop."

Dorie grinned. "Yeah, and be sure to wear your cute Amish outfit, okay?"

Jenny heard little Anna stirring in the playpen. "I'd better get going—thanks for coming to visit."

Pamela said, "We're staying at the Hampton Inn over on Greenfield Road if you want to do anything this afternoon."

"Wish you'd given me a heads-up. I'm busy all day today."

"Well, if you change your mind, just text us," Pamela said. "Oh, wait, I forgot—"

"No cell phone," Jenny reminded.

Dorie grimaced. "You're really cut off, Jen."

"It's not so bad."

Dorie shook her head. "Maybe not for you."

Pamela gave her a sad little smile. "Nice seeing you, Jen. Take care."

They embraced quickly, instinctively.

Jenny sighed. It was no fun saying good-bye to her faithful friends. This was the hard part of separating oneself from the world. Samuel Lapp had read aloud from the English Bible on this very subject just last evening. *"The tearing away is never easy,"* he'd added while looking over his spectacles at her. *Tearing away from the English world . . . and from my wicked self.*

She smiled and waved as her friends looked back at her, the shock still evident on their fair faces. She watched them go for what might be the last time, a lump in her throat. But what gave her even more pause was the fact that her family hadn't had the nerve, or the interest, to come visit themselves.

Chapter 27

With a bit of trepidation, Marnie Lapp waited for her beau beneath a cluster of willows near the road Tuesday evening. Roy Flaud brightened when he jumped out of the passenger van wearing his Sunday-go-to-meeting clothes. He helped her in with a silent grin.

They talked quietly in Deitsch as the paid driver pulled forward. Marnie felt the energy between them when Roy reached for her hand. "I didn't bring along a Bible," she told him. "S'pose that's all right?"

He removed a small Testament from his coat pocket. "We'll share."

She thought he might kiss her cheek right then, Roy seemed so pleased. Was it being with her or anticipation for the meeting he was so impatient to attend?

"I'm reading chapter eleven in Luke's Gospel, the part about lighting a candle and hiding it under a bushel basket," he said. "Have ya seen that verse?"

"Can't say I have."

He opened his New Testament to a bookmarked page. "Here, read it for yourself." He pointed to verse thirty-three.

She wondered why this was so important, but she took time to look at it all the same. Then, nodding, she handed the Testament back. "'Tis *verninfdich*."

"Jah, I agree. It *does* make sense to display a light for all to see." Roy's eyes brightened and he slid closer to her.

"Why did ya want me to read that?" she asked.

"The Lord's shown me truths in the four Gospels that I've missed my whole life."

Marnie didn't know what to think of this. Weren't the ministerial brethren supposed to be the ones to impart the knowledge of Scripture?

Roy leaned back, still holding the thin little book. He said no more on the topic, and Marnie hoped that was the end of it.

Turning off Hickory Lane, they drove down a meandering road, past meadows where black-and-white heifers roamed. In the distance, a yard light illuminated a graceful row of poplars that served as a windbreak for a nearby redbrick farmhouse, and Marnie began to wish for the first lovely snowfall. Now that wedding season was in full swing, she could also start to dream of her own wedding day . . . next year.

"You're awful quiet, Marnie." Roy pressed his shoulder against hers.

"Just thinkin'."

"'Bout us, I hope."

She looked at him, smiling. "Always."

"*Gut*," he whispered. "Me too."

She thrilled to his words as he searched her face. Leaning in next to him, she whispered, "We'd best behave ourselves in public, ya know."

He bobbed his head right quick and let go of her hand, folding his arms over his chest. "*Gut* idea."

She suppressed a laugh and turned to gaze out the window, so happy. "Where are we goin', anyways?" She had noticed some familiar terrain along the way, but here there were no streetlights.

"Ever hear of Daniel Fisher?" Roy asked as the van turned into a driveway.

"There's a bunch of 'em." She had to smile. "But sounds Amish, ain't?" She looked outside again, then noticed the little porch light and gasped. "You've brought me to my shunned relatives' house?"

He shook his head. "Who do ya mean?"

"Dan and Katie—they're my first cousins." Oh, she could've cried, and now the driver had turned around, gawking at them but thankfully not able to understand what they were saying. Yet he could surely see her downturned face.

Marnie pressed her hand to her heart. "I can't go in there, Roy. I just can't."

"We'll talk outside." Roy reached for the door.

Marnie shook her head. "I think we best be stayin' right here."

"Sweetheart, please."

She had been taught to obey her father, older brothers . . . and her fiancé, too. So, reluctantly and with a heavy heart, Marnie followed Roy and stepped down, out of the van. Roy went around and paid the driver, instructing him to return in two hours.

He must not care how I feel, Marnie thought.

The van backed up slowly, then pulled out onto the road and sped away while she and Roy stood off to the side of the driveway by a tall tree. Marnie bit her tongue and tried her best not to argue with her beloved. As much as she knew she'd be in terrible trouble with her father, she did not want to spoil the evening, although she feared she already had.

"No one will ever know you're here," Roy coaxed. "I promise."

"My cousins will know . . . and so will God."

"But your cousins won't tell on ya, and the Lord will be mighty pleased."

"And you really think my father won't hear 'bout this?" she asked in what she hoped was a meek voice.

"Just follow me, love." He kissed her forehead. "You won't be sorry."

Marnie walked to the front porch with him, fretting the whole way. Was she doing the right thing? And what on earth was she to say to Cousin Katie?

Jenny took mental notes while Samuel balanced his old German *Biewel* on his knee, sitting there in the front room with Rebecca. It was Samuel's idea to read one verse first in German and then in English. *"Reading from the Psalms that way is something he likes to do,"* Rebecca had mentioned earlier.

Jenny's guilt tore at her heart. She could not bring herself to look at Rebecca during the reading. She had offered her silence up to God, praying to be forgiven. She wondered if Rebecca was also compelled to ask for mercy each time she hurried off to see Katie against the bishop's wishes. By the looks of her, the woman was under tremendous strain, perhaps even losing weight. Jenny felt moved to pray for her during the silent prayer time, offering her entire entreaty on behalf of poor Rebecca.

When they were finished, Samuel rose with some effort, put the Bible on a nearby table, and headed back through the kitchen to the door. In a few minutes, though, he returned to tell Jenny she ought to go out and observe Andrew unhitch one of Samuel's road horses. "Andrew's the one to watch," he said, and Rebecca, in turn, encouraged Jenny, as well.

"I'll get my scarf and gloves." Jenny felt odd about going. After all, it had been eight days since she'd encountered Andrew down at the springhouse pond, which must be frozen over by now, with the cold weather.

When she'd put on Rebecca's old work coat and boots, Jenny made her way outdoors and across the yard to the driveway. The cold pricked her face and she adjusted her scarf. She realized Samuel had returned to the barn to finish cleaning the milk house, since Andrew was working alone to unhook the straps on the back of the horse.

"Samuel suggested I come to watch," she said as she neared the horse.

Andrew chuckled. "Actually, it was *my* idea," he was quick to say. "Go round to the other side of the mare, won't ya?"

She followed his instructions, trying extra hard to do things correctly this time. Jenny concentrated on helping him unhook the traces and tuck them into the harness around the back of Star.

"Have ya been outdoors prayin'?" Andrew asked casually.

"It's been too cold." She hoped that would lessen any fears he might have about being caught with her.

"I haven't gone there to pray lately, either," he said.

Yet I've been praying more than ever, she thought, though naturally she didn't wish to reveal why.

"There were some Englischers lookin' for ya here lately."

"That Amish grapevine is astonishing, jah?"

"Well, I didn't hear this secondhand," Andrew said, still working on his side. "A red sports car stopped, and the lady driver asked me for directions."

"Must have been my friend Pamela Kennedy," she volunteered.

"She was real chatty, I'll say."

Jenny smiled. "That's Pamela, all right. Her sister's quite personable, too."

"They did seem nice. Not like some tourists who manage to find their way to Hickory Hollow." Andrew paused and looked over at her. "Did they come to take ya home?"

"I think they would have liked to, but it wasn't the main reason they came."

"Oh?"

She nodded slowly. "My parents sent them."

Andrew sucked in a breath and straightened. "Your family misses ya, then?"

She laughed. "I wouldn't say that exactly."

He didn't press further.

"The truth is, no one back home can believe I've walked away from my former life." She sighed. "I doubt it's the last trick my parents will pull."

He didn't respond. Did he think she was disrespectful?

Andrew asked her to help him hold the shafts and lead the horse out and away from them. For some reason, the maneuver was easier than her previous attempts, even though this time it was by lantern light.

Andrew pushed the carriage over a ways, and together they walked the horse to the stable. As they went, Andrew took a sugar cube from his pocket and handed it to Jenny. "Here, give her this, all right?"

"Denki."

He added, "The more you bond with the horses, the better."
It wasn't the first time she'd heard this. "I don't have a lot
of free time," she told him. "Rebecca—and Mary—keep me
very busy."

"Well, every chance you get, come out to the stable and
help groom or feed the horses. Eventually, they'll become
more accustomed to you and actually work with ya, makin'
it easier to hitch up."

She thanked Andrew for the advice and stepped back,
waiting for him to lead Star into her stall. Once the horse
was secured, she held out the sugar cube on her flat palm.

"No need to be afraid," Andrew said, holding the lantern.

She's so much bigger than I am. . . .

"Go ahead . . . talk to her," Andrew gently urged.

Jenny felt silly, even awkward. "That's a good girl," she
whispered.

"Don't be shy," Andrew said. "Go on."

"But I am shy."

He tilted his head, sizing things up. "All right, then, maybe
you can practice when no one's round. Will ya?"

"Sure, I'll try it."

Andrew grinned. "There's something else you might like
to help with." He explained that his uncle Chester Lapp's
golden Labrador, Posey, had followed Marnie down the lane
earlier and hadn't returned. "Chester's worried she might've
gotten hit by a car, up near Route 340. I've already looked all
along Hickory Lane searchin' for her," Andrew said, concern
in his voice.

"I'd be glad to help you look."

Andrew raised the lantern a bit. "It's not too late, is it?"

"I might need something to warm me up first. How about some hot cocoa or coffee? Would you care for something?"

"I sure would."

His enthusiasm surprised her. And Jenny hoped Rebecca wouldn't be too shocked to see Andrew following her into the house, all smiles as he was right now.

Chapter 28

Why'd I let Roy talk me into this? Marnie froze in place and glanced at her beau standing next to her. What on earth would she say to Cousins Dan and Katie?

It's been so long. . . .

Her mouth was cotton, and she trembled at the thought of breaking the church ordinance. *I'm taking a big risk.*

The front door opened and Cousin Katie appeared, wearing a gracefully long print dress, her hair in a bun covered by a formal Mennonite veiling. Her pretty face broke into a smile and soft brown eyes widened when she realized it was Marnie. Without hesitation, Katie stepped down onto the porch and reached to hug her. Roy moved aside, giving them some privacy.

"Cousin Marnie . . . oh, sweetie," Katie murmured into her ear. "I've missed you just terribly."

Marnie nodded her head, scarcely able to speak. Oh, the happiness of this reunion! "I thought I'd never see you again," Marnie whispered. And she felt it might be the one and only time, so she let herself enjoy this precious moment.

They looked into each other's beaming, tear-streaked faces.

The Bann kept us apart, thought Marnie, won over as always before by Katie's warmth and love.

"Are ya happy, cousin?" asked Marnie with a glance at the door, which had been closed.

"Oh goodness, incredibly so, and counting my blessings every day! Wait till you see our little boy, Sammy, and baby Kate."

"Well, I'm really not s'posed to be here, ya know," Marnie said, not that she had to explain.

"You've come for the Bible study, then?" Katie's eyes still glistened.

"It was my beau's idea."

"Well, it doesn't matter whose it was; I'm so glad you're here." Katie turned and welcomed her inside. "Come and take a seat next to him."

As resistant as she'd been to attending, Marnie experienced such comfort talking with her dearest cousin. It was all she could do to keep her mind on the Scripture reading, at least for the first few minutes. She also noticed two other Amish courting couples present—one of the girls was the bishop's niece Naomi Beiler, but none of them looked at all ill at ease. Marnie was curious to know what Roy thought of that.

Katie's husband, Daniel, hadn't changed much since she'd last seen him. His hair was still quite fair and, oh goodness, those blueberry eyes Katie had always referred to. Marnie couldn't help remembering what close friends Katie and Mary Stoltzfus Beiler had been in years past, since they were tiny girls. *"Friends for life,"* they'd always said of each other. Now to think Mary was the bishop's wife and mother to his children . . . and Katie was far removed from the People.

She sighed as Dan read the entire third chapter of the Gospel of John. Katie sat next to him in the circle of chairs.

Marnie couldn't help also watching her auburn-haired cousin, whose proper Mennonite head covering looked so different than the Amish one Katie had once worn—a squared-off cup shape with pleats ironed in on the sides.

Does she adhere to any of her Amish upbringing? Marnie wondered, trying not to stare at the darling couple.

Just then Roy held his New Testament out before her so she could follow along. She'd better pay closer attention, but it was ever so hard, considering the years she'd lost with her cousin and friend.

"'The Father loveth the Son, and hath given all things into his hand,'" Cousin Daniel read again, his face radiant. "'He that believeth on the Son hath everlasting life. . . .'"

Marnie drank in the verse as if she were hearing it for the first time.

A sermonlike talk followed. Daniel reminded her of a preacher, without the singsong approach. It was surprising how relaxed and conversational he was as he spoke. He seemed to know just what to say about the chapter he'd read, focusing primarily on the final verses.

How can this be? Marnie wondered, nearly in awe.

"The verse means precisely what it says," Daniel emphasized, leaning forward in his chair and folding his hands between his knees. "We have eternal life through Jesus Christ alone." He continued, his eyes shining as he shared the "great joy and amazing peace" he'd found in "accepting this truth and receiving Jesus as my own Savior and Lord." He paused to look around the circle, compassion on his handsome face. Dan's deep voice grew softer then. "I have found a love I'd never known before, my good friends. And I'm thrilled to share it with all of you."

Marnie noticed one of the Amish girls struggling not to

cry, her lower lip quivering as Daniel continued his testimony, sharing his personal background in the Old Order Amish community . . . and later, his excommunication. There was scarcely a dry eye in the room. Even Marnie had to hold her breath to keep from being overwhelmed. Anyone could see that Dan's and Katie's experience with God had changed their lives.

When Daniel asked them to bow their heads while he led in prayer, Marnie felt a great yearning to be alone in her room to pray privately. The incredibly tender way she felt just now, there was so much she wanted to tell the Lord God.

Afterward, Katie and Dan played their guitars, leading the group in a slow version of "Amazing Grace." Now it was Marnie who could scarcely keep her tears in check as she blended her voice in unison with the others. To think the bishop had renounced their expressive playing.

Following the final prayer, Katie invited all of them to the cheery kitchen for homemade refreshments: carrot and nut cake, vanilla ice cream, and root beer. Marnie was surprised how the folk there kept talking in hushed tones while they mingled—some of them praying for each other aloud. Clearly, they were eager to linger.

When everyone was served, Katie silently motioned for Marnie to follow her upstairs. Still profoundly touched by Daniel's words and the Scriptures he'd shared, Marnie looked fondly down at Katie's darling children, an auburn-haired boy and a girl with blond ringlets, both sleeping soundly.

"Oh, honey-girl," Katie said as she slipped her arm around Marnie's waist. "Go ahead, my sweet cousin. It's all right to cry. . . ."

Unable to speak, Marnie wept for the pain Katie and Dan had suffered for the sake of their obvious love for Jesus. And yet immense joy was written on their dear faces.

Later, when she'd composed herself, Katie opened her arms and hugged and kissed her. "I hope you'll come again, Marnie. You're always welcome here."

"Denki," she eked out.

Katie leaned down and peered into her eyes. "Are you baptized, cousin?" she asked softly.

"Not yet."

Katie seemed to sigh. "Then you can't be reprimanded for visiting us."

"Pray for me, won't ya, Katie?" Marnie told her how harsh her father had been toward Marnie's older brother. "If I'm found out, I'll be in trouble."

Katie promised to pray daily. "You can count on me." She wiped Marnie's tears with both thumbs. "All right?"

Katie had such an appealing way about her—she stirred up the atmosphere with her love of people. Only a woman like Katie could believe the cure for her own sadness due to the Bann was in making others happy. She remained the cousin Marnie had always loved, even though they were not blood kin. Truth be known, folk had been drawn to Katie since she first arrived in Hickory Hollow as a rosy infant with Uncle Samuel and Aunt Rebecca, who'd claimed her as their own nearly thirty years ago.

"Our home is open to you, if you ever just want to come and stay awhile." Katie told Marnie that one of the bishop's nieces was considering doing the same thing.

Marnie nodded gratefully, knowing in her heart that, with or without Roy's wanting to return, there was nothing anyone could do or say to keep her away from the next meeting.

Chapter 29

A ndrew Lapp's flashlight paved their way with a white circle of light as Jenny kept pace with him. "How long has your uncle had Posey?"

"Not long, which might be the reason she's run off. You see, Uncle Chester's a real stickler for obedience, not excluding his pets."

"So Posey must be a pup?"

"Jah, the runt of the litter. She comes from a long line of pedigreed Labs owned by my Dat's family for several generations."

"Interesting."

Andrew nodded and looked her way. "My uncle also has two golden retrievers for hunting small game, Skip and Sparky."

Trying to be helpful, Jenny asked, "Could Posey have followed Marnie?"

"I doubt that, 'cause Uncle Chester said Marnie left in a van, headed somewhere. It's a mystery why Posey's still missin'."

Jenny purposely breathed through her nose and tried to keep from shivering as she walked. The moon was a delicate light behind a stream of clouds, but the night was very still. She listened for anything that might sound like a puppy.

Up the road, they heard the fast trot of a horse with an enclosed buggy behind it, bright lights on both sides. "Someone's late for supper," Andrew joked.

"Can you differentiate between one neighbor's buggy and another's?" she asked.

"Sometimes, jah . . . after you're around the different road horses."

Jenny wondered if she'd ever reach that point and, intrigued by this, forgot to call out for Marnie's father's dog. She liked Andrew's willingness to answer her questions and his free and easy style, much like his casual stride.

Another horse and carriage approached now and began to slow. "Can you tell whose horse it is from here?" she asked Andrew.

"If it was daylight, I could."

"Hullo there" came a low male voice.

Jenny looked closer and could see an older man waving through the windshield.

"Who's there?" Andrew called, stepping closer to the shoulder with Jenny.

"It's Preacher Yoder." The horse halted in the middle of the road. "You two headed somewhere?" The man had slid over and was looking out at them from the passenger side of the front seat. •

"Just out searchin' for Uncle Chester's Labrador. Did ya happen to see a small yellow pup anywhere?" Andrew asked.

"Wasn't payin' any mind, to tell the truth."

Andrew chuckled. "Aren't you usually in bed at this hour?"

"Bishop sent me out on an assignment."

"Well, don't let us keep ya, then."

"That's all right—got what I needed." The preacher nodded his head.

"Gut Nacht," Andrew said, and Jenny repeated it.

After the horse pulled forward and headed on, Andrew said, "Wonder why he's out after dark."

Jenny wondered the same, as well as what reason the bishop might have for sending the preacher. *Bishop Beiler's nice enough,* she thought, thinking back to their brief meeting and having seen him around the farm on days she baby-sat there. It was still hard to imagine that Bishop John was as stern as Marnie and others made him out to be.

"I've been wantin' to mention something, Jenny," Andrew said after they'd walked awhile without speaking. "I daresay you're paying us Amish folk a big compliment."

"You think so?"

He paused a moment and looked at her, his flashlight still shining on the road. "I don't know any other Englischers who'd give up everything to do what you're doin', or fight so hard to be Amish."

She didn't know what to say.

"It can't be easy for ya. And I admire your courage."

"With the Lord's help, I'm doing my best." She never would have thought she'd feel comfortable talking like this with him, especially as attractive as he was. "I appreciate your prayers."

"It's the least I can do, Jenny." He laughed again. "That, and help ya learn to hitch up."

"I must be a slow learner."

He asked her to count for him in Deitsch and she smiled, happily able to get to *zwelf*—twelve.

"Lots of Amish folk mix up their numbers with English, did ya know that?"

"I'm not surprised."

"My own brother would have to think a second to say the Deitsch for, say, ninety-five."

Jenny wondered if that had come about because so many men now worked among Englishers, away from the Amish community.

Andrew asked her to run through some of the easier sociable questions, the same ones Rebecca had gone over with her, and Jenny remembered each one. It struck her funny that Andrew seemed so pleased about it, even energized by her small triumph.

"You're doin' very well, Jenny. Won't be long and you'll be talking up a storm like the rest of us."

"Deitsch is slowly starting to make sense. I just wish some of the other things would, too."

"Like what?"

She wasn't sure she should say. After all, he wasn't sharing *his* inner struggles. And, too, they hardly knew each other.

"Well, if you really want to know."

"I do," he said quietly.

"I'm not sure how well I'm emulating the seemingly ingrained attributes I've observed in the People." She thought suddenly of Rebecca's visit to her daughter, Katie. "Well, in *most* of them."

"Not sure who you're talking 'bout, but I don't know anyone born into this world with a pure heart."

His words echoed in her mind as they continued walking farther away from the Lapps' farm. *"We're not perfect,"* Rebecca had once said.

In the distance, Jenny thought she heard a shrill whining, and she stopped walking to listen more closely. "Did you hear that?"

Andrew pitched forward, cupping his ear.

Jenny held her breath for a few seconds. There it was again. "Sounds like there might be a lost pup over that way."

They turned off the road to hurry through a pasture in the direction of the crying. According to Andrew, this was Nate Kurtz's meadow. She was thankful for the large flashlight, not wanting to step in a cow pie!

Jenny glanced at Andrew as they picked over the uneven ground and nearly tripped. He put his arm out and reached for her gloved hand.

"You all right?" he asked, still holding her hand.

"Jah." She laughed. "I'm fine, thanks. Denki," she said and slid her hand gently out of his.

Self-conscious now, they walked in total stillness. And Jenny almost forgot to listen for the puppy's cries.

Chapter 30

J enny left with Andrew Lapp after makin' hot cocoa for him," Rebecca told Samuel as they sat at the kitchen table that evening.

"'Twas the oddest thing, Andrew askin' for her like that." Samuel went on, indicating that he'd thought their nephew only wanted to help her learn the unhitching process. "Tricked me, I guess."

"Oh now." Rebecca sprinkled a few more miniature marshmallows on the hot chocolate in Samuel's big brown mug.

"You just don't know, do ya, with these young folk?"

"Jenny's not someone he should be takin' a shining to, is she?"

"May God grant him wisdom if he does." Samuel stirred in the marshmallows with his spoon. "They'd best be waitin' till she's safely baptized before any formal courting."

Safely baptized.

Rebecca tensed up and wondered what Jenny would reveal when Preacher Yoder asked her the *most* important question, after the six weeks of instruction for baptism next summer. *If she's invited to take part.* She shivered and her husband looked up, his brow furrowed.

"What is it, dear?" Samuel raised his sturdy mug to his lips. She tried to calm herself. "What are the chances Jenny Burns will last round here?"

He drank slowly and lowered his cup. "That's one question I'll leave with the Good Lord." Samuel locked eyes with her. "He alone knows the intent and purposes of the heart."

"'Tis best, jah." She suddenly felt almost too weak to sit there as Samuel's eyes continued to probe hers. *Does he suspect?*

"I've noticed some tension between you and Jenny here lately," Samuel added. "I think it's wise you keep her at a cautious distance."

She said nothing to that.

"I approve of the way you're heedin' my advice, dear."

Lowering her gaze, Rebecca felt all the more guilty.

"I hope ya don't think I was too forward back there," Andrew said as he and Jenny stood in Nate Kurtz's field. They'd stopped walking when Jenny heard another sound in the distance.

Jenny blushed and was thankful the flashlight wasn't shining in her direction. "Listen," she said. "I just heard it again."

Andrew turned off the flashlight. The moon skimmed out of a translucent cloud, brightening the landscape somewhat. Then the piercing cries came once more, and Jenny darted off in that direction, not waiting for Andrew.

Posey sounds hurt!

When Jenny found her, the poor thing was trapped, her collar caught on a raised tree root. "Quick, Andrew! Help me pry her loose," she called as he approached. She worked the thin root back and forth rapidly, trying her best to break the pup free. "Do you have a pocketknife?"

He did, and when Posey was free at last, she held the whimpering pup close, carrying her back across the field, toward the road. She snuggled her face into the pup's downy body.

"Posey's shivering," she told Andrew, feeling the cold seeping out of the furry pet.

"And you must be cold, too, Jenny." He took off his heavy outer coat and draped it gently over her, tucking the pup underneath. "Uncle Chester's place isn't too far from here," he assured her. "We'll get warmed up there before I take ya back to Uncle Samuel's. How's that?"

She was shocked that Andrew would shed his coat in such cold, but it had been a long time since Jenny had felt so cared for. How could she object?

Three buggies were parked alongside Marnie's driveway when Jenny and Andrew arrived. The puppy had stopped crying as they hurried around to the backyard, toward the house. Jenny was anxious to take a closer look at Posey in the light of a gas lamp.

The house was abuzz with the sounds of Deitsch and people eating. Marnie's robust father turned and gawked at them when they entered the kitchen, which looked very much like Rebecca Lapp's with its linoleum flooring and long trestle table and wooden benches.

Spotting the pup, Marnie's father nearly leaped out of his chair at the head of the table, coming quickly to greet Andrew and Jenny. But it was the pup that Chester wanted, and he reached under Posey to lift her out of Jenny's arms.

Tall Chester Lapp smiled and shook her hand firmly. "Denki

ever so much." His face beamed as he cradled Posey in his strong left arm. "She ain't hurt, is she?" He looked the pup over and stroked her head. Posey's pink tongue gave Chester's cheek a lick, and he grinned again.

"A happy outcome for one vivacious pup," Marnie's mother, Peggy, said, coming over to thank Jenny, as well. She glanced suspiciously at Andrew as he removed his coat from around Jenny's shoulders. "Denki for your help." She looked up at Chester. "I can't tell ya how happy you've made my husband—and all of us."

Jenny smiled. "I'm glad Posey didn't get stuck out in the cold all night." Based on the reception, she felt like she'd accomplished something important here.

"Won't ya join us for some warm apple betty and coffee?" Peggy asked, a bright expression on her plump face.

Andrew accepted without conferring with Jenny, which tickled her. "We've been walkin' all over creation," he told them, offering Jenny a seat at the far end of the table. "So this'll be right *gut*." He, in turn, sat across from her, on the side with his middle-aged uncles.

In a few short minutes, they learned that everyone present had been out looking for Posey. "Till the womenfolk turned into popsicles," Chester Lapp said, sitting back in his chair, still holding his pup with one hand. He forked up some dessert and smacked his lips. "I would guess Marnie'll be home here fairly quick," he said, then began introducing Jenny to his relatives.

Peggy explained that Marnie's younger siblings were already tucked into bed. "For school tomorrow. You'll just have to come another time and meet them."

Jenny said she would enjoy that. But it was the delighted expression on Andrew's face whenever he looked her way that stayed in Jenny's mind long after Andrew drove her home in a borrowed carriage.

··· ≻ ≺ ···

When Jenny slipped in the Lapps' back door, she was surprised to see Rebecca still up, lifting a pie from the oven.

Straightening, Rebecca said, "You've been gone a *gut* while."

Jenny realized the late-night baking was probably an excuse to be there when she arrived. She explained she'd gone to help Andrew look for Chester Lapp's dog, Posey.

"Ah, that silly pup—he's gone head over heels over her." Rebecca seemed to know.

"That's the one." She said they'd found Posey and taken her home.

"You must've seen Marnie, then?"

She didn't think she should reveal that Marnie had just been coming home in a van from a date. "Right as I was heading back here," she said vaguely.

"You two are getting along nicely, ain't so?"

Jenny nodded and said they were. "Say, I was wondering . . . did I happen to get any mail earlier?" It had been a while since she'd written to her parents, but Jenny wasn't certain they would actually write, especially when her mother had sent Dorie and Pamela after her. All the same, she could hope.

"No letters that I've seen." Rebecca placed the pie on a cooling rack and moved to the sink to wash her hands. "Are ya lookin' for something in particular?"

Jenny shrugged, not saying more. Her mind was overflowing with many pleasant things—she wanted to savor the evening rather than lose herself in small talk. She excused herself, eager to go upstairs and write in her journal.

Okay, this may sound earthshaking, but I think I might be falling in love again. The trick is that before I can be of real interest to anyone here in Hickory Hollow—including the very likeable Andrew Lapp—I must first be baptized into the church. At least, before I can be courted officially.

On the buggy ride back to Samuel Lapp's farm, would you believe that it began to snow softly, just like in the movies? I sat on the left side of the seat and watched Andrew handle the horse out of the corner of my eyes. We had several heavy woolen lap blankets tucked around us to keep us warm. I've never experienced anything quite like it. Something more ethereal than romantic, but I'm getting way ahead of myself!

It was especially nice bumping into Marnie and her beau, whom she introduced to Andrew and me, although she was a little reticent about doing so, there at the end of her father's lane. Marnie's eyebrows soared when she saw Andrew at the reins and me sitting in the buggy with him.

All in all, it's been an incredibly interesting day. If only it didn't have to end!

Now I need to get myself settled down after that coffee— don't I know better than to have caffeine so late? Time to read my Bible and pray for God's guidance. And to sleep . . . if I can!

Marnie felt it coming.

"You know better than to let the puppy out of the utility

room," her father scolded, raising his voice even as Marnie's uncles and aunts were out on the back porch saying their good-byes to Mamm. "What were ya thinkin', daughter?"

"I'll be more careful," she replied with a slight bow of her head.

"You'd better be," her father muttered, heading toward the stairs.

"I really am sorry, *Daed*." She followed him.

He kept going, ignoring her.

Part of her heart was broken anew each time he turned his back on her—more times than she could remember to count. *I'll be more careful with your precious pet*, she thought sadly. *But you won't keep me from Cousin Dan Fisher's meetings*.

Going to the kitchen to see cute little Posey, Marnie leaned down and lifted her into her arms, then slid onto her regular spot on the hard bench. She stared at the dark sky through the window—her relatives were still talking outside. Tears threatened to spill as she snuggled with the puppy. "Nosy Posey," she whispered. "You just had to see where I was goin' tonight and who I was with, didn't ya?"

Did Daed see Roy, too?

She worried that, because of her father's involvement in helping to start up the Bank of Bird-in-Hand, which appealed to Plain folk, he knew many Amish farmers and businessmen over where Roy and his family lived. Still, it was far better for Daed to recognize Roy as one of the prominent, progressive Flaud family than for him to hear where Roy had taken her this most inspiring night.

Chapter 31

Jenny was delighted when Rebecca invited her to go along to the Bird-in-Hand Farmers Market the next morning to help tend the cash register at Groff's Candies. The vendor, a friend of Rebecca's, was sick at home with the flu. So it was decided that Jenny would do the financial transactions and Rebecca would help the customers find what they were looking for among the homemade fudges, nuts, dried fruits, and brittles. Jenny asked if Rebecca was going to sell some of her jams and jellies, as well.

Rebecca shook her head. "The vendors don't work that way," she explained. "I'll just sell them at the house, like always."

Jenny was glad for the opportunity to get out for a good part of the day, wanting to clear her head. Today had her second-guessing why her mother hadn't written back. Not even a Thanksgiving card, the perfect excuse to get in touch.

Is she just waiting for me to fail . . . and return home?

This being the day before Thanksgiving, the marketplace was packed with patrons—young and old, couples and singles, and a number of families. The air smelled of fudge and freshly popped popcorn and, around certain men, sweet-smelling pipe tobacco.

Jenny had been told by both Rebecca and Marnie that Amish folk did not observe Thanksgiving Day, *"not like the English."* Instead, the day was typically taken up with all-day weddings, one of which Samuel and Rebecca would be attending tomorrow, in honor of their niece Susannah Lapp.

So I'll spend the day by myself, Jenny thought, reliving the many times she and Kiersten had helped debone the turkey for their mother after dinner, always searching for the wishbone. *Will I miss being there this year?*

Jenny worked nearly nonstop ringing up dozens of purchases. She didn't bother to look for Emmalyn Lapp this time and was relieved when a few hours passed and Andrew's sister had not appeared.

She did notice, however, a tall, brown-haired young man who very easily could have passed for Kyle Jackson's brother or cousin. She felt momentary surprise, then scolded herself, quite positive Kyle was nowhere near Lancaster County. *He's long gone from my life.*

Later, Ella Mae Zook and Mattie Beiler came by to say hello, each taking a small sample of homemade fudge. They stood there oohing about it, and Ella Mae's eyes danced at the rich taste. The Wise Woman appeared to be more spunky today than the last time Jenny had seen her, and Jenny smiled as she artfully reached for another piece while Mattie was talking with Rebecca.

"Do you know how *gut* this is for the arteries?" Ella Mae said with a chuckle. "'Specially if ya eat enough of it?"

Jenny played along. "So . . . how much is enough?"

"Oh, just let your sweet tooth decide."

The woman was adorable, and Jenny wished she had the opportunity to bump into her every day. "It's fun to see you, Ella Mae. Come by anytime." Jenny smiled at herself—she was starting to sound like Rebecca.

"I think it's time *you* dropped by for some tea again, Jenny." Ella Mae turned things around as she was known to do. "Will ya?"

"When I'm able to get free, sure."

"How 'bout tomorrow? Or are you goin' with Samuel and Rebecca to the wedding?"

"I haven't been invited," she replied, glancing at Rebecca, who was still gabbing with Mattie. "Do you know if anyone serves turkey on Thanksgiving Day around here?"

"Only if it's Amish roast—ya know, cooked turkey or chicken mixed with stuffing. Same as what's served at the wedding feasts." Ella Mae blinked her small eyes. "But now, if it's turkey you want, I could make ya some."

She felt silly for saying anything. "Oh, I don't want you to go to any work! Especially not on my account."

"Well, you just make sure ya come for dinner tomorrow, hear?"

Rebecca turned away from Mattie to focus on them. "What's this?" she said. "Did I hear you two makin' plans?"

"She's comin' for the noon meal tomorrow," Ella Mae informed Mattie. "We're havin' us a Thanksgiving feast!"

Rebecca's eyelashes fluttered. "I beg your pardon?"

"We can't have the poor thing all alone on an English holiday, now, can we? She's gonna have family back home enjoying turkey and mashed potatoes and gravy and whatnot all. The least we can do is give her some turkey roast, ain't so?"

Mattie shook her head, and Jenny had the impression the midwife wasn't surprised at anything her mother proposed.

"What can I bring to help?" Jenny asked, hoping she wouldn't suggest a loaf of homemade bread, knowing her own track record.

"Just yourself." Ella Mae's white head bobbed up and down. "Leave everything to Mattie and me."

Rebecca's smile spread to her ears, and Jenny could hear her trying to squelch her snickers. "So we'll have a feast at the wedding, and so will yous."

"And why not? It's mighty close to a month since Jenny came to us. I daresay a celebration's in order."

Jenny blushed.

"Goodness' sake, Ella Mae," muttered Rebecca as she went over to help a customer. The young woman's cozy red sweat suit reminded Jenny of one she'd once had, and for that single second, she missed wearing sweats.

"There'll be pecan pie and pumpkin, too. I know what Englischers like to eat," Ella Mae said, her face beaming mischief. "Drop by round eleven-thirty—come hungry."

"Denki," said Jenny, her mouth watering.

Mattie went over to her mother, and the older woman reached for her arm and headed off. A few steps forward and she turned to wink at Jenny.

She's got something up her sleeve. Jenny was very sure.

After supper, Jenny slipped outside under a canopy of stars. She had missed her peaceful prayer time at the springhouse. The night was mild, and since Rebecca wasn't on the list of kitchen workers for the wedding tomorrow, both she and

Samuel were relaxing in their rocking chairs by the heater stove in the kitchen. Jenny wanted to give the couple some time alone, especially because she'd heard them talking in an obvious code during the meal, Deitsch words and phrases mixed in with English. Unknown to them, she'd managed to piece together some of it. Evidently, the bishop and the deacon had pulled together a short list of young people who'd attended a Bible study last evening. Jenny recalled the note on the fridge at the bishop's house. Was this talk about Dan and Katie's meeting?

She was glad the evening was so temperate compared to last night's tromp through Hickory Hollow to look for Posey. She thought of the Wise Woman's visit at market earlier and her generous invitation. Why had Ella Mae seemed to seek her out, and in front of both Mattie and Rebecca, no less? And what was all the talk about celebrating? Jenny didn't feel she deserved it. *I haven't yet accomplished what I've set out to do.*

Jenny carried a lengthy mental list as she walked down the lane to the springhouse steps. She needed to pray for guidance. She no longer had the confidence of her first days at the Lapps', uncertain she was able to do all that was needed to make her Amish dream a reality.

Chapter 32

Thanksgiving morning, Jenny spent the first couple of hours trying to make two loaves of bread that wouldn't collapse like a sinkhole. Much earlier, even before breakfast, she'd gone out to groom Ol' Molasses and narrowly missed being kicked. The day was off to quite a start.

She had started long before Samuel and Rebecca left for the wedding to gather the ingredients, mix them, and punch down the dough. Jenny needed all the practice she could get, and while she waited for the dough to rise the second time, she sewed.

The thought occurred to her that she might write to her mother again, or to Kiersten for the first time. But she didn't want to appear desperate. The silence on their end was becoming deafening, but she couldn't blame them, could she? She was the one who'd left without saying what she was up to. *Neurotically guarded.*

With every stitch she made, her prayer was for wisdom in following her heart here. Jenny didn't want to think she was second-guessing her resolve, but she knew she was. "I'm only half Amish, if that," she whispered. "When will it register on the inside?"

When it was time, she carefully patted the dough into the loaf pans, hoping for success. When, oh when, would it happen? If she couldn't even make a decent loaf of bread, how would she ever manage a kitchen as an Amish wife and mother?

If I'm fortunate enough to ever marry.

Marnie wished to goodness her parents had reserved their criticisms for a different day. The three of them had ridden together in one buggy to Susannah Lapp's wedding earlier that morning. Her father's sharp words on the way there had spoiled the service for her, and she'd fretted and stewed ever since. Presently, her head throbbed, and her thoughts were spinning at the revelation that someone had seen her and Roy over at Dan and Katie's.

And if that wasn't enough, her father's spy, whoever he was, recognized Roy as the son of a progressive Amish businessman. Marnie sighed, knowing she was in twice as thick a stew. *"You are a very poor example to your younger siblings. Des is arig—bad!"* her father had said, his face red with anger. *"You must not continue seein' that Flaud fella, and you will stay away from the Fishers' place, too."*

She could hardly hold her head up the rest of the morning, even when it was time to file out of the house before the wedding feast and cluster with the single girls, all of whom had serious beaus.

How quickly things had come to a halt. And worse, the precious feelings she'd had at Cousin Katie's must be left to flicker away. Marnie was a captive in her own home, cut off from her beloved and prohibited from following her newfound faith. What could she do?

Suddenly, Katie's invitation to stay with them began to look like an actual possibility . . . a place of refuge. Her mind turned around the idea again and again, but there was no easy answer.

The crisp air felt good as Marnie stood with the other young women her age under the overhang of the stable. Her cousin Mandie glanced at her, then gave her a closer look.

"Are you ill?" Mandie asked as they waited.

"Do I look it?"

Her cousin nodded her blond head. "I've been worried 'bout ya all mornin', Marnie. You all right?"

Oh, the questions! They only served to make her feel sorry for herself. "I'll be fine," she told Mandie, but she knew she wouldn't. If Marnie was to submit to her father, she would be miserable the rest of her life. And if she defied him, she might lose the love of her family.

It was close to eleven o'clock when Jenny opened the oven and removed the steaming loaf. But as before, the bread had flopped in the middle. "What am I doing wrong?"

Disgusted, she refused to give up. Tomorrow she would try again, and she would leave extra money with the weekly rent payment for Rebecca to replace the wasted ingredients.

Jenny ran upstairs to change into a clean dress, having spilled milk and flour on both her apron and her dress. "I'm a sight," she said, trying to put the baking disaster out of her mind.

It was going to be the strangest Thanksgiving ever, but hadn't she counted the cost before coming here? It was her choice, after all, to separate from her world in an attempt to live a life in unity with God and the People. In so doing, Jenny had lost her family.

Just like Katie . . .

— ➤ ◄ —

"Ach, are you sure?" Rebecca asked Rachel Stoltzfus, the bishop's mother-in-law, who had ridden along with her and Samuel to the wedding. They were sitting alone at the table, having just finished their dessert of delicious white cake, and the topic of Katie and Dan's invitation had come up.

Rachel removed a lace-edged hankie from beneath her sleeve and leaned close to Rebecca, whispering. "Word has it your daughter's offered to open up her home to two of our teenage girls."

"You don't mean it!"

"Just ask Lovina Yoder."

Rebecca found it difficult to consider talking to their preacher's wife about such a matter. "Ach, this is *greislich*—dreadful."

"Jah, indeed."

"Why would Dan and Katie do such a thing?" She could not for the life of her understand what they were thinking.

"Well, when ya believe in something so strongly that you're willin' to leave family and home to pursue it, ya never know what's next." Rachel wiped her brow with her hankie. "Once this gets out, I'm afraid we could see a whole bunch of young folk movin' away."

"Why's that?"

Rachel turned to glance over her plump shoulder, then

looked back at Rebecca. "Some are sayin' the bishop's gonna empty out the church. You can read between the lines, ain't?"

"Too strict?" Rebecca bent near Rachel's ear to say it.

"Seems so."

"Well, we've always known that. What's different?"

"Modern ways are creepin' in—smartphones and iPads and whatnot all. Word has it the young folk are talkin' privately amongst themselves about their questions—and the bishop. Something 'bout goin' viral."

Rebecca shuddered to think her own daughter was paving the way for an exit, if that's what was happening. Could it be true? It was ever so hard to believe that more than just a couple of girls might want to leave Hickory Hollow. "Are ya sure this isn't tittle-tattle?"

"Ain't gossip." Rachel shook her head. "Like I said, if ya don't believe me, go an' talk to Lovina."

"Oh, dear me." Reaching to cover Rachel's wrinkled hand with her own, Rebecca knew it was high time to write Katie a letter. And she would do so the very minute she returned home today.

Jenny was surprised to see Emmalyn Lapp already there at Ella Mae's when she arrived. The Amish teen was down on the floor playing with three young children, whom Ella Mae quickly introduced as Mattie's grandchildren—Ella Mae's "greats."

Did the Wise Woman know Emmalyn was coming? Jenny wondered. *Did she plan this?* Jenny offered to help set the table in the larger house, but Ella Mae insisted that Mattie had already finished doing that. "You just relax and enjoy the family atmosphere," Ella Mae said with a smile. Yet how could Jenny, with Emmalyn there?

Eventually she learned that Emmalyn had chosen not to attend the wedding today, so at Ella Mae's invitation, she'd come to help entertain the children.

Interesting, Jenny thought.

After spending time in Ella Mae's kitchen and carrying over several hot dishes to the main house, Jenny was relieved when Mattie called all of them next door to be seated. Emmalyn went to sit with the youngest children at the far end, away from Jenny.

David and Mattie Beiler and their grandchildren were there, as well as the bishop's wife, Mary, with six of the bishop's children still living at home. It surprised Jenny to see Mary Beiler without her husband, but someone said that the bishop had gone to marry Samuel and Rebecca's niece to her longtime beau, Adam Miller.

All the same, Jenny wondered why Mary and the children were there and not at the wedding. *What's going on?*

Marnie felt altogether blue by the time the wedding feast was finished. It was hard not to remember how happy she'd been at Cousin Linda Ebersol's wedding with Roy two weeks ago. How she'd loved spending the day with him!

Naomi Beiler, who had also gone to the Fishers' Bible study, smiled from across the room. Marnie rose and went to her, and Naomi suggested they go for a walk. "I can't breathe in here anymore," Naomi whispered.

Agreeing to go, Marnie hoped she wasn't in for more bad news. The day had been fraught with enough emotion. "Are you enjoyin' yourself at all?" she asked as they made their way up the road.

"Not much." Naomi sniffled.

"You too?"

Naomi nodded slowly. "I had such wunnerbaar-*gut* plans, but they're upset now 'cause I got found out. Did ya know Preacher Yoder was over there in the shadows watchin' all of us file into Dan and Katie's Tuesday night?"

"Jah, I heard someone was spyin'. Didn't know it was Preacher Yoder, though."

"What're you gonna do, Marnie?"

She shrugged. "What *can* I do? We'll just have to quit goin', is all."

"Well, you might not know it, but I've decided to take Katie up on her invitation to move in over there." Naomi was fuming.

Marnie stopped walking, shocked. "You'd do that—you'd up and leave your family?"

Naomi jerked on her Kapp strings till one of them popped right off. "Just look what I did," she said and burst into tears. "Just look. . . ."

"Maybe it's a sign." Marnie wished she could comfort her.

"I want a different life, one like Katie's and Dan's," Naomi insisted. "Don't ya see how happy they are?" She paused to brush back tears. "Just think 'bout it. Most of the men I know are sour faced, and the womenfolk, well, the happiest times are when we're all workin' at a quilting bee or whatnot." Naomi started walking again.

Marnie listened but did not agree. "Maybe you're only seekin' out the miserable ones. Could that be?"

Naomi said she didn't know. "*Gut* thing I ain't baptized. I can fly away . . . if I get the gumption to."

Marnie didn't comment. Still, she felt awful bad for Naomi. She would have the ministerial brethren breathing down her neck now for sure.

"Don't let me sway you, though, Marnie." Naomi slowed her pace in spite of the cold. "You've got your own mind to make up."

"Does the bishop know you're movin' to Fishers'?"

"How can he not know?" Naomi whimpered. "The way the grapevine goes."

"Well, this is the first *I've* heard it."

Naomi merely bobbed her head, her face wrinkling as if to cry, and Marnie reached for her hand.

Chapter 33

After the memorable Thanksgiving feast, Jenny helped Emmalyn dress Mattie's three small grandchildren, putting on their coats, knit hats, scarves, and mittens. They dashed out the back door, along with Emmalyn and Jenny, too, into the big yard, where mature trees rimmed the area to the north. One in particular had an inviting circular wooden seat built at its base. Though the air was brisk, the sun was strong and warm. The lone boy and two little girls ran around the tree, flapping arms held high, then would sit down for a few seconds on the wooden seat before popping back up to run again.

It looked to Jenny like they were pretending to be either birds or butterflies. Perhaps the boy was the bird and the girls were young butterflies fresh out of cocoons. She stood just a few yards back from Emmalyn, unsure if she dared subject herself to Andrew's sister again. *So far, so good,* she thought, looking at the sky and wondering what her family was doing today, besides eating themselves into oblivion.

"It was awful nice of Ella Mae and Mattie to celebrate an

Englischer's holiday with you," Emmalyn finally said, her eyes meeting Jenny's.

"It certainly was."

"Never saw that happen before round here. Prob'ly never will again."

"It really wasn't necessary," Jenny said. "But I appreciate it."

"Well, you've given up a lot to come here, I 'spect."

"In some ways, yes . . . er, jah."

Emmalyn fell silent and the children's playful sounds filled the yard. The boy had no problem fitting in with his sisters, Jenny noticed, and she remembered her own brother's futile attempts to mesh with her and Kiersten when they were kids. It had basically been Cameron against the two of them from early on. Then later, Kiersten had teamed up with Cameron against Jenny. *Someone was always on the outside looking in,* she realized, feeling sad as she watched the Amish youngsters play so delightfully together. Rebecca might say it was all in the upbringing, and Jenny had to agree.

"Have ya learned the shortcut for makin' butter?" Emmalyn asked unexpectedly.

"No," Jenny said, not sure where this was coming from.

"You just pour some fresh cream in a canning jar and make sure the lid's on real tight, then put it in the washing machine."

After the trick Emmalyn had pulled after the first shared meal, Jenny looked at her skeptically. "You're not pulling my leg, are you?"

"Just ask Ella Mae—she does it sometimes, too."

Jenny still wasn't sure if Emmalyn was actually serious, so she changed the subject to baby-sitting. "Looks like you're having fun today with the Beiler grandkids."

"Oh jah. But 'tween you and me, it all depends on *die Kinner*—the children." Emmalyn glanced back at her. "How do ya like takin' care of the bishop's youngest?"

"They're very sweet."

Emmalyn nodded. "I've kinda wondered how ya got that job, considering . . ."

Emmalyn's words always had a way of jabbing. "I really don't know," Jenny replied softly, gently, the way Rebecca had taught her. Above all she wanted *"the ornament of a meek and quiet spirit."*

Soon, the bishop's eleven-year-old son Jacob and five-year-old daughter Mary Mae came outside to play, too. They had not even the slightest hesitation to join the others, and they all swooped and darted about like barn swallows in flight.

Why can't I merge into Amish life like that? Jenny wondered, a little envious of the fluid motions of their interaction.

Emmalyn went to sit on the seat at the base of the tree, and the children clapped their hands and treated her like a princess. Sunbeams dappled the front of Emmalyn's hair, making it look like spun gold. Was there such a thing as Amish royalty? Jenny imagined that if there were dandelions to decorate Emmalyn's hair, the girls might have made a crown with them.

They adore her. . . .

Jenny turned to go inside, contemplating the odd dichotomy. Was it true that children often sensed whom they could trust and who was real or fake?

Is Emmalyn only difficult around me?

Naomi's cheeks and nose were red with the burning cold as she and Marnie approached the bride's parents' home. "Do you think of me as a person who'd openly disobey?" Marnie probed.

"Well, if you're thinkin' thataway, then maybe so. Are you planning to?"

She couldn't tell Naomi her plans, because she wasn't sure of them herself.

"What if Roy asks you to leave the Amish with him—I mean, if *he's* leavin'?"

"He's never confided that." Shaking her head, Marnie felt sick at the thought. "I look at what's happened with the breach 'tween Cousin Katie and her parents and brothers. It's awful sad, ya know. And it's not changin' anytime soon. Dan and Katie aren't comin' back to bow their knee and repent. Prob'ly never," said Marnie.

"It's like I said: They're happy in their new church community. God is their King, not the bishop."

Marnie gasped. "You think like that?"

"Sometimes it seems like that." Naomi said it straight-faced. "I've heard a lot of the other youth are getting fed up, too."

Marnie didn't want to defame their bishop's position. "They'd better be careful what they say. Bishop John was chosen by divine lot—God ordained."

Naomi didn't bow her head in shame, but she nodded slowly. "It's all so hard to understand. But Dan Fisher's teachin' from the New Testament makes sense to me."

"I agree, but it's all woven together like a well-made basket. Don't forget, you can't have one without the other—faith without family. And vice versa."

Naomi hissed, "That's silly, Marnie, and you know it. It's the Lord who's the center of our faith."

Marnie didn't say more. She felt nearly frozen from their long walk and was anxious to get warmed up.

"I'll be prayin' for ya," Naomi said as they went.

Marnie thanked her and hurried around to the back door, surprised to see most of the young couples had disappeared from the bride's house. *Must be in the barn or the stable.*

Her parents, however, were sitting in the front room speaking with Bishop John Beiler. When Marnie spotted him, the man of God looked at her with fiery eyes, and she was helpless not to meet his gaze.

He knows everything!

Ella Mae was dropping a sugar cube into her coffee cup as Jenny returned to the Beilers' large farmhouse. Emmalyn had gone over to pick up the toys at Ella Mae's.

Mattie motioned Jenny back to the table, where the adults had settled in for coffee and another helping of pumpkin pie. Two of the bishop's children, Levi and Susie, were playing dominoes at the far end of the table.

"Is it getting colder out?" asked Mattie.

"It's pretty nice in the sun," Jenny told them.

"And the little ones are bundled up, so they should be all right," Mattie replied.

Ella Mae scooted over next to Jenny. "Mary has something she'd like to say," she said softly. The frail woman leaned forward to get Mary's attention. "Tell Jenny what ya told me earlier."

"Well, sure." Mary looked like she'd been put on the spot. "Bishop John has been askin' me to talk to you."

Jenny tensed up.

"There's something goin' on . . . well, how should I say

this?" Mary paused. "The bishop's aware of one of our former church member's interaction with—"

"Just come out and say it," Ella Mae interrupted.

Please, no, thought Jenny, clasping her hands beneath the table. Oh, she felt nauseous, recalling that fateful night, following Rebecca in the dark, up the long road. Then, discovering the secret and wishing for all the world she'd never known the forbidden pull between mother and daughter.

"Have you met Naomi Beiler yet?" asked Mary. "She's our niece . . . the bishop's blood kin."

"Jah, once." Jenny's heart pounded. Was this about Naomi or Rebecca? She held her breath.

"Would ya like to befriend her, maybe?" Mary continued, explaining that the bishop was concerned about her and thought Jenny's fervor for the Amish life might benefit his "rather wayward" niece. "We're concerned she's planning to leave the hollow."

Jenny was startled by the request, just as she'd been surprised at being entrusted with the bishop and Mary's little girls so early in her Proving time. "What would you suggest?"

Mary went on, saying she'd thought about perhaps having Naomi over to show Jenny how to do piecework for quilting on one of the days when Jenny was caring for the girls. "How's that?"

"That'd be great—I've always wanted to learn to piece a quilt."

"*Gut* then, I'll let John know. I'm so glad I got the chance to talk with you today. Denki, Jenny. This will mean so much to him—to us both."

"If Jenny can work a miracle, that is," Ella Mae piped up, a half smile on her face.

Jenny offered a smile of her own to Mary, her heartbeat

slowing again in relief that Rebecca Lapp wasn't going to be the topic of conversation. But she was very curious about what the bishop thought she as a seeker might do for his niece.

Naomi has grown up Amish, so how can I possibly be of help?

Chapter 34

J enny relished her time with Ella Mae's charming family, as well as everyone else present. She learned from Mary that she and the children hadn't been invited to the wedding where the bishop presided. "I imagine there were enough folk there without our brood," Mary chuckled.

All of them divided up in groups and played Dutch Blitz for an hour or more, and she quickly understood why David Beiler called the game habit-forming. Jenny would have stayed longer, but an idea had come to mind that she was eager to pursue. Somewhere in a nearby field, there was a phone shanty, she'd been told—one concealed by a clump of tall bushes. Assuming Jenny could locate it, she would try to get in touch with her family. *If I can keep up my courage.*

She wanted to share a little with them about her exceptional Thanksgiving Day. *Remarkable in every way,* Jenny thought as she again thanked Ella Mae, and David and Mattie, too. She felt like she was actually part of the Amish community here at last.

The lengthy walk back across the field toward the Lapps' was a haze of delight. These people really cared about her.

And that dear, sweet Ella Mae—the special meal really had been her doing.

Today would have been perfect, if it weren't for my jumpy conscience. Jenny relived her initial fearful reaction to Mary Beiler's comments. "What will I say if I'm ever confronted about Rebecca?" she whispered into the cold air, breath spiraling up. Her stomach turned, but at least for now, she would continue to honor Rebecca's plea for silence.

… ➤ ◄ …

Jenny had been home for only a few minutes when she heard a knock at the back door. Looking out, she saw Andrew Lapp with a wrapped package in hand. She opened the door. "Hello, Andrew," she said, hoping she didn't seem overeager to see him.

"I have something for ya," he said, inching the present toward her. He was dressed as if he were going to church.

"Is it my birthday?" She laughed a little, feeling awkward but pleased.

"Just got to thinkin' you might be a little homesick, ya know . . . today." He looked quite serious. "I hoped I'd catch ya before Samuel and Rebecca returned home, maybe." His smile was as addictive—if not more so—as the fast-moving game at the Beilers' earlier.

"I don't know what to say," she replied.

"You don't have to say anything—just accept it." He grinned.

"Denki, Andrew." *How sweet is this?*

"I'd invite you in, but . . ."

He agreed and nodded. "I understand, and I'll be on my way."

"Oh, before you go," she said, "do you happen to know where the nearest phone shanty is located?"

He removed his black felt hat, then glanced back at her, eyes twinkling. "You know what? What if I just took ya over there?"

"Oh, would you mind?"

"*Gaar net*—not at all!"

"Okay, I'll just grab my coat." She set the gift on a small table near the door.

"All right, then." He held her gaze for a second longer than necessary, then stepped back and headed for the waiting horse and buggy.

Closing the door, Jenny donned Rebecca's old coat and outer black bonnet. She tied it quickly beneath her chin and looked curiously at the gift with the card attached. *I'll wait to open it*, she decided before hurrying outside.

··· ➤ ⬳ ···

Jenny felt each movement of Andrew's trotting mare. *Or is it a gallop?* Certainly the horse was going faster than any she'd encountered before. Maybe it was just Andrew's way of showing how adept he was at handling his beautiful ebony horse.

"I should've opened your present back there," she blurted out. "I'm really sorry."

Andrew shook his head and smiled at her. *Always smiling.* "No hurry. It'll still be there when you return."

She thought of his sister's strange butter-making shortcut and almost asked Andrew if he'd ever heard of such a thing, then thought better of it.

He turned off Hickory Lane and headed north a little ways before pulling over onto the shoulder. The horse came to a halt close to a thick cluster of bushes that nearly obscured the phone booth. "Here 'tis. And if you plan to make a call out of state, you'll need my code." He explained that he would receive the bill later, and she could pay him back at some point. "Least if it's a long chat." He winked at her.

He suspects what I'm up to!

"Oh, I'll reimburse you, no matter what." Thanks to his flirting, she felt like a schoolgirl.

As she made her way around the bushes, Jenny suddenly wondered if making the call was a good idea after all. Besides, why would she risk spoiling such a wonderful day?

In spite of that, she felt compelled to place the call. She opened the wooden door and slipped into the narrow space, where she picked up the receiver and gave the code, then dialed.

Her heart in her throat, she nearly hung up at the sound of the first ring. One . . . two . . . and three.

Where was everyone? Hadn't they had their usual celebration?

Then, just as she was feeling dejected to be missing out on whatever it was her family was doing, Kiersten answered. "Burns residence."

"Hey, sis . . . it's Jenny."

"Jenny who?" Kiersten laughed.

"Happy Thanksgiving to you, too," she said. "Just wanted to greet you and everyone."

"Cool . . . thanks." Kiersten paused. "The same to you, Jen."

"Did the family get together?"

"Yep, and Cameron's here with his new girl and her baby."

"A child?"

Kiersten sighed. "It's a long story."

"Well, I hope he's happy."

"Yes, and happiness always counts, doesn't it?"

"I mean it," Jenny said.

Kiersten seemed to whisper to someone else. "It's Jen, calling from Amishville."

Feeling strange at this, Jenny said, "Kiersten, is Mom there?"

"She's in the kitchen, but I'll get her. And don't break her heart again, okay?"

"What's that supposed to mean?"

"You should know—you wrote the letter, right?"

"Kiersten . . ."

"Well, I hope you're calling to say you're done with your super-crazy stunt."

Jenny couldn't speak. Was it always going to be like this? It was all she could do to remain meek and mild with her sister. *Like boot camp for the emotions,* she thought.

"You *are* coming home, aren't you?" Kiersten added.

Maybe for a visit someday . . . if I survive this call.

"Jenny? Are you there?"

"Jah . . . er, yes."

"Oh, that's just great—now you're talking Amish, too?"

"Kiersten, just please get Mom, okay?" Talking to her sister was as exhausting as she remembered.

There was a silence broken by muffled talking here and there, and what seemed like an endless wait for her mother. Was Kiersten filling Mom in on everything she'd just said?

At last, Jenny heard her mom's voice. "Hi, sweetheart. Are you all right?"

"Hi, Mom. Yes, I'm fine. It's wonderful to hear you. And happy Thanksgiving!"

"The same to you. How nice of you to call."

"I've been wanting to talk to you. Kiersten said you received my letter."

A long pause. Then, "It was a complete shock. No matter how you look at it, Jenny, I never saw it coming."

You should have . . . all my life. "I didn't mean to hurt you." She thought she might choke up. "I wanted you to know where I am . . . that I'm safe and very happy."

"Just not here, honey." Her mother sighed into the phone. "Pamela and Dorie seemed to think you were . . . well, doing okay."

"I wish you hadn't sent them, but it was good to visit." She forced a laugh. "I think they were sorry they came, though."

"Oh no . . . no. They never said that."

They reported back?!

"Jenny, darling, when are you coming home?"

"I don't plan to, Mom." Hadn't she made this clear in the letter? "Not if I'm accepted as an Amish convert."

"What are you thinking, dear?" Her mother sighed. "You're not Amish."

"Not yet, no." Jenny's patience was being put to the test. "I'm sorry this is upsetting to you, Mom."

"More than you know, honey."

"Is Dad upset, too?" She had to ask.

"Oh, you know your father. It takes a lot to trouble him."

"Well, tell him I called, okay?"

"Sure, dear. And please keep in touch."

Jenny nodded, tears threatening as she squeaked her response.

"Call anytime," her mother said. Then, before Jenny could fully find her voice, "Good-bye."

What a disaster. Gently she put the receiver back, buried her head in her hands, and sobbed, glad for the privacy of the closed door. For all the years Jenny had tried so hard to be known and accepted, she wept.

Chapter 35

Jenny wished she'd had the sense to carry a hankie under her sleeve, like Rebecca. She had no other option but to lift her apron hem and wipe her eyes and face on the back, then dab at her nose. "I'm a mess," she muttered. She'd indulged her pity party for too long.

Once she felt more composed, she pushed the phone shanty door open and was startled but pleased to see Andrew a few yards away, looking concerned. "Guess my call took longer than planned," she said with a weak smile.

"Jenny?" He tilted his head, eyes searching hers. "Are you all right?"

She couldn't tell him without more tears, so she shook her head and moved out of the phone booth. She fell in step with him out to the road, where he accompanied her to the opposite side of the buggy and helped her up, holding her hand. "Denki," she said when she was in and straightening her black apron.

Andrew hurried around the front to hop in on the driver's side. "How 'bout a short ride—see the area?" He seemed to read her and know that she needed some tender care.

"Sure, but I don't want to take up your time."

"No problem. I took off work for Adam and Susannah's wedding—same one Samuel and Rebecca attended." He looked at her then, a concerned expression on his face. "I'd really like to make ya smile today, Jenny . . . somehow or other."

She felt her cheeks redden. "That's very nice of you."

"I'm not just sayin' that," he added.

Jenny felt the familiar thrill of being pursued—and wasn't Andrew doing just that? She was comforted by their small talk as they toured Hickory Hollow. Oddly, all of this seemed more real to her than the frustrating phone call home. And far more pleasant.

"Adam Miller, the groom, is a cousin to Tessie, a relative of mine. Tessie was also at the wedding with her four older sisters and all their husbands, and she was askin' about you, Jenny. Awful curious, I daresay." He shrugged sheepishly before adding, "Anyhow, Tessie's wonderin' if there's anything she can do to help you get better adjusted here. She'd really like to."

"That's so thoughtful—please tell her I appreciate it."

"Why don't *you* tell her? She'll be at the quiltin' bee over at Mary Beiler's next week."

"Perfect, then, I will." Jenny was dying to ask why his own sister wasn't as considerate. "I had dinner today with the bishop's wife and children at David and Mattie Beiler's house. Ella Mae was there . . . Emmalyn, too."

He nodded as if he'd known.

"It was Ella Mae's idea to cook a Thanksgiving Day feast for me," she explained.

"Not surprising."

Jenny agreed and folded her hands. "Everyone likes the Wise Woman."

"Well, and you can see why."

She really wanted to talk further about Emmalyn, but since he didn't go there, she dropped the idea.

They rode all the way up past the Hickory Hollow school-house on the right side of the road before getting to Route 340. "I want to show you the school where I attended as a boy," Andrew said, slowing the horse to a stop. "Several of my girl cousins were in the grades below me, but they were more like sisters. And growin' up around so many girls and other young women in the church district, I had plenty of opportunity to get to know them. But none of the suitable girls appealed to me . . . for a bride." He was quiet for a moment, his head forward, eyes on the road. "I've been accused more than once of bein' too picky."

She wondered where he was going with this, and there was a long moment as he seemed to measure her, as though judging whether he should continue in a similar vein. "Do you mind if I'm frank with you, Jenny? I mean, I don't want to offend you . . . or give you the wrong idea."

"Honesty's good," she managed to say, suddenly feeling a bit tense.

Andrew coughed nervously. "I respect your courage . . . actually everything about you." He turned to face her. "I admire how you stick to your chores and practices that have to be foreign to you, doin' so with kindness—and even *gut* humor. But most of all, with a gracious spirit. Truth be told, you're the kind of girl I've been lookin' for." He stopped for a moment, frowning a bit. "But you prob'ly won't be here a year from now, will ya?"

She was completely taken aback and had to scramble to gather her wits. "Only if I don't learn to bake a better loaf of bread." She tried to laugh but it came out as a sigh. How had they arrived at such a serious discussion? "You know, all the other girls around here can cook and can and bake and think like an Amishwoman. They have me beat hands down."

"But they don't have your sweet personality, or your determination—least not the girls I know." His expression was solemn. "So many of our young folk are mighty curious about the modern world, tryin' to get out of the church. And here you are, trying to get in."

"Maybe they've taken their Plain heritage for granted." She looked at the barns and the dairy cattle, envying anyone who'd grown up here. "I have so much catching up to do, beginning with the language."

"But that's comin' along much better."

"Well, slowly."

"And you're learnin' to hitch up, ain't so?" he said kindly. "For that matter, I've been thinkin' we could have ya try hitching up a pony to a pony cart, to make things easier. What do ya say?"

We . . .

"Whatever works best for someone who's all thumbs with a harness," she replied, pondering this. "Any ideas on bread making, as well?"

He chuckled. "Whoever said a girl has to be an expert in the kitchen?"

"*Amish* girls, of course!" Now she was laughing with him.

Andrew looked down at her folded hands and then back at the road. "None of the things you mentioned are as important as a person's heart," he said, pausing. "I'd like to get to know ya better, Jenny . . . if that's all right."

The day of her baptism had never seemed so distant. "*You're not one of us,*" Emmalyn had pointed out that day at market. "As a friend?" she asked softly.

"Of course."

"Will it be a problem for you, spending time with a seeker like me?"

"If young couples see each other secretly, why can't we?" He smiled at her, so striking in his black felt hat and black coat. "We could meet at the springhouse once a week . . . to pray, then to talk or walk, depending on the weather."

She thought again of Emmalyn. "I probably shouldn't say this. . . ." Her voice trailed off.

"Say whatever you like, Jenny."

Her heart warmed to this thoughtful man. "Your younger sister seems leery of me."

He nodded, his expression reflective. "S'pose she is, jah."

Jenny held her breath. Had she spoken out of turn?

"I take it Emmalyn hasn't told ya why."

Jenny shook her head. "We *did* chat this afternoon while watching Ella Mae's great-grandchildren playing outside." *And she was nicer today. . . .*

"I may tell you 'bout all that someday," Andrew said quietly. "When you and I know each other better."

Jenny acquiesced but remained very curious.

When Jenny saw that Samuel and Rebecca were already home, she suggested Andrew let her out on the road. She thanked him for the ride and for the gift, promising to go in and open it right away.

"Will ya meet me next Thursday evening at the springhouse pond, then?"

She smiled. "I'll look forward to it."

"Till then," he said, getting out of the carriage to help

her down. His smile touched her heart, and he released her quickly before she hurried through the front yard and around to the back of the house.

Her heart fell when she stepped inside and noticed the present was missing. Had Rebecca found it? Oh, Jenny wished she'd taken it directly to her room. What was she thinking, leaving it out?

Going into the utility room, she removed her outer clothes and hung them on the specified wooden pegs. Then she looked to see if Rebecca was anywhere in the kitchen, which thankfully remained empty. Tiptoeing in, she spotted Andrew's gift on the kitchen table, the card still tucked under the ribbon, with only her name printed on the front. *Whew*, she thought, taking it upstairs to her room and closing the door.

What will I tell Rebecca if she asks?

An impious thought crossed her mind. After all, she was keeping Rebecca's secret, so wasn't it fair to expect her to do the same?

Jenny unwrapped Andrew's gift and was tickled to see a hardcover devotional book, *Streams in the Desert*. She opened to the front page. Andrew had written an inscription: *To Jenny Burns. May God grant you the peace your heart craves here in Hickory Hollow—for always. Sincerely, Andrew Lapp.*

"For always," she whispered, realizing it was his way of saying that he hoped she would still be here in a year, if not forever.

"How considerate," she murmured as she paged through the devotional book. It surprised her that he seemed so in tune with her spiritual yearnings. He, too, enjoyed communing in prayer with God.

Andrew's card was next, and she purposely hesitated to open it. Didn't she already care too much for him?

She held the envelope and stared at her name in his strong, flowing handwriting. What could he possibly have written inside?

Chapter 36

Y ou simply cannot do it!" Marnie's friend Tessie Miller
said, shaking her head as they walked home late that
night from the barn Singing after Susannah's wedding. "You'll
be sorry—I just know it."

Marnie refused to cry, afraid her tears would freeze on her
cold cheeks. "But I love him. I'd follow Roy anywhere."

"To Bird-in-Hand, then? To his progressive church?" Tessie
bit her lip. "You'll be the next Katie Lapp."

"Naomi Beiler and I might share a room over at Fishers',
till we're able to get out on our own."

Tessie wrinkled her pretty little nose. "You mean till you're
married. But why not just stay home till then? It'd spare your
family the heartache."

"Oh, Tessie . . . I'm in a fog. No matter what, I'm cooked."
Marnie wrapped her scarf closer to her mouth and tried not to
breathe in the frigid air. A half moon glistened in the heavens. "Since the preacher knows—and the bishop, too—soon
everyone will. I don't think I could bear bein' looked down on."

"Just be thankful you can't be shunned." Tessie shivered
noticeably.

"Small comfort."

Tessie went on, urging Marnie not to move in with Katie and Dan, insisting it would be a blight on her. "It'll look like you're in favor of their leavin' the People."

"Maybe so."

"Just bide your time. Please don't go an' live at Fishers'."

Marnie hugged herself, glad for a warm coat and scarf. She looked at the clear sky. "Isn't it peculiar, really, how someone like Jenny Burns can come in and be so devoted after only a month's time?"

"Does it make ya feel guilty?"

"Something awful." Marnie pondered that. Oh, the irony of it all, when she'd played such a big part in Jenny's life-altering choice. "Makes me wonder what's wrong with me."

"Well, it's not like you're going fancy. You'll still be Amish."

"Daed won't think much of the difference. He'll say I'm scarcely Amish, wanting to attend Bible studies with my beau and all."

Tessie nodded. "And I still say you'll be honoring the Old Ways, no matter."

"If only my father could look at it the way you do." *The way I do . . .*

"Besides, wouldn't he want you to marry for love?" Tessie asked.

"I'd hope so." Marnie wished the night weren't so cold and the walk home so far. And she wished, too, that she might see her sweet beau again. But how?

Maybe Ella Mae will have some ideas, she thought, determined to visit the Old Wise Woman, and soon.

It was late when Jenny reread the card wishing her *A happy English Thanksgiving.* Andrew had also printed the reference to a Scripture verse at the bottom, below his name. She didn't even have to look it up, because it was one she had memorized a few years ago.

"Psalm 84:11," she murmured. "'The Lord will give grace and glory: no good thing will he withhold from them that walk uprightly.'"

She bowed her head and thanked God for bringing so many new and wonderful Plain friends into her life. *Especially Marnie and Andrew,* she added with a smile.

Then she sat down on her bed and wrote a short note of thanks to Andrew, determined to mail it in the morning.

The atmosphere in the house was so tense by Saturday that Marnie hurried through her chores, not saying much to Mamm. As soon as she was finished dusting and dry mopping, she went to her room and locked the door, longing for solitude . . . and to be held in Roy's arms.

She pulled out a page of stationery and began to share her thoughts with him.

Dear Roy,

   I hope you are doing well. How I miss you!

   You must know that I love you dearly, and nothing has changed, except our present circumstances. I've been found out—Preacher Yoder saw me at last week's Bible study. Honestly, though, I can scarcely handle the pressure here at home—the disapproving glances, the harsh words from Daed. Mamm struggles not to say much, yet I see the pain in her eyes. My parents are sorely disappointed, and that's the hardest of all.

The Fishers' meetings are off-limits for the time being, so I cannot go with you, at least not as long as I'm living here.

Ironically, Katie has invited me, along with another girl, to stay with her family until you and I wed next year. Can you believe this? It would be against my parents' wishes, and I don't know what to do. My heart belongs to God, and soon to you, my dear Roy. What do you suggest?

When you write back, please send your letter to Ella Mae Zook, who will get it to me. She'll soon know about this plan . . . and I appreciate your understanding and prayers.

> *With all my love,*
> *your girl, Marnie Lapp*

··· ➤ ➤ ···

The Wednesday after Thanksgiving was blustery with snow and arctic wind. Jenny headed across the field to baby-sit for the bishop's youngest girls. She'd taken Rebecca's advice and worn an extra layer of long underwear beneath her dress. *"Lots of the womenfolk do, at least this time of year,"* Rebecca had said, indicating that some of the younger women even wore leggings under their skirts if they worked out in the barn.

She leaned into the bone-chilling wind, fondly recalling Andrew's gift, which she'd been reading daily. She found it most interesting that Rebecca had not mentioned the gift or card, though she assumed both Rebecca and her husband must have surmised who had dropped by in their absence. *Who else?*

When Jenny arrived at the bishop's, she removed her boots and coat and put them neatly away in the utility room. The farmhouse was becoming familiar to her, and she cherished her time there with the girls.

Emily raised her arms to be picked up, saying, "*Aendi*," and patting Jenny's cold cheek as Mary came smiling into the kitchen.

Jenny twirled Emily around and set her down to play on the floor with some blocks. At the playpen, Jenny leaned down to tousle Anna's silky hair, cooing at her in Deitsch, "*Mei lieblich Boppli*—my adorable baby."

"You're getting more confident with our language, I see," Mary said.

"It's about time, jah?" Jenny laughed softly, and Emily looked up at her, chattering in Deitsch, asking what their snack would be.

"Chocolate *Millich*," Jenny replied.

Emily grinned back at her.

"You're makin' *gut* strides forward, Jenny. Wunnerbaar!" Mary reached for her purse. "By the way, Mary Mae is over at my sister's house playin' with her preschool cousins this morning."

"Okay, be sure to tell her I missed her."

Mary nodded. "I surely will. And I won't be gone more than a few hours—Naomi should be here very soon." She kissed each child, then smiled at Jenny. "I hope you'll get along nicely with Naomi."

"I'm looking forward to it," Jenny said, wondering just how far on the fringe the bishop's niece really was.

After a few minutes, Naomi Beiler arrived at the back door, carrying a big quilted bag. Jenny went out to greet her, playing hostess as Mary and Rebecca always did. "Did you walk over, too?" she asked.

"Jah, but not very far . . . just from up the way." Naomi pointed east. "Feels like a snowstorm comin'."

"I noticed that fresh, crisp smell hanging in the air."

"Jah, we'll get it when it comes," Naomi said, grinning. "Mamma always says that. My father likes to walk through the field in the springtime and pray, 'Lord, give us all the rain we need, and not one more drop.'"

Jenny liked hearing that, another example of the People's profound trust.

When Naomi had hung up her coat and scarf, she came into the kitchen and sat on the opposite side of the table, her back to the window. She talked in Deitsch to Emily, who smiled brightly and jabbered about her block tower.

With the children happily settled, Jenny poured some hot coffee for Naomi and herself. And Naomi shared some pumpkin cookies she'd made before coming, offering them to Emily, too.

"Aunt Mary Beiler urged me to get acquainted with ya," Naomi said with a glance at Emily, who wasn't paying attention and couldn't understand English, anyway. "She hopes you and I might become friends in due time."

Jenny nodded, smiling. "She told me that, too."

"How long have you wanted to be Amish, if ya don't mind me askin'?" Naomi leaned her elbows on the table, her fists under her chin.

"Since I was fairly young."

Naomi wanted to know what triggered it, and Jenny said she thought that at first it had come from an appreciation for the culture and a craving for a simpler life. "Things changed, though, as I grew older. I became disillusioned with modern society . . . felt I belonged in a different era." She studied Naomi, who began removing colorful squares of fabric from her bag, placing them on the table. "Can you understand that?" Jenny really wanted to know.

"Makes me all ferhoodled, really." Naomi stared at the ceiling and shook her head. "Honestly, I must be just the opposite of you."

Jenny glanced over at baby Anna, who was babbling softly and playing with her toys. "We're all different," she told Naomi. "I know that much."

"Ain't that the truth?" Naomi slowly began to open up. "I really just hope to learn how to make it out in the fancy world . . . someday. With a little help, though."

"So you're leaving Hickory Hollow?"

"When it's time."

Jenny watched Naomi move the cloth squares around to her liking. "What would make you change your mind? Anything?"

Naomi looked up suddenly, her pale blue eyes meeting Jenny's. "I can't imagine what."

"Well, until you do go, I like the idea of being friends."

Naomi reached for two squares, trading them with two others. "Ain't that I'm ungrateful . . . I hope ya understand." She again raised her eyes to Jenny. "My beau wants to leave, too." She said it softly, almost reverently, like it was a well-guarded secret. "And here you are, Jenny . . . from the outside and wanting to be . . . well, like us."

"Remember, it's human nature to want something other than what we already have, right?"

"I guess that's true. Rarely are we content with what we're given." Naomi smiled. "For example, I'd like to wear pretty necklaces and learn to drive a car." She fixed her gaze on Jenny. "I think everyone's curious to know how you gave up your wheels."

"Oh, it wasn't easy," Jenny admitted. "I sometimes wonder if one reason I have such trouble hitching up is that I subconsciously miss my car. Actually, I've never voiced that to a soul."

"Not to worry. I won't make a peep."

Jenny helped Naomi rearrange the squares an assortment of ways. "It's always seemed to me that Amish folk are the salt of the earth, you know."

"Well, sometimes we're more earth than salt," Naomi replied, laughing. "As you're finding out."

Naomi's remarks echoed in Jenny's mind until well after Mary Beiler returned from her errands.

Chapter 37

Rebecca got up much earlier than usual the next morning, not knowing where to keep the letter Katie had sent. Well, now there were *two*—both private responses to Rebecca's earlier one saying she'd heard from Rachel Stoltzfus that Dan and Katie were causing a stir with their Bible studies. Katie, bless her heart, had jumped to the conclusion that the bishop must be "under conviction from God," putting such clamps on the youth who were in Rumschpringe and entitled to decide spiritual things for themselves. Katie had even gone so far as to encourage Rebecca *and* Samuel to come to their Tuesday night Bible studies, which were growing so rapidly Daniel had to borrow more folding chairs from their church. *Forget the bishop's demands, Mamma . . . please! Trust the Lord instead,* Katie had written.

Thus things had begun to change between Rebecca and her daughter—she'd felt it clearly the last time she'd gone over there, during the dark phase of the moon. Rebecca had felt so guilty during her walk there, fearful of being caught by someone other than Jenny, she'd nearly returned home, shaken. All Katie had talked about during the visit was the spiritual renewal they, and those who were attending their Bible study, were experiencing.

Presently, Rebecca sat in the front room near the heater stove to reread Katie's most recent letters while the house was ever so still. She'd considered destroying them, but wouldn't she be wiping out the last remnants of their relationship in doing so? *What's it matter whether we're seeing eye to eye?*

It was truly peculiar to think that Katie and Dan were praying just as hard for her and Samuel to "see the light of God's truth" as Rebecca was for them to return to their Amish heritage, "to stay in Jesus."

In the end, she went and hid the letters upstairs in the sewing room, in a drawer where she kept extra pillowcases. Knowing him, Samuel would never look there.

Jenny awakened with the pleasant thought of seeing Andrew Lapp later that evening. How quickly the week had passed, yet she still struggled with concerns about not measuring up to the People's standards, domestic and otherwise. She was beginning to wonder if her own yardstick was perhaps too high, considering she compared her cooking ability to Rebecca Lapp's. She felt it was a good idea for her to meet with her new prayer partner to continue to ask for divine help and patience in her struggle.

As for the secret she carried, Jenny had convinced herself that it was best to turn a blind eye to Rebecca's nighttime comings and goings. In fact, Jenny now closed her shades at dusk to keep from spotting her. She did, however, want to know more about Rebecca's daughter. Shockingly, the shunned young woman had somehow managed to convince

Marnie Lapp to move in over there sometime after the New Year. Marnie had told her yesterday afternoon, only hours after Jenny had returned from talking with Naomi about *her* wishes.

Jenny and Marnie had walked down near the springhouse, as Marnie had been anxious not to be overheard. She was experiencing mixed emotions, she'd said, loving her family—and not wanting to hurt or disappoint them—and wanting to do what she believed was God's will. The whole thing put Jenny on edge, and she'd told Marnie so. She didn't want to lose her closest friend. Jenny wondered if Marnie had been influenced to make this decision by Katie and her husband. But Marnie was her own person—Jenny knew that to be true. So, hard as it was to grasp, it must be that Marnie actually *wanted* to live with the shunned couple until she married Roy Flaud.

"I won't be able to visit you there," she'd told Marnie, who promised to visit Jenny at Samuel and Rebecca's. Yet Jenny wasn't convinced things would ever be the same.

Getting out of bed, she put on her slippers and strolled to the windows to pull up the dark green shades. She looked out, glimpsing the first rays of dawn on the far horizon, and suddenly realized if she positioned herself in the window just so, she could see all the way down to the springhouse. There was a dusting of snow on the pond, and her heart warmed once more at Andrew's surprise invitation. *He's willing to take a chance on me.* She wondered if meeting him had been providential, as Ella Mae liked to say.

Jenny went to the dresser for her brush. When she pulled back her hair, she noticed her bangs had grown enough to pin back more easily. She reached for one of her newly sewn dresses, glad for Rebecca's treadle sewing machine. Funny, but working the ancient contraption was already old hat to her. *Who knew?*

At least she was making some progress, because Jenny's talks with Andrew made her all the more determined to pass her Proving with flying colors.

··· ➤ ◄ ···

As Andrew had indicated, Jenny was glad to meet several of his female relatives at the quilting circle that morning at Mary Beiler's, including his own mother, Maggie Lapp. Andrew's tall, slender cousin Tessie Miller was present, too, her pretty reddish-blond hair parted down the middle and pulled back on both sides like Jenny's. Tessie smiled gaily when she spotted Jenny and hurried over to talk with her.

Jenny was quick to say how grateful she was for Tessie's offer to help her get her bearings in the community.

"Cousin Andrew must've told ya, then?" Tessie asked, her delicate blue-green eyes questioning.

Jenny wondered if it was okay to confide that Andrew had spoken with her. Glancing about, she nodded and noticed the other women still appeared very curious.

Tessie stepped near. "I think he's got his eye on ya, Jenny. I guessed as much your very first Sunday." Her eyes sparkled with fun. "I saw you two talkin' out on the porch—remember?"

Jenny certainly did but wasn't about to say so.

When it was time to sit at the quilting frame, Tessie and Marnie decided to "share Jenny," as they said, with one sitting on either side of her. They guided her patiently as they demonstrated how to use the small needle.

As they worked, Jenny still sensed the gaze of the other women, especially Rebecca and her quilting partner, Maggie

Lapp, Andrew's attractive mother, who kept one eye on the quilt—and the other on the seeker in their midst.

... ➤ ◄ ...

The evening air was icy, but without snow, and Jenny easily made her way down the lane to the springhouse steps. It crossed her mind that Andrew might not remember their prayer appointment. Even if he didn't show up, she would pray alone. Whether she bowed her head and heart in the privacy of her room or outdoors, this quiet time was the highlight of her day.

Christmas was coming soon, and she wanted God's direction on how to connect with her family back home. This had been on her mind for days now because, for the most part, gifts weren't typically exchanged among Amish adults, and she wanted to respect that. On the other hand, she doubted her family would understand not receiving gifts from her, just as they didn't comprehend any other aspect of her choice to be Plain. She wanted to honor them in some special way, as well as demonstrate her love. But how?

"Hullo, Jenny," Andrew called quietly to her from the murkiness.

She followed the steps to the entrance of the springhouse, where he stood with his flashlight shining on the ground. "You're early," Jenny remarked.

He nodded and motioned her inside. "I've just been here a few minutes."

She hesitated about going into the small space with him; it seemed nearly too intimate. "We could pray outside, too."

"Jah, but you'll be warmer in there."

Not wanting to dispute him, Jenny stepped inside, where he

offered her the only wooden ledge, with just enough room for one. He insisted she sit and be comfortable while he stooped across from her, near the waters of the spring.

"Is this a good idea?" she said, thinking suddenly of Emmalyn. With the flashlight lighting up the space, could their shadows be seen from outside?

"All's well." He hunkered down as he folded his hands.

They began to pray, silently at first and then aloud, with Andrew leading in prayer "for wisdom on the part of the restless youth in the church." He prayed a while about that as Jenny offered her silent agreement.

Later, Jenny gave praise for God's many blessings, large and small, and then asked for help in knowing how to respectfully approach her family over the Christmas holidays.

Their prayer time was short and to the point, and even though she'd felt a bit uncomfortable about letting Andrew hear her prayers, Jenny soon realized she no longer clenched her folded hands. Praying with Andrew was quite exciting, and very sweet, too, although she did still feel somewhat anxious about being alone with him, not wanting anyone to mistake their intentions.

"I received your thank-you note," Andrew said as he reached for the flashlight and rose to open the door. "You didn't have to do that, ya know."

"And neither did you," she said, referring to his gift. "I've been reading the devotional book morning and night and really enjoying it."

He smiled, looking even more handsome tonight. "It's a timeless classic. My older brothers and their wives use the same one each morning."

"I can see why." She loved talking with him but thought they should be going.

"I'll see you here next week, if you'd like," he said.

"If it's milder weather, we should pray outdoors, jah?" She knew he'd understand.

He agreed, smiling. "Do ya mind if I write to you between our prayer visits?"

Just the way he said it made her heart smile. "Okay."

"I won't put my name or return address on the envelope . . . for obvious reasons."

"*Gut* idea," she said. "And before I forget, how much was the long-distance phone call?"

"I haven't gotten the bill yet, but let's just forget about it."

"Um . . . we had a deal." She didn't want to renege.

"I'll let you know when it comes."

"Denki, Andrew. Gut Nacht." She headed out the door as he held it open. Without looking back, she hurried toward the stairs as she heard him go in the opposite direction.

As she walked toward the house, she decided that their prayer rendezvous would probably seem peculiar to anyone but the two of them. And she wouldn't enter Rebecca's kitchen before removing the pleased smile from her face. From her current vantage point, she could see Samuel and Rebecca presently having their own devotional time.

Jenny slipped into the stable to see the driving horses again, as she had been doing at Andrew's suggestion. She realized once more how fond Andrew was of her, even though the pretext for their relationship was friendship. *That, and prayer partners.*

Chapter 38

Marnie knew just the person to confide in on Friday afternoon. It was either that or burst. Besides, she was dying to know if Roy had sent a reply, and today was the first chance she'd had to ask.

"I can't think of not bein' with my beau," she told the Wise Woman, trying to contain her emotions at the pretty tea table with yellow rose paper napkins and matching placemats.

"'Course ya can't, Marnie. Your heart's all bound up in him, ain't so?"

Marnie wiped a tear from her cheek. "Did ya feel that way, too, when you first met your husband?"

"Oh jah . . . ages ago." Ella Mae leaned nearer. "And ya want to know a little secret?"

Marnie quickly nodded her head.

"Every single one of us feels that way in the blush of first love. I did, so did your Mamma and Dat—same with your grandparents, too. It's the way the Good Lord made us."

Marnie thought on that. "So what happens when we're told we can't be with the young man we love . . . what then?"

"Are ya grown-up enough to make your own decision about

love? Are ya trustin' God for that important choice?" Ella Mae stirred the peppermint tea in her delicate cup. "Are ya, dearie?"

"I have no doubt Roy's the one for me," Marnie said, meaning it.

Ella Mae shrugged her slight shoulders. "That's your answer, then. Ya know what you must do."

She bowed her head. "Why's it such a struggle?"

"Believe in God's Word and live your life accordingly . . . however the Lord leads."

"Even if that means disregarding my father's wishes?"

"Well, it ain't like your father was the most obedient young man there ever was."

"What are ya sayin'?"

"Your father went up against his own Dat—your Dawdi Lapp—back when he was a young fella."

Marnie had never heard this.

"I'll just say there was quite the *Uffruhr*—uproar—in the woodshed, and for days at a time, too." Ella Mae blinked her eyes and squinted into the window's light, a mask of memories on her wrinkled face.

"Now ya've got me wonderin'."

"Had plenty to do with your father courtin' a girl he loved."

"My Mamm?"

Ella Mae nodded. "Your Dat won out, too . . . which was a mighty *gut* thing, jah?"

Marnie sniffed and agreed.

"I daresay you've got some of his fine stubbornness in ya, dearie."

For some reason, hearing this made Marnie feel better. "Denki, Ella Mae. I think I needed to come see ya today."

"Believe ya did, too, Marnie."

Ella Mae rose and brought the teapot over. "I've been wondering 'bout your friend Jenny Burns. How's she doin'?"

Marnie tittered. "Honestly? I think better than most of us."

"Why's that?"

"She just seems so settled, despite what she calls 'some botched attempts' to do what comes naturally to the women-folk."

"And learnin' to speak our language?"

"Inches forward at a time, she likes to say."

"How's her sock darning comin' along?"

"Well, she hasn't sewn any shut this week, she said. I'm only tellin' ya because you asked . . . not to make fun." Marnie explained that she felt sure Jenny would keep trying. "She wants to meet Aunt Rebecca's standards for everything."

"Well, that'd be hard for any of us, jah?" Ella Mae was grinning.

"Ach, for sure. But I've never heard her say anything 'bout giving up or turnin' tail and running home."

"If ya don't give up, you haven't lost. Tell her that, won't ya?"

Marnie smiled. "I've always liked that proverb." She sipped some more tea.

"I'd hate to see her get discouraged," Ella Mae added.

Marnie nodded, feeling exactly the same.

"Someone whispered she's got herself a fella already," Ella Mae said, surprising her.

"Ach, I really doubt it—she's not a church member."

Ella Mae smiled thinly. "Best not be sayin' more, then."

"But you must!" Marnie said, knowing she could trust Ella Mae. "What do you know . . . and who told ya?"

"My lips are sealed. See?" Ella Mae pressed her lips tightly together and blinked her little eyes.

Marnie groaned.

"Jenny'll tell ya when she's ready, jah?"

Marnie knew better than to ask again. But then, thinking back to seeing Jenny with Cousin Andrew the night Posey had gone missing, she had a glimmer of an idea. Could it be Cousin Andrew might open his heart, even a crack, to let in someone like Jenny?

Later, when they'd had some delicious finger cakes, Ella Mae gave her Roy's letter, addressed as Marnie had suggested. "I wouldn't tell just anyone this, but by the looks of his handwriting, this is one determined young man." Ella Mae chuckled. "I believe your little ones will be mighty strong willed, too . . . a *gut* thing, mind you, when they're molded and shaped for the Lord."

"Do ya think it's a problem he's not as conservative as we are?"

"Pity's sake, Marnie, there're many kinds of Amish." Ella Mae waved a wrinkled hand in the air. "Those of us who love Jehovah God worship Him alone, ain't so?"

Marnie pondered that as she walked toward home, realizing what the Wise Woman meant. And, unable to wait a minute longer, she tore Roy's letter open and savored each word, tears threatening as she learned that he was in favor of her moving in with Dan and Katie Fisher. And not once did he refer to the Fishers' Bann.

That afternoon Jenny did her best to darn another sock, practicing her very lacking skill. She sat with Rebecca in the cheery sewing room, soaking in the warmth from the windows like a cat in a sunbeam.

But the more she tried, the worse things got, and her

pinpricked fingers hurt. *I'm fooling myself if I think I'm leaving this sock in better shape than I found it!* Still, she was determined. "Do you know of an Amishwoman who can't darn socks?" she asked Rebecca with a deliberate shake of her head.

"Well, to be honest, no."

Rebecca reached across the table. "Here, let me have a look-see." She examined the sock this way and that, even lowering her reading glasses to better scrutinize.

The elongated inspection frustrated Jenny further, and she got up and stood near the window. "This is ridiculous," she muttered. "How long have I been here, and I still can't do this chore?"

"Well, you do very nicely with other sewing, and your embroidery's coming along, too." Rebecca put her glasses back on. "Mustn't forget that."

"But I can't embroider my way through life here."

"Well, you must keep at it." Rebecca slid the sock and needle across the table. "Mustn't be too hard on yourself, Jenny. Remember, you haven't been doin' this for very long yet."

"Some days it seems like it's been forever."

Rebecca's head bobbed up. "Ach, Jenny . . . you're discouraged. That's all."

The last thing she wanted to do was return to her chair and keep darning.

"Try 'n' relax, all right?"

Reluctantly, Jenny returned to the table and sat down, leaving the sock where it was. She leaned back and sighed.

"Just give yourself more time, won't ya?" Rebecca removed her glasses and wiped her eyes. "I daresay you're doin' your best—trust the Lord God." She stopped for a moment, turning to look out the window. "Don't forget the Old Ways are

worth learnin', Jenny. I can't impress that on you enough."
She nodded her head. "Worth their weight in gold."

Somewhat encouraged, Jenny reached for the sock and
picked up her needle, wanting to keep trying . . . and at more
than just this task. And as she began again, she asked Rebecca
what she might do to support herself.

"Ya mean, if you stay single?"

Jenny nodded.

"Well, you could embroider some." Rebecca smiled, glancing over at her. "And ya haven't cracked any eggs yet, now,
have ya?"

"Maybe I could raise chickens."

"Or get some tips from one neighbor up the road—she
made out perty well runnin' a greenhouse. Of course, she
rented out her land to an Amish farmer, too."

I have no land, Jenny thought, glad she had saved more
than a year's worth of income. She hadn't known, however,
that she'd be so reliant on it. She'd definitely need to make
a living of some kind here in Hickory Hollow.

Rebecca had gone over to see Ella Mae late in the afternoon, leaving Jenny to make supper. But Jenny became
distracted with mashing potatoes, forgetting to keep an eye
on the creamed chipped beef. By the time she smelled the
burning, it was too late. Stopping what she was doing, she
turned off the gas and removed the ruined main dish. She
carried the smoldering mess to the trash, hoping to get the
burn out of the pan before Rebecca returned. If only the
scorched smell in the house would dissipate before Samuel
came in for the meal.

I'm losing ground, she thought, aggravated with herself. *I'm getting worse instead of better!*

That evening, after a supper of mashed potatoes and reheated stew, Jenny allowed her mind to wander during Bible reading and silent prayers. She needed to write in her journal—she might feel better if she dumped her annoying thoughts . . . got the negativity off her chest.

> *Hard as I try, I'm still a failure compared to the other women here. Even the bishop's school-age daughters can cook better than I can!*
>
> *Marnie came by this afternoon, and when I told her about my woes with bread baking, she was very kind, as always, and suggested that I might be trying too hard. But how is that possible?*
>
> *Marnie was happier than last time I saw her. I think she has a new lease on life, because her fiancé has given his blessing on her move to Katie and Dan Fisher's, whenever she's ready. I can't wrap my brain around this. Roy must be drifting away from the Amish himself, to encourage this. It's inconceivable to think my first Amish friend might soon be fancy!*
>
> *The Amish teens who do seem more settled closely follow in their parents' footsteps. Marnie and Naomi seem more interested in exerting their own wills, though. Most adults disapprove, including Rebecca . . . and the bishop and Mary. If Samuel Lapp opened up and spoke his mind, I'm sure he'd be opposed, too. It's odd how he reminds me of my own father in that way.*
>
> *I sometimes wonder if this business with Marnie, especially, has affected me on some level.*
>
> *There is much for me to contemplate while Rebecca keeps*

me busy. To top things off, we're hosting the Preaching service here on December 16, and there is a long list of chores to accomplish. All the walls must be washed down, the windows cleaned, and Rebecca said at supper tonight that some of the upstairs rooms will need a fresh coat of paint, as well. She announced this while the residual odor of my burned chipped beef was still strong in our noses. My mother and sister would think this is an omen, and maybe it is—at the very least it's a sign that I need to work harder at reaching my goal.

Sigh . . . why is it so hard to be Amish?

Chapter 39

Jenny didn't know why she was startled when she got the
Saturday mail, especially when Andrew Lapp had said he
would write. It was a remarkable experience to read Andrew's
journal-like letter, a chronicling of his daily welding work and
his various English and Amish customers. And she anticipated
her next visit to the springhouse with her unexpected prayer
partner even while she spent time with Naomi at her parents'
house, once Jenny's chores were finished.

She considered Andrew's letter, newsy and interesting.
Only slightly romantic. *As it should be*, she told herself as she
leaned over the sink to dig out black spots in a large potato.
A committed church member like Andrew would follow the
ordinance to a tee.

She found herself feeling very happy he'd written, choosing
to take time for her. And couldn't help being a little hopeful
that courtship might follow someday.

Jenny experienced a week of fewer bread-baking fiascos,
thankful Rebecca was encouraging and even seemed to be

warming to her again. Had Rebecca stopped visiting Katie, perhaps?

This early December morning was exceptionally sunny and not as chilly as previous days. The sun played across the snowy fields, casting regular shadows along the horse fence and nearby trees.

Jenny was struck with an idea as she stood on the back steps and waved to Rebecca, who left in the family carriage to visit her daughter-in-law Annie, Daniel Fisher's sister. Samuel, for his part, was hitching up the spring wagon to go help his youngest son, Benjamin, haul a large quantity of feed bags from the nearby mill.

As Jenny observed the experienced Amishman, she wondered if she dared attempt what she was thinking. Nevertheless, why *not* practice what she'd repeatedly been taught?

She waited until Samuel pulled out of the driveway to dress warmly, yanking on boots and a heavy coat and scarf. Then she hurried to the stable and chose her favorite black pony, Josie, and curried her, just as Samuel always did before taking a horse or pony out on the road. She led the pretty young mare down the driveway and tied her to the hitching post before heading back for the cart stored in the upper level of the double-decker barn.

When she was ready, Jenny followed the same instructions she'd been given for hitching a road horse to the family carriage, thinking this should be a good test of her ability. And without anyone prompting her, either!

The process took longer than she'd hoped, but Jenny refused to give up as she hooked up the pony to the cart. *I can do this,* she told herself, giving Josie a sugar cube for being so patient.

At long last, when Jenny was ready to take a spin, she double-checked every aspect of the process one more time.

Then, smiling at her accomplishment, she untied Josie and brought the driving lines back, climbed into the pony cart—and off she went.

... ➤ ◄ ...

Annie was busy in her sun-drenched kitchen making egg noodles when Rebecca arrived through the creaky back door. Her dark chestnut brown hair peeked out from beneath her Kapp. "Hullo, Annie dear!"

"Come on in," Annie called, her cheeks white with soft dustings of flour. "Well, and it looks like you already are." She gave a mellow laugh and opened her slender arms to Rebecca, offering a hug. "You're just in time to help me, if you'd like."

"Sure, anytime," said Rebecca, removing her winter layers. "That's why I'm here . . . and for the company, too."

Cheerful and lovely as always, Annie nodded demurely as she waved Rebecca inside. "Awful nice seein' ya, Mamm."

"You too."

They exchanged comments about the bright, sunny day, and how young Daniel was off to school, enjoying first grade. Rebecca wondered but would never inquire why he was still their only child. *Thus far.*

She and Annie worked to roll out the stiff, smooth dough onto an old tablecloth. As each layer of rolled dough was complete, they let the noodles continue to dry, turning them over and later cutting them with a sharp butcher knife to make fine strips. Afterward, Rebecca shook the noodles apart so they did not stick together.

Rebecca had always liked Annie—like a daughter in many ways, and ever so pleasant. *No wonder my son was head over heels for her when they started courting,* she remembered, smiling even now. Annie was the kind of girl who was just plain good-natured.

"Mamma's aunt Miriam isn't too well these days," Annie confided. "Mamma says she came to visit her the other day, and Miriam couldn't remember if she was comin' to see her or leavin', the poor thing."

"Ach, that is sad. Painful to see, ain't?"

Annie nodded. "Hard to understand why some elderly folk are clear-minded right up to the end, and others, well . . ." Her voice trailed away. "But the dear Lord knows."

Rebecca agreed, struck again by how tenderhearted Annie was and always had been.

They talked of the quilting bee at Mary Beiler's house for a while. Then, during a lull in the conversation, Rebecca asked, "Have ya heard 'bout your brother's Bible study groups?"

Annie said she had. "Elam thinks it's mighty bold of Daniel to invite anyone who wants to come, knowin' plenty of our young folk might wander over there."

"Well, if they ain't baptized yet, what's the worry?" Instantly Rebecca froze. *Did I really just let that fly out of my mouth?*

Annie gave her a startled look but didn't say more on the subject. "Heard Katie's expecting a baby again. Wish we could see her and the children . . . and Dan." She said the latter in a whisper, with a little catch in her voice.

The dear girl.

"We've been prayin' the bishop might ease the Bann on Katie and Dan—even lift it entirely." Annie bowed her head. "Would be such a help to the family, ya know."

Rebecca sighed, not daring to discuss it. She did wonder, however, exactly who'd shared the news of Katie's coming babe with Annie. Could it be Annie's mother knew? Surely that was so. It was hard to imagine the elder Fishers not knowing something so important. Like Annie, surely they, too, were missing the chance to know Dan and Katie's little ones.

Before leaving, Rebecca handed Annie a basketful of peach and pear jams.

"Come see us anytime," she said, giving her a quick hug.

"Oh, we will. Denki for stoppin' in, Mamm."

"Why don't yous come for Christmas dinner?" Rebecca said quickly.

"Well, we would, but Mamma's been askin' us to go *there* this year." Annie's eyes were sad. "Ach, sorry. We'd really love to . . . but maybe for Second Christmas instead?"

Rebecca agreed, glad their church district observed the visiting holiday right away after Christmas, on December twenty-sixth. All the Amish shops in Hickory Hollow and surrounding areas would be closed for the occasion. "Jah, it'll be nice to look forward to that." *Ever so nice.*

"I can't promise till I talk to Elam, of course, but I'll let you know. If not Second Christmas, then for sure New Year's."

Rebecca assumed the latter was the soonest they'd make it over, which was fine. Between Annie's parents and grandparents, and all of Elam's and her siblings, she and Elam would have many invitations. Rebecca couldn't help wondering if Dan and Katie had ever invited them over there.

She waved and made her way out the door to the waiting horse and carriage.

··· ➤ ➤ ···

Jenny was excited to be riding down Hickory Lane in the pony cart. She did feel a bit strange, though, a grown woman sitting cross-legged like this, the black strings from her outer bonnet fluttering over her shoulder.

Jenny admired the sky, delighting in the day. Across the way, horses silently milled about the pasture, two of them trotting now, long tails flying.

Suddenly—*crack, snap*—and a lurch!

Josie galloped off free, away from the pony cart!

"Oh no," Jenny muttered, disgusted. "How'd that happen?"

There Jenny sat, stranded in the middle of the road and feeling embarrassed and upset. Scrambling out of the cart, she called to the spirited pony only to watch her trot through a hole in the neighbors' horse fence.

And if that wasn't bad enough, she could see Andrew Lapp and his sister Emmalyn coming this way in Andrew's open buggy. He was waving as he slowed the horse, apparently ready to jump down from the carriage and onto the road.

"For pity's sake, Jenny . . . what happened to ya?"

She explained quietly, painfully aware of Emmalyn, who was still perched there in her brother's buggy. *More fuel for ridicule,* Jenny thought miserably.

"Here, let's get the cart off the road some," said Andrew, pulling it over to the shoulder.

Then, before either of them could say more, Emmalyn got down and offered to bring the pony back. "Is that Josie over there?" She pointed beyond the fence.

"Jah." Jenny wondered how she knew. As Emmalyn hurried off to catch the pony, Jenny turned back to Andrew, relieved there wasn't a hint of mockery on his face. "I did everything I've been taught about hitching up," she declared.

"Never mind all that," Andrew said, brushing it away. "I'm just glad we came along when we did."

Jenny mustered a smile. "I am, too."

"And not just to help you, neither." A slow grin crept across his face. "I'm very happy to see you in the daylight again." He chuckled. "I mean that."

She blushed a little as she realized their secret meetings would always be under the covering of night. "It *is* kind of nice, I admit," she said as she shaded her eyes and glanced at the sky.

"You mustn't get down on yourself over this, okay?" He assured her that it could happen to anyone who was still getting used to hitching up, though Jenny knew he was being kind. "With enough practice, you'll be an expert soon enough."

"That's what you think!"

They both had a good laugh, and when he reached for her hand, standing in front of her as if to block his sister's view, Jenny was the one trying not to smile too much.

"I look forward to our prayer time this evening," he said, releasing her hand as he stepped back.

Jenny agreed, watching Emmalyn bound across the snowy meadow with the pony, coming this way. She led Josie around to the break in the fence, then out to the road. With both Andrew and Emmalyn to talk Jenny through it, the three of them had Josie hitched up solidly in no time.

When it was time to part, Jenny and Andrew simultaneously said good-bye in Deitsch, and they laughed again, more softly this time. And as he returned to his horse and buggy, Jenny noticed a hint of a smile on Emmalyn's face. It seemed Andrew's youngest sister was no longer an adversary.

Chapter 40

Rebecca slipped out to the back porch after evening Bible. She wondered where Jenny had gone. Here lately on Thursday evenings, she'd noticed her missing from the house. Not that she cared one way or the other—she guessed the poor thing needed to get outdoors alone, perhaps to sort out her thoughts. The seeker was spinning her wheels some, and it was clear that she might be questioning her resolve. Was the Amish life really what Jenny wanted? Of course, it didn't help that she'd become disheartened due to Marnie's and Naomi's sudden interest in moving away. *And my own shortcomings, as well, no doubt,* Rebecca thought sadly.

One thing was sure, the half moon was a glimmering splendor tonight, and Rebecca drank in the sight as she admired the stars, taking a deep breath of frosty air out on the back porch.

Later, when she heard Jenny's soft steps coming up from the springhouse, Rebecca slipped back inside.

For each and every day that week, Rebecca felt like she was doing the same things over and over again. Did Jenny feel it, too? That is, until Katie's letter arrived with an idea she wanted to explore. Her little boy's one and only Christmas wish was to meet his Dawdi Samuel, and Katie wanted Rebecca to think about that.

> *Talk it over with Dat. After all, he is Sammy's namesake. Please pray about it, too.*
>
> *We'd like to come for Christmas dinner at your house. I would prepare a meal for you and Dat here, but Dan and I have already gone over that and realize it's out of the question, given the rules of the shunning. Don't ask Dat—just tell him. Okay, I'm smiling at that last line, but please do think about it.*
>
> *With our love,*
> *Katie*

Rebecca shuddered at the very notion of telling Samuel, who didn't even know she'd been corresponding with their daughter, let alone met and held their darling Fisher grandchildren. Knowing her husband was a stickler for the Ordnung, Rebecca couldn't see how he would bend even this far. And if by some marvel he did so, what would the ministerial brethren think of it?

Of course, if she and Samuel could meet all the requirements for having Dan and Katie there for a meal—eat at separate tables and not pass the food directly from their own hands to Katie's and Dan's—perhaps Samuel might just agree. Oh, she hoped so. With all of her heart, she did.

Still, Rebecca was certain that, just because it was permitted

in the letter of the law, such a visit—even at Christmas—
would not be looked upon favorably by their stern bishop.

···➤ ◄···

Jenny wasn't sure how it came up at the springhouse pond
Thursday evening, but she and Andrew had been talking
about the Amish way to celebrate Christmas, and she found
herself confiding in him. They sat on the stone wall, watching the moon's likeness glitter on the pond's partially frozen
surface. "I've been freaking out lately, Andrew," she told him.
"Do you know what that means?"

He chuckled a little. "Only that you need more encouragement, ain't?"

"I feel like I'm on the edge, unable to cut it here." She
paused and sighed. "It's everything I want, but—"

"Jenny, listen. Samuel wants to shepherd you a bit—show
you how to hitch one of the ponies up to the pony cart. It's
like you've passed some sort of test with him, I'm thinkin'."

"Samuel? Are you sure?"

"He wants to help you, Jenny. Hitching up is just the first
step in his, well, fatherly role with you."

She'd never had a word alone with the man . . . wasn't
sure he could actually conduct a conversation with her. "I'm
astonished but really glad to hear it."

"Samuel Lapp's a mighty fine mentor. Do you trust me
when I say this?" He reached for her mittened hand. "I know
you will be a *gut* Amishwoman someday. And now, clearly
Samuel believes it, too."

"Denki," she managed, thrilling at her hand in his.

"And, since you shared with me, I'd like to tell you why
Emmalyn is so protective."

He hadn't let go of her hand, and she was intrigued by the urgency in his voice. They certainly were not doing much praying tonight!

Andrew began by saying he'd once fallen in love with a sweet Amish girl, whom he'd courted for some time. She was devout and they'd planned to marry. "In fact, it was just three weeks from our wedding—three weeks to the day—when she told me she'd set her eyes on the world and wanted to leave the hollow." He paused briefly. "And of course, me."

"I'm so sorry." She shook her head. What else could she say?

"That was several years ago."

"So thus your sister's concern over an outsider—*me*—spending time with you."

He nodded, cupping her hand in both of his. Finally he released it, saying it was time they started to pray, but he began by reciting the Lord's Prayer, first in English, followed by his first language.

Andrew lingered much longer than ever before, and after they said good-night, Jenny considered why he was still single: Marnie and Naomi weren't the first young people to grumble over joining church. And knowing how pressed to the wall she'd been recently, unsettled and on the periphery and not fully Amish herself, Jenny was scared. She did not want to break Andrew's heart . . . again.

During a breakfast of Rebecca's tasty mush made from cornmeal and sausage the next morning, Samuel asked Jenny to go out with him to hitch up the pony cart. *Just as Andrew said,* she thought. *Should've waited to do this with Samuel!*

Jenny was surprised at how patient, even nurturing, Samuel was with both the frisky pony and with Jenny herself.

"You've had quite a time of it here, ain't?" he said, petting Josie's mane. "Farm life is a big adjustment for a city girl." She smiled, pleased he was actually talking with her.

"Well, and not only that." He held the short shafts and backed the pony into them.

Of course, Samuel didn't need to point out her English upbringing, but she knew he meant as much. "I'm looking forward to your hosting church here this Sunday," she said, making small talk.

"'Tis a big responsibility, and one not to be taken lightly. We believe this old farmhouse will become the house of worship for the day. An honor and a blessing, to be sure."

"I understand Rebecca's sisters are coming Saturday to help prepare the food to be served at the meals."

"Including the pies." Samuel grinned and then his face turned solemn. "It is our desire to be at peace with Gott and the church."

Jenny understood by now that the unity of the congregation was highly desired—even necessary—before each Preaching service. "I pray it will be so," she said.

The sky was speckled with cotton-ball clouds, and the wind began to pick up as, with Samuel's assistance, she helped where she could. The weather had turned colder overnight, marching toward deep winter, and it reminded her of the passage of time.

Jenny felt the familiar pang of disappointment as she watched Samuel's hands move expertly through the process. It was as if the Amish world was a complicated tango, moving here and there in perfect rhythm, and she still didn't know the steps.

When they were finished, Samuel suggested she hop in and go up the road a piece. "Chust *fer Schpass*—for fun."

She got in and picked up the lines. "Like this?" she asked, recalling her own short-lived jaunt up the road, thankful the grapevine hadn't spread word of the mishap to the Lapps' ears.

"You'll do fine if ya stay on the *rechts* side of the road."

"I can remember that. Denki," she said and was off.

Although the ride was satisfying and fun, Jenny had a hard time thinking of anything but Andrew's rescuing her the last time she'd done this. To think last night he had shared so personally with her about his heartache. *Especially the reason behind it.*

He'd asked if she trusted him, but she wasn't sure she trusted her own heart anymore.

Marnie strolled to the barn, carrying a weight of worry. She'd spent all morning cleaning house with her mother and mentally rehearsing what she wanted to say to Daed. And she questioned why God had planted this powerful longing to know Him better if it was so frowned upon.

"I wish I had no heart, it aches so." The words from *Little Women*, which she'd just recently reread, resonated in her mind.

She pushed open the barn door and crept inside, but when she asked her older brother where Daed was, Jacob pointed to the milk house. Nodding, she headed across the way and approached the doorway. She could hear her father muttering as he scrubbed down the bulk milk tank.

"Daed?" she said. "Can I talk to ya?"

He raised his head. "What's on your mind?"

She froze.

"Marnie?" He looked at her with searing gray eyes. "Speak up if you're gonna talk."

She'd dreaded this and now she wished she hadn't thought she was so brave. "Maybe you've heard from the grapevine."

"For pity's sake, you're gonna have to talk louder, Marnie!"

She wished he wouldn't talk so, at least to her. "I want to move out," she declared in her strongest voice. "After Christmas, I'll go an' stay with Dan and Katie Fisher . . . just till Roy Flaud and I wed."

"Well, if you're that determined, why wait?"

She gasped, but he couldn't have heard, not with his head halfway into the tank. *So that's his first response?*

"Thought it'd be nice to stay round for Christmas, is all." She felt all in and close to tears. "I don't want to disobey you, but I love Roy. I truly do."

Daed kept on cleaning, not looking up.

"I thought it'd bring less shame on you and Mamm this way."

"Shame on *us*? But not on yourself, Marnie?" Daed rose and straightened to his full height. "Daughter, you are not behavin' at all the way your mother and I raised ya to be." He shook his head and stared her down.

She saw the crow's feet near his eyes, the wrinkle lines around his chapped lips. She remembered Ella Mae's comments about her youthful father, so long ago. Still, it made her sad that she was the reason for Daed's somber face just now.

"You're such *gut* friends with that seeker-girl. Why can't ya be more like Jenny Burns?" he bellowed, his face brighter than a red beet. "That's all I have to say!"

Marnie turned and left the milk house, running as hard as she could through the meadow, aware of the snow-laden earth beneath her feet. She ran till she had no breath left in her before stopping to rest, panting and leaning against the coarse tree bark on Samuel Lapp's property. *I came all that way,* she realized, turning to look back but refusing to think poorly of her father. No, she put herself right into his old work boots and knew, without a doubt, that she would feel the selfsame way if her daughter stood up to her like this.

Poor man, as staunch as he is, he does deserve a daughter like Jenny!

Chapter 41

After the Preaching service and the shared meal, Jenny and Marnie worked up a sweat with Rebecca and her sisters in the assembly line in the steamy kitchen. Jenny's mind was still reeling, attempting to understand both German sermons that morning, although she'd caught a few more words and phrases than two weeks ago. She was most impressed by the fervency of the People's singing from the *Ausbund* hymnal—it would take some time for her to learn the Gregorian-like chanting of the melancholy songs of the Anabaptist martyrs.

"You're lost in thought," Jenny whispered to her friend.

"I am?"

Jenny smiled. "I think we need to talk . . . alone."

Marnie agreed. "You don't know the half."

Cringing, Jenny passed the newly dried dishes to Rebecca's younger sister, who carefully stacked them in a large box with padding for each plate. Rebecca had explained that this same enormous set of dishes was transported from house to house for weddings, funerals, and the shared meal following church.

Once they were finished cleaning up and the place looked

as spotless as it had last night, Jenny invited Marnie upstairs to her room until Chester and Peggy were ready to leave for home. "You look like you might burst," Jenny said when they'd closed the bedroom door. "Are you all right, Marnie?"

Staring down at her folded hands there where she sat on the bed, Marnie shook her head. "My father chewed me out the other day in the milk house." She quickly told everything to Jenny, who felt sadder with each word. "I should've known better than to spill the beans on myself," Marnie said as she raised shimmering eyes.

Jenny didn't know how to console her but moved to sit next to her, head bowed. "You wanted to tell him where your heart is, jah? Wanted him to understand."

"Right. I wasn't there to ask his blessing. I knew he'd never give that."

"I'm so sorry," Jenny said as Marnie sniffled. "Maybe in time, things will change between you and your father."

"I'm not holdin' my breath."

They talked quietly a while longer. Then Marnie asked, "It's prob'ly none of my business, but do you have a special fella?"

Jenny frowned. "Why do you ask?"

"Well, not sure I should say."

"Why not?" Jenny was astonished.

"It's just that Ella Mae said something 'bout it."

"The Wise Woman?"

Marnie glanced at her, smiling. "There is someone, ain't so?"

Jenny knew she couldn't let things go any further now with Andrew. Not with her situation still so up in the air. If Marnie and Naomi—even Katie—weren't cut out to be Amish, how could she as an Englisher ever hope to belong? She sighed.

Thankfully, at that moment, Jenny heard Rebecca calling through the door. "Marnie's family is ready to leave."

Marnie reached for Jenny's hand. "I'd better get goin'."

"Keep in touch, okay?"

Nodding, Marnie wiped her eyes, promising to do just that. "Christmas is comin' fast now, and I wanted my last days at home to be happy ones." She sighed as she stood and straightened her pretty white apron. "I really did."

"Let's not give up hope for that." Jenny rose and joined her, heading down the stairs and out the back door with her dear friend, a lump in her own throat. She closed her eyes for a second in the glare of the sun.

Marnie gave her a quick hug, whispering in her ear, "I'll see you again soon."

"*Zimmlich glei*—very soon." She watched Marnie hurry to the waiting carriage.

The low buzz of a plane made her glance up, and Jenny remembered the fit she'd thrown as a young girl, about to take her first flight. It struck her, even then, as so very wrong to defy nature—hurtling through space in a canister with wings.

Sighing now for Marnie, she turned to go back to the house and spotted Emmalyn on the porch in her black woolen shawl, her head cocked just so. When Jenny approached her, she actually smiled.

"Thanks for bringing Josie back," Jenny said.

Emmalyn shrugged. "'Twas nothin'."

"And for keeping it to yourself, too," Jenny added, smiling back at her.

··· ➤ ◄ ···

After the long day, extended by all the visiting that followed that afternoon, Rebecca was glad to get off her feet and sit by the heater stove with Samuel. They'd had their evening

Bible reading and prayer, and Jenny had gone upstairs for the night. It was just the two of them, rocking away their cares and keeping toasty warm.

"'Twas a *gut* Lord's Day." Rebecca looked over at her husband's relaxed profile, the peppery gray flecks evident in his beard.

He nodded in rhythm with his hickory rocking chair. "'Twas inspiring to hear the bishop preach on the young folk heedin' the call of Christ, jah?"

"Seemed like he was pickin' on them from where I sat."

"Aw, now."

"No, seriously, Bishop John's got it in for the youth."

"Well, and for *gut* reason, ya know."

Oh, she knew. "Hate to see Chester Lapp's family go through what we did with Katie."

Samuel shook his head right quick. "But it won't be anywhere near the same, Rebecca, with Marnie yet to be baptized."

She quit talking about it, thinking now might be the time to tell him about Katie's latest letter.

"What if we did something different this year for Christmas?" she heard herself say.

"You mean the boys and their families ain't comin' for dinner?"

"Elam and Annie are goin' to *her* folks'." She paused. "All our sons and their families are welcome, sure . . . but what about our grandson Sammy . . . and his baby sister, Kate?"

Samuel grimaced. "What do ya mean?"

"Dan and Katie's little boy wants nothin' more than to meet you for Christmas this year. He told his mother so."

Samuel pondered that, rubbing his chin and threading his fingers through his beard. "How old would this youngster be now?"

"Four—and with a hankerin' to see his Dawdi for the first time." She held her breath. *What will Samuel say?*

"You said that already." He was either miffed or glib.

"Ain't like we're shunning *him*," she added, then waited. He'd have to say something, one way or the other.

"How do ya know this, Rebecca?" His voice was stern, yet there was also a note of something else. Was it curiosity?

She told him about Katie's letter.

Samuel rocked all the harder and she braced for the whole thing to fall back into her lap. *Katie should've known better than to get her hopes up. Or poor little Sammy's, either.*

Rebecca forced her mind away from what she dearly hoped for, trying her best to set her thoughts on today's main sermon again and how heated Bishop John had been. Not a single head was nodding to sleep during *that* two-hour sermon, for sure, though the small children had gotten fidgety. Rebecca had passed a dish of crackers to all the families with little ones before going later to fetch a tall glass of cold water for the same children. Then she'd carried up a fresh glass of water for Bishop John Beiler, too, who rarely preached except at weddings and funerals. Today, however, he'd had plenty to say.

Samuel coughed a little. "Tell Katie that's all right with me," he said at last. "And not a word 'bout this to anyone, ya hear?"

Rebecca tried not to act surprised. "All right," she replied, her heart hammering happily. "I'll write her back first thing tomorrow."

Or better yet, I'll tell her in person!

Chapter 42

J enny stood in the utility room at the bishop's house the following Tuesday morning, hanging up her long coat and scarf. She was uncertain if she ought to enter the kitchen, because Bishop John and Mary were arguing, obviously unaware Jenny was within earshot. She'd come to baby-sit as planned but was mortified to be stuck there eavesdropping.

"How many young people are we goin' to push away, John?" Mary asked, her voice pinched.

"There's a standard to be upheld under God. You know it as well as I do, dear. The tradition of our forefathers is part of our very foundation" was the unyielding reply.

"But think 'bout it this way—these are God-fearing youth. Marnie and Naomi have been raised in the faith, just as you said. All they want is to seek God and to read the Scriptures in order to understand for themselves. Times are a-changin', John. You and I both know it."

"Righteousness must be utmost, Mary. Are ya listenin' to yourself?"

"You surely realize there are more of our young people who are spiritually hungry."

"Jah, I reckoned as much from the preacher's list."

"Well, and there're even more folk interested in studyin' the Bible." Mary no longer sounded desperate but sad. "I can't even see Katie, and she was my very best friend. It's been too many years, John. *Years!*"

"We're not talking 'bout the Bann now."

"Maybe not, but isn't it all wrapped up together?" Mary said, a catch in her voice. "I daresay it is."

There was a long pause; then Mary said more quietly, "If I may be so bold, John, I wonder sometimes if you put the severe shun on Katie Lapp because she stood you up on your wedding day. Ach, but is that possible, love?"

The bishop sighed audibly. "Mary . . . I . . ."

Another pause ensued.

"Have you held a grudge against Katie—and Dan, too—all these years?"

There was no response from the bishop.

"This is all I'll say about this, John. But honestly, it might be time to let go of past hurts, ain't so?" The words were brave, but Mary sounded so meek in the way she spoke to her husband.

The sound of chair legs screeching against the floor made Jenny jump. Apparently the discussion was over. She wondered when she could make her entrance without giving away that she'd overheard them. Or should she simply leave and come back later?

Too late—she heard footsteps coming and realized the bishop was heading for the utility room. *Oh no!* Her moment of escape had passed. Her teeth were clenched, heart pounding . . . and just that quick, she was standing face-to-face with the man of God.

"Well, I forgot you were comin' today," John Beiler said,

leaning over to grab his brown work coat. He stood up, a quick smile on his face. "And I'm mighty glad ya did, Jenny."

She stood there awkwardly, waiting for him to continue, wearing what must have looked like a ridiculous kind of smile.

He gave her the most scrutinizing stare as he leisurely buttoned his coat. Then he said something about a "peculiar sighting" last Sunday evening. "I won't say who saw her, but it seems Rebecca was headed somewhere in the direction of Dan and Katie Fisher's place, and in an awful big hurry."

She took a small breath and slowly let it out. *So Rebecca has visited Katie again. . . .*

Jenny remembered following Rebecca through the shadows toward the very doorstep of her shunned daughter's home . . . and Rebecca's heartbreaking plea for silence later that same night. *She's a loving mother . . . how can she be expected to stay away from her only daughter?*

Jenny nearly gasped with the weight of her knowledge. Was this the moment of truth?

John Beiler took a step closer, his words falling with slow deliberation. "If you know something 'bout Rebecca, I'd expect you to tell me." His eyes were so piercing, she stepped back slightly.

Does he know? Jenny swallowed hard, wishing she might keep her secret, to defend poor Rebecca. Yet how could she do so and fulfill the conditions of her Proving?

Lord, please help me. . . .

Unexpectedly, she heard a giggle and Emily appeared in the doorway, her blond hair braided all around her petite head. "Aendi Jenny," she said, lifting her arms up.

Jenny leaned down to pick her up and squeezed her tight. Had Mary sent her? Emily wrapped her arms around Jenny's neck and hugged her back, jabbering in Deitsch.

The bishop locked eyes with Jenny for a second, then headed out the back door toward the barn. *He's testing me.* Jenny was certain.

In order to succeed in her Proving, Jenny must confess what she knew—which would betray her hostess's secret and trust. What a horrid quandary!

She carried Emily into the warm kitchen. Mary's face was crimson as she placed more Cheerios on Anna's high chair tray, but she didn't look at Jenny. "Looks like you're right on time, Jenny." Mary came to give Emily a kiss in Jenny's arms. "This one's been anxiously waitin' for ya."

"We'll have fun together," Jenny said, feeling jittery. She set Emily down at the table near Mary Mae, who was doing a maze from a book of activities.

Mary gathered up her purse and a carryall, still not making eye contact. "'Jenny, Jenny,' is nearly all Emily talks 'bout these days."

Forcing another smile for sweet Emily's sake, Jenny slipped her arm around the little girl, angry at the bishop for putting her on the spot, and upset at Rebecca for asking her to promise.

She worried for her own and dear Rebecca's future. *What will happen to her?*

"Is something wrong, Rebecca?" her husband asked later that week while they dressed for bed.

"Well, I wonder if I shouldn't have told Eli and Benjamin that Dan and Katie are comin' for Christmas dinner."

"Why's that?" Samuel pulled on his blue corduroy bathrobe, his face anxious. Surely he suspected something.

"They're concerned 'bout it."

"What the bishop'll say if he gets wind, ya mean?"

She nodded and sat on the side of the bed. "Oh, Samuel, this is one sorry situation."

"I'm beginning to think the same thing. I mean, if a man can't grant his own grandson's Christmas wish, what sort of Dawdi is he?"

Rebecca was relieved to hear it.

"Er dutt mir leed!" Samuel said, referring to the bishop.

"I'm sorry for him, too . . . in a peculiar sort of way."

Samuel got into bed and propped himself up with a pillow before leaning his head back. "Kumme, Rebecca, let's have a word of prayer 'bout this. Look to Gott to work things out."

"I don't think it'd be the worst thing that ever happened if Dan and Katie and their babes are the only ones at our table Christmas Day."

"And Jenny, too, don't forget."

"Jah, and Jenny," she said, smiling at Samuel.

"She's almost like family, ya know."

Rebecca couldn't help but agree. "It'd be so nice for her to meet our long-lost girl, ain't?"

Samuel coaxed her next to him, patting the side of the bed. "I was just now thinkin' the same thing." Once she was situated there, rutching around to get her pillows plumped just so, he reached for her hand.

Thank the dear Lord in heaven. Rebecca sighed as her husband began to pray.

Chapter 43

Jenny slogged through the next few days before Christmas. She had never attended more fun-loving "frolics and doin's" in her life—cookie exchanges and pie-baking bees galore, as well as helping the bishop's youngest children make colorful paper chains to decorate the windows and string across the doorjambs. She lost herself for a full week in a party atmosphere that seemed only more wonderful because it lacked the razzle-dazzle of the modern world. And each night, she wrote about the day's quaint and meaningful activities in her journal.

She also wrote about the bishop's stern remark—and how it was eating her alive.

In lieu of gifts, she sent pretty cards to her family, with long handwritten letters. And two days before Christmas, she received a store-bought card in the mail from Andrew. He'd written at the bottom about a special gift planned for her, wanting to know the best day and time to give it. *Sometime alone with you, Jenny, just the two of us. Maybe we could meet at the springhouse on Second Christmas, instead of waiting till Thursday?*

She hadn't given her answer yet—she felt nervous about it, although she cherished every spare minute he offered, and his letters, too, which came more frequently. *And now this exquisite card. I don't deserve this . . . now especially.*

On the afternoon of Christmas Eve, she helped Rebecca kill the fatted goose. Together they worked to pluck the feathers and clean it "right *gut*," as Rebecca liked to say. When the bird was ready for stuffing and baking, they carried it down to the springhouse in a sealed container and set it in the ice-cold water inside. Early tomorrow, they'd make Rebecca's tasty dressing and get it all set for baking.

There was plenty of opportunity for dessert making, and Jenny assisted Rebecca with tapioca pudding, bread-crumb pudding, and two kinds of pies—pecan and Dutch apple— careful to measure the ingredients, hoping not to spoil a single part of tomorrow's feast. She had much to make up for.

The intent look on Rebecca's face made Jenny realize again how very important this meal and the reunion were to her. Samuel, too, had talked of removing the hard wooden benches and bringing over some more comfortable chairs from the empty Dawdi Haus. Of course, a separate table would be necessary for their shunned family members, in keeping with the Ordnung.

Will the bishop find out—and then what?

Jenny was experiencing some unanticipated emotions, as well—stressed on the one hand, yet also wanting everything to be perfectly polished and prepared for Katie, whose room she had inhabited all these weeks now.

As soon as the breakfast dishes were cleared off and washed and dried Christmas morning, Jenny laid out a green table cloth for the meal. The day thus far had been a far cry from the holiday of her upbringing, but she had not missed the mountain of gifts beneath a shining artificial tree, or the mess of wrapping paper and ribbons piled high in the corner.

Instead, Samuel had talked of the Christ child, the dear Lord Jesus, and had taken time to read the Gospel of Luke's account of Jesus' birth. "'And so it was, that, while they were there, the days were accomplished that she should be delivered. And she brought forth her firstborn son, and wrapped him in swaddling clothes, and laid him in a manger; because there was no room for them in the inn,'" Samuel read, his voice gentling on the last line.

Jenny tried not to tear up as she considered the Savior who'd come to offer redemption. She listened along with the Lapps' eldest son, Elam, and the cousins who had come as usual to help Samuel with the morning milking. The fact that they had stayed this long was a treat for Samuel and Rebecca, who knew the men's families were waiting for them back home.

Jenny hoped with all of her heart that it was the start of an extra-special day for them. And she prayed the same, trusting that Bishop John wouldn't see the car parked in the driveway, or hear eventual rumors and spoil things.

Families are precious. . . .

Everything was ready for Daniel and Katie's arrival with the children, including a small wrapped gift on Sammy's and Kate Marie's dinner plates. Rebecca felt her cheeks flush, yet refused to be on pins and needles over this longed-for reunion.

Jenny, meanwhile, was still cutting pickles at the kitchen counter and placing them prettily on a red-hued Carnival glass relish plate. Rebecca went over and slipped her arm through Jenny's and whispered, "I think this might be a day to remember." Tears filled her eyes, and she smiled through the veil. "I'm so glad you can meet my Katie-girl."

Jenny nodded, and then they heard the car turn into the driveway.

"They must be here," Rebecca said, moving forward to the window, eager to get a glimpse.

Just then Samuel came downstairs, all spiffy like it was a church day, and he and Rebecca moved swiftly to the utility room, where they stood like excited children. *Our hearts on our sleeves . . .*

Jenny hung back in the kitchen to observe, undoubtedly not wanting to interfere, and Rebecca hoped she didn't feel strange about being present.

Rebecca noticed Samuel's chin quiver as he opened the door without waiting for the knock. And, oh, such happiness on little Sammy's face as his tall, handsome Dat carried him inside and presented him to Samuel, who reached out his big callused hand. "Hullo, Sammy," she heard Samuel say. "*En hallicher Grischtdaag!*"

Merry Christmas, thought Rebecca. *Ach, so very true!*

Tiny Kate Marie, in her mother's arms, reached toward both Samuel and Rebecca, stretching her chubby hands to Samuel's big beard. Samuel's hearty laughter made Rebecca blink back tears as she took her granddaughter from Katie and motioned all of them into the kitchen. Ah, the feel of this darling child in her arms!

Katie removed the children's coats, hats, and scarves as all the while Samuel and little Sammy held hands. The blond boy stared up silently in awe at the grandpa he'd never met.

Jenny couldn't pull her gaze from the tender scene, riveted by it. What she was witnessing was a family's heart mending before her eyes. She wanted to rejoice in this major step forward, and she prayed that the man of God might pay attention to his wife's encouraging, even convicting words, especially at Christmastime. Was it possible that a family man like John Beiler might soften his heart at this time of year?

And then she recalled his pointed words to her and trembled.

"I've heard so much about you, Jenny," Katie said when Rebecca introduced her, and Jenny had stepped out of the shadows. "Such nice things, too," she added, the brightest smile on her lovely face.

"Merry Christmas to you and your family," Jenny said as she shook Katie's slender hand. "It's wonderful you're here."

Rebecca stood nearby, nodding and smiling.

It must seem like forever, Jenny thought.

Katie was looking all around the kitchen, observing what Jenny assumed she hadn't seen since the advent of her shunning. "It's so good to be home again, Mamma. It truly is." Her voice broke and she turned to reach for Rebecca, embracing her mother as her shoulders heaved with silent sobs.

Daniel, meanwhile, was holding baby Kate Marie over near the doorway to the kitchen, with little Sammy near, his mouth puckered and his big blue eyes regarding everyone.

Soon they were seated at their separate tables, although no one would have known, considering the tablecloth stretched all the way down and over the larger one. Tiny Kate was propped up safely in a booster chair Rebecca kept in the pantry for her other young grandchildren, playing with the bouncy red ribbon on her present.

Jenny and Rebecca brought over the large serving plate with the goose, browned perfectly, and all the steaming hot side dishes. There was dried corn casserole, green beans with ham bits and diced onions, mashed potatoes and rich gravy, chowchow, the relish dish with two kinds of homemade pickles—sweet and dill—and rolls still warm from the oven.

The silent prayer was longer than usual, and Jenny supposed it had much to do with the celebratory spirit of the day . . . and the homecoming of this cherished family.

At the end of the prayer, little Sammy got down from his chair and went to sit on his Dawdi Samuel's knee, sitting there for the longest time while Samuel beamed. It looked like the youngster had his heart set on remaining there for the entire meal, until Dan intervened when the chowchow was being passed around, coaxing Sammy back to his plate with the small wrapped present, which Jenny knew was a set of washable markers.

The table conversation was scarce at first as everyone enjoyed the spectacular meal. But later, when appetites were satisfied, the talk turned almost urgent, as if the principal players were all too aware of the space of time between now and their last visit here. Dan and Samuel, especially, filled in any existing lulls, as if determined no moments be wasted.

After the dessert dishes were cleared away and the children's faces and hands were wiped clean, Katie spoke quietly to Jenny over near the sink, where she and Katie were washing and drying. Katie had urged Rebecca to go into the front room with Samuel and Dan and the children, insisting on helping clean up.

With hands deep in the sudsy water, Katie asked Jenny what had made her interested in living in the Amish community. "Did you have some experience with the People prior to coming?"

"Some." She nodded. "I've been studying the Plain people since I was a girl. And I met Marnie, your cousin, at a roadside stand a few years ago, as well—my first personal link. I guess you could say I've always had a big hole in my heart . . . growing up English."

Katie's eyebrows rose. "How interesting." She brought up the fact that while she herself had loved her Amish childhood, she had never felt a deep connection to the Old Ways. "But I guess you know by now I was adopted." She laughed softly. "If you think about it, I was born fancy."

Jenny said she understood.

"I just hope you're not trying to find the ideal setup, you know." Katie frowned as she handed Jenny the next washed plate. "I mean, in the church and the community here."

"Your mother warned me the same way."

Katie dried her hands. She touched her white cupped prayer cap and smiled. "A person can live for the Lord Jesus anywhere, really. The Amish don't have a corner on piety, as I'm sure you know."

Jenny listened—Katie was certainly outspoken.

Later, when they'd finished, they wandered over to the window and stood there looking out. "People can embrace the simple lifestyle just about anywhere." Katie went on to say she and Dan had encountered searching souls from many walks of life. "Folk reexamining their entire approach to life . . . everything from wanting to downsize to rejecting materialism, or less modest ways of dress."

Jenny agreed but wondered why Katie was making such a point of this. For Jenny, the attraction to Plain living had to do with all those things, but especially faith. *There's no place else I'd rather be.* . . . Which made the thought of what was to come all the harder.

Chapter 44

T he morning after Christmas, Andrew came to breakfast for the first time, along with Samuel's other nephews. Jenny took pause at the irony of it all. She had not slept much the night before, knowing what she must do . . . today.

After breakfast, Andrew asked if she could walk out to his buggy. "I'd like to give you something. I didn't want to wait till tonight."

Another gift, she thought, feeling unworthy and guessing this must be the Christmas present he'd mentioned recently.

Today he demonstrated no hesitation about being seen alone with her, although they went to the side of his enclosed carriage opposite the house, where he offered the gift more privately. She thought of apologizing for not having a gift for him, but then, she hadn't given anything but cards to anyone this year, her family included.

"This is something I wanted myself for a long time," he said as she removed the festive bow and gift wrap to find a Deitsch version of the Bible. "I have one just like it."

She was stunned. "Andrew, this is priceless!" She opened it reverently to see her name printed there and the date.

"It's been more than twenty years in the makin', I'm told. Wycliffe Bible Translators have been working on this important project in Sugarcreek, Ohio—first came the New Testament, and now the rest of the Bible. They got the help of Pennsylvania Dutch linguists to double-check every word, every sentence."

Jenny pressed the Bible to her heart and held it there. "This is the best present ever, Andrew. Denki so much."

He smiled and shook his head. "A blessed Christmas to ya, one day late." Andrew walked around the buggy with her, then got in and waved. "I'll see ya tonight for our prayer time."

She nearly choked, realizing she might not be there. Still, it was impossible to tell him here and now, to reveal that she had decided that she was leaving as soon as she could get a bus ticket home. "Oh, before I forget, I want to pay you for the phone call."

He shook his head and insisted she not worry about it.

"I really want to," she argued.

But he refused, smiling infectiously in the way she had come to know so well.

"Denki again, and have a good day, Andrew." She turned to head for the house, her spirit dismayed. *Thanks for everything.*

"Till then," she heard him call softly.

Jenny's heart ached as she shuffled back inside. She sat with Rebecca at the kitchen table, painfully aware she was letting everyone down—especially herself. And Rebecca had no idea, which was best for now, since she was still caught up in reliving yesterday's reunion, her face shining with the lingering joy of it.

Struggling with her emotions, Jenny had to look away. She could not bear this.

Rebecca wiped tears from her plump pink cheeks. "Ain't

many Christmases I'll keep close in my heart like that one," she said. "For always."

Jenny wanted so badly to say how happy she was for her, but a dark, nearly suffocating curtain of anxiety hung around her. "I need to make a phone call," she said at last. She would miss the bright and sunny kitchen, and Rebecca, too. But she would not miss her failures here.

"Must you right now?" Rebecca's expression revealed more than curiosity.

"I'll be back to help you prepare the noon meal." *Then I'll start packing.*

"Ach, take your time, dear. Looks like a perty day, in spite of the cold," remarked Rebecca. "A nice mornin' for a long walk."

Jenny glanced at the sky, where snow clouds hovered on the northwest horizon. "We might be in for a storm," she said, stating it the way Marnie liked to. *Oh, Marnie,* she thought. *We're leaving the very same week. . . .*

When she'd finished her coffee, Jenny hurried up to her room to get her purse. Back downstairs, she took time to layer up for the trek to the phone shanty, aware of Rebecca's inquisitive looks, though they were indisputably more about Jenny's earlier visit with Andrew than anything else. She walked to the back door with one look back at Rebecca, who sat staring absently at her second cup of coffee, plump hands curved around it.

It's wrong of me to keep enjoying her good graces! Jenny convinced herself once more of that as she walked down the drive, past the heavenly little springhouse and pond, then turned onto Hickory Lane. And suddenly, she remembered the cabbie's words as he dropped her off at that very spot. *"In case things don't work out, here's your ticket out of Plainville . . .*

back to the real world." She hadn't taken his business card at the time, thinking she'd never need it.

No matter how much she wished and prayed, the Lord wasn't coming down to help her make a decent loaf of bread or successfully hitch up a driving horse. Nor would He stop Marnie and Naomi from leaving, or protect Jenny from having to be honest with the bishop. *God's not lifting the Bann from Dan and Katie, either—nor will He keep it from Rebecca.*

She attempted to keep her emotions in check. Hadn't she become more adept at that, wanting to emulate the other women here—their generally stoic approach?

Only a few more hours remained . . . then she could release her sorrow.

Jenny took her time heading for the phone shanty, remembering all too happily walking that way with Andrew to search for Chester Lapp's beloved pup. Today was definitely colder, and dense gray clouds were rolling in quickly. If she was to get out of here before the storm hit, she needed to keep moving.

She loved Hickory Hollow, here for only two months, yet it felt like nearly a lifetime. *The life I always dreamed of . . .* She had met the most wonderful people—Rebecca, Ella Mae, Marnie, and Andrew—and learned things she never would have learned elsewhere. She had planned to stay forever but hadn't even made it to the new year.

At that moment, she noticed a car coming this way, a tan Ford. Stepping off onto the right shoulder, she lowered her head as she'd seen Amishwomen do when a vehicle approached.

The car slowed and then stopped. "Excuse me, miss," a male driver said, the window down. "I wonder if you might help me locate the Lapp residence."

The voice sounded surprisingly familiar, and Jenny glanced

up to see a dark-haired man, his face shielded partly by the visor. Her heart pumped hard.

Can it be?

"Which Lapps are you looking for?" she asked, her voice shaky. "There are quite a few around here."

The man held up an envelope. "Samuel and Rebecca Lapp," he replied, smiling.

Her breath caught in her throat as she recognized this very handsome young man.

Marnie had a serious case of cabin fever. She'd stayed home yesterday cooking and serving Christmas dinner, then helped her mother get caught up on some much-needed sewing for Daed, once the kinfolk cleared out and left for home. Now she was in the process of making a list of things she wanted to take over to Fishers' in a few days. She also wanted to see Jenny, feeling bad about how she had complicated her seeker-friend's life. *I should be more supportive.* She also had a wall hanging she'd made and planned to give as a belated gift.

Marnie got her warmest coat and scarf and headed down Hickory Lane to visit Jenny for a while that Wednesday afternoon, assuming that if her friend was busy redding up after the Christmas festivities, she might just stay and help.

But almost as soon as she left the front yard and was making her way onto the road, Marnie spotted a tan vehicle stopped in the middle. The dark-haired driver was leaning out the window, talking to Jenny!

What the world?

Marnie hurried her pace, but when Jenny walked over to the car, Marnie hung back a bit, not sure what she was seeing.

Thinking better of it, she turned and went to look in the mailbox and discovered a letter from Roy. *How bold of him— he's honestly dared to send one directly here?* Her heart fluttered with happiness, and glancing down the road again, she decided to go back to the stable and warm up a bit while reading the letter. Oh, was she ever glad she'd found this before Mamm came to check the mail, although Marnie was sure her mother would never keep one of Roy's letters from her, disappointed in Marnie though she was.

She perched herself on an old bench near chestnut-colored Willis, her favorite driving horse, and read the letter. Roy wanted Marnie to think about meeting him at his church in Bird-in-Hand, once she'd settled in at Fishers'. *I'm trying to decide on the right one for us to join. As you know, I want God's will in all of this*, he'd written.

His church? Marnie put her head down on her knees and gritted her teeth. Like Roy, she yearned to seek the Lord more fully, but this would only compound problems. After her father's reaction in the milk house, she knew that for certain.

Something had to give, but what? And on this day after Christmas, with Jenny down the road talking to an Englischer, Marnie had an ominous feeling some very big changes were coming. And fast.

Chapter 45

K yle?" Jenny was shocked at the sight of her former
fiancé.

Kyle Jackson's brown eyes searched hers; then he studied
her Amish dress and apron. "Looks like you did it," he said
quietly. "You pulled it off, Jenny."

She approached his car. He looked the same, although
his brown hair was longer than she remembered. Suddenly
feeling ill at ease, she slipped a hand into her coat pocket.
"What are you doing here, Kyle?"

"I just happened to be in the area. . . ." He grinned at his
own joke, the same old bravado, only now it felt out of place.

"I'm serious. How did you find—" She stopped. "Wait. Did
my mom give you the address? Or was it Pamela or Dorie?"
She was upset. "Oh, maybe it was Kiersten."

"Jenny." He hesitated a second, glancing toward the road,
then back at her. "They're all concerned, of course. But that's
not why I'm here."

She let that sink in. "So . . . my *mom* sent you?"

"No, Jen. It's not like that."

He explained that he'd contacted her mom a few weeks

ago and was told Jenny had "made the leap to the Amish," as he put it. "Then, when I said I wanted to visit you, she was excited and gave me the envelope you sent her, with the return address for the Lapps."

Taking a step back, Jenny took a deep breath—*why today?*—and slowly let it out.

Kyle indicated that he wanted to pull over and park, which he did before quickly getting out. Tall and wonderfully appealing, he wore dark jeans, a striped button-down shirt, and a black leather jacket. Leaning on the driver's side of the car, he put his hands in his pockets and exhaled a plume of moisture. "It's cold out. Can I drive you somewhere?"

It *was* cold.

"I was headed for the phone shack up the road," she said, still amazed he was here.

Kyle turned, shielding his eyes as he looked into the sun. "May I at least walk with you?" he asked, his dark eyes pleading.

She shrugged, not pleased at the prospect but uncertain what to say. She gestured to his car. "We might as well drive, then."

He broke into a smile, going around with her to open the front passenger door. She got in and was immediately aware of the familiar scent of car leather and the plush surroundings. For a second or two she felt disoriented.

"I hope you don't mind my just showing up." He settled into the driver's seat and started the ignition. "But there wasn't any way to let you know."

There's always the mail.

"So why did you call my mom, anyway?" she asked as he turned the car around and drove slowly up the road.

"It's a long story, Jenny."

"Try me."

He hesitated for a moment; then a look of resignation crossed his face. "I've missed you, okay?"

She was a sitting duck. Here was the man she had adored and loved to laugh with—and oh, how they'd laughed, enjoying every moment together. She'd wanted it to last for a lifetime.

She spotted the crystal praying hands hanging on the rear-view mirror, a birthday gift from her. *He kept it. . . .*

"Jenny . . . I was wrong about us. I've been kicking myself for almost two years."

"Kyle, please."

"Is that the phone booth?" he said, pulling the car over in front of the shack.

She turned in her seat. "Why now, after all this time?"

He smiled. "Why not?"

That's his best answer?

Go home, she was tempted to say.

"I'm not asking you to give up your dream, Jenny."

No, she thought. *I'm giving that up on my own.* Her cheek twitched.

"Want to get something to eat?" He touched her arm. "I'd really like to spend some time with you."

Her heart was in her throat. "What then?" It was hard enough seeing him again, but hearing him talk like this threatened to reopen old wounds.

"We can catch up on old times," he suggested.

"Why?"

Kyle looked exasperated. "Fine. You want me to just say it? I thought maybe we could talk about *us*. How things used to be."

She was dumbfounded. "Isn't it too late for that? You left *me*, remember?" She realized her response sounded anything but meek and mild. She was definitely not Rebecca Lapp.

"I mean, we were together one minute, and you were gone the next. That quick." She wouldn't tell him how long it took her to recover.

"You were changing so radically, Jenny." He shook his head. "I just flipped out, okay? I don't deny it." He said he'd pondered everything and no longer cared anymore how she dressed. "I respect your Plain yearnings. None of that matters anymore."

She was actually relieved he hadn't made fun of her Amish clothes, though she didn't know why she even cared when she was leaving the People.

Jenny looked over at the phone shed, suddenly feeling claustrophobic. She needed to breathe, to be outside. "I have to make a call before it gets too late."

"I'll wait for you," he said.

Now he'll wait. She bit her lip at the sarcasm.

Nodding, she opened the car door and headed around the brushwood to the phone. Inside, she dialed the number and reached a clerk for the bus company. She asked for their bus schedule to Connecticut and received unfortunate news. Due to weather delays in Philadelphia, the earliest available seat was the day after tomorrow. She exhaled in frustration, and then the thought occurred to her: *What if Kyle drove me back?* He was heading there, anyway.

But would that lead him on?

She thanked the woman and hung up. Returning to the car, she spotted Kyle's expectant face and determined to nip *all* hope in the bud. "Let me say this just for the record."

"Yes?"

"I don't see us getting back together."

He flinched. "I don't blame you—"

"But . . . if you want to do me a really big favor . . ."

Without missing a beat, he nodded. "Say the word."

She asked him where he was staying, and he told her the Bird-in-Hand Family Inn on the Old Philadelphia Pike, not far from here.

Jenny made her request and Kyle seemed pleased. *Too* pleased. Then his eyes squinted nearly shut. "Wait a minute, why are you going home?"

"I'll tell you tomorrow." She directed him back to Samuel and Rebecca's, where they parked on the road near the mailbox at the end of the long driveway. "Tomorrow morning, seven o'clock. Please don't be late."

"I'll be here," he promised.

Jenny saw him wave through the window, and she hurried up the lane to Rebecca. It was time to fulfill her promise to help make the noon meal.

Chapter 46

When Jenny returned from the phone shanty, she and Rebecca kept busy at their separate work spaces in the kitchen, Jenny glancing every now and then at her friend and hostess. She had no idea how to say what she must.

Once they had the large chicken potpie nearly ready to place in the oven, Rebecca began to talk about the coming snowstorm, going on about how Samuel had complained of his knees aching something awful yesterday from his rheumatism. "He seems to know nearly right on the dot just when a storm'll hit," Rebecca was saying.

Jenny listened, still surprised at Kyle's appearance. Was it a sign from the Lord? After all, he had always been a prayerful man.

Jenny knew she couldn't put off the moment any longer—it was time to tell Rebecca that she was going home. "Rebecca, I want to tell you how much I appreciate everything you've done for me," she said. "You've given me so much." Her voice broke and she paused in dicing apples for a Waldorf salad. "I'll never forget."

Rebecca stopped what she was doing. "Ach, Jenny, what're ya sayin'?"

"I'm leaving Hickory Hollow tomorrow . . . with an old friend of mine." She sighed heavily.

The blood drained from Rebecca's face. "I don't understand."

"I don't see how I can meet the expectations of the Proving . . . not now. Not when I must eventually confess what I know about your visits to Katie." She bowed her head. "And I don't feel good about betraying that, considering all you've done for me."

Rebecca was quiet for a long while, her eyes downcast. When she finally spoke, she merely nodded her head. "If you must, then go with the Good Lord's blessing."

"Denki" was all Jenny could say.

The two of them remained awkwardly silent until they heard the sound of the back door screech open and Samuel tromp in.

Rebecca looked devastated during the noon meal, and Jenny cringed all through it. *If only things could be different!* she thought miserably. *The last thing I want to do is leave here.*

After dishes were done and there was still no conversation between them, Jenny escaped to her room to write Andrew Lapp a letter, which she gave to him when they met at the springhouse pond that evening. He accepted it but was clearly taken aback by her not wanting to stay and pray as planned.

"When you read the letter, I hope you'll understand," she told him, her voice quivering.

His eyes held hers, his expression concerned. "Wait, Jenny . . . you seem—"

She shook her head. "I'm sorry . . . I really can't talk about it."

He nodded and reached for her hand. "Something's wrong."

She looked down at their entwined fingers. "Jah, everything's wrong, Andrew." Her voice cracked and she reluctantly slipped her hand away.

"I'd like to talk to you," he said. "Will ya stay awhile?"

Tears rolled down her cheeks. "I can never succeed in my Proving. It's not possible."

"Why do you say so?" He moved closer. "I don't understand."

She sniffled. "I just can't . . . not without jeopardizing the peace of someone I care deeply about."

"Is it Rebecca?"

Andrew's words shocked her. How could he possibly know? She ignored his question. "I'm not the type of person who could—" Her voice broke and she had to pause a moment before continuing. "Please, will you trust me when I say this is for the best?"

"That's what's special about you, Jenny. And I appreciate you not sayin' anything amiss 'bout Rebecca, too." He reached for her hand again. "You're ever so trustworthy."

She was unable to choke down the lump in her throat. *I need to leave now, before I come to care for you even more than I do.*

"Please read my letter, all right? Good-bye, Andrew." And with that, Jenny fled, holding back her tears as she headed back to the farmhouse.

··· ⤛⤜ ···

Jenny could not sleep again that night. She gave up trying to rest at all and instead wrote yet another letter—this one to dearest Marnie. In it, she avoided revealing Rebecca's devastating secret but told her friend she would miss her very much and hoped that she and Roy would be happily married next autumn.

I'd like to stay in touch, she wrote, giving Marnie her parents' phone number and street address. *Your friend always, Jenny Burns.*

Rebecca lay wide-awake, listening to Samuel's irregular snoring, forcing her mind toward happier thoughts: little Sammy's visit. Such an adorable child, sitting like a wee angel on his Dawdi's knee at the table all that while on Christmas Day. It was as if he'd intended to take his meal right there with Samuel. And if she wasn't mistaken, Daniel's blueberry eyes had glistened about then. Samuel's too. And then again tonight, when she told him that Jenny Burns was leaving in the morning. He must've steeled himself, poor man, unbuttoning his shirt without speaking, his actions deliberate and methodical. Then he'd gone to kneel at his bedside and remained there for the longest time, his heart obviously broken.

Like hers.

Marnie arrived at Uncle Samuel's back door with her handmade wall hanging Thursday morning. She could hardly wait to present this particular gift to her friend and could not believe her ears when Aunt Rebecca told her Jenny was gone. "Left just an hour ago or so," Rebecca said. "She said to give you this."

Marnie stared at the letter her aunt handed to her, biting her lip. *Did Jenny leave because of me?*

She had no right to protest, did she? After all, she, too, was packed and ready to move. But to think her friend hadn't told her in person or bothered to say good-bye. Why?

"Denki," she told Rebecca, deciding to take the wall hanging home with her and wondering if she might simply mail it to Jenny.

"Won't ya come in for some hot cocoa, get warmed up?" Rebecca's eyes pleaded.

Marnie accepted and removed her boots and coat before following Rebecca into the warm, inviting kitchen.

They talked around Jenny's leaving, never addressing it outright, but Marnie could see Aunt Rebecca was greatly troubled.

Jenny was so exhausted she slept for the first two hours while Kyle drove. When she awakened, she was startled at the sight of her own clothing . . . the English outfit she'd worn to Hickory Hollow back in October. In the haze of waking up, she'd nearly erased the last two months.

She wondered if Rebecca would be surprised that she'd packed all of her Amish dresses and aprons. But of course, she'd left Rebecca's black shawl and outer bonnet, and Katie's former things. The room she'd shared with Katie's memory was fast fading in her own mind—or was she simply pushing it aside . . . letting the time in Lancaster County die away to nothing?

"You're tired," Kyle said when she glanced over at him there in his navy blue pants and tennis shoes.

She nodded. "It's been a couple of rough nights."

"Want to talk about it?"

Must I?

"Let's talk about *you*, Kyle."

He smiled, eager to do so. She learned that he'd continued to work as a computer tech at the same company in Hartford but was thinking of buying a large parcel of land near Frankfort, Kentucky. She wondered if this was to impress her. But before she could ask, he volunteered that he'd been thinking of paring down to live a simpler life. "Besides, who wants to live in fear of the national grid going haywire?" He laughed.

"And on that note, let me help out with the gas," she offered as they stopped off to refuel and grab some snacks.

"Don't be silly. The trip's on me."

When they returned to the car and got back on I-95, she asked about her family and was given an ambiguous response. This brought it all back—there wasn't anything to tell, as usual—and she dreaded the thought of going home.

He asked where she would live, since her mother had mentioned she'd left her condo and job. "Well, if my parents haven't disowned me, there's always the guest cottage behind the main house." *Like a detached Dawdi Haus,* she thought, wondering how Ella Mae Zook would take the news that she had left so hastily. *And poor Marnie, too . . .*

She asked Kyle if she could use his cell phone to call the antique shop in Essex. She wanted to see if she might work part-time, perhaps, maybe even eventually get her job back. Not that she expected the owner to agree, but if there was a chance, she preferred to work there. *With old things cushioning me,* she thought, picturing dear Rebecca sitting in her sewing room on her grandmother's cane chair, watching the snow fall.

Does she despise me?

Chapter 47

The snow became heavier the farther north Kyle drove, and Jenny prayed silently for God's protection. Kyle brought up the church he was still attending, mentioning a men's prayer breakfast group he enjoyed. He asked her about the Amish church, but she skirted the question. The reality of what she'd done, leaving Hickory Hollow so suddenly and without giving anyone but Rebecca or Andrew a heads-up, became increasingly more painful as the hours passed. And in spite of Kyle's attempt to make her think he wanted to live a tranquil, uncomplicated life, he continued to talk about his job and Hartford. She knew he must care for her a lot to want to give that up to move to a big spread of land in Kentucky. It was sweet and she appreciated him for it, but she needed time to get her head straight.

"I have an idea," he said when they were closing in on the turnoff for Essex. "Let's catch the train in New Haven and go to Manhattan for New Year's Eve."

They'd enjoyed this excitement-charged event once before, and the following month he'd taken her home to meet his parents, close to Valentine's Day.

He looked over at her, beaming. "So . . . what do you say?"

Jenny knew the trip would merely be for old time's sake, because nothing could take her and Kyle back to those days. If anything, he was attempting to reignite something romantic between them, which meant everything would have to be on a brand-new footing. But for him to even suggest a trip to the Big Apple confirmed for her that they were out of sync, and she told him so. "I'd rather not," she said politely. "I'm sure you can understand."

He nodded, but she could tell by his eyes he was disappointed.

Hickory Hollow had altered Jenny forever.

Jenny's mother was astonished to see her, and her dad actually stood up and came over to greet her as Jenny walked in the front entrance. They said absolutely she could stay in the small guesthouse until she got settled elsewhere. And they went with her to the living room and sat there, managing some awkward small talk and getting caught up a little. Jenny asked about each of them—and about her sister and brother—and soon the conversation centered on Mom's various upcoming social events . . . and Cameron's "pretty new girlfriend." No mention of the former one, or the child belonging to the new girl.

After a half hour or so, Dad rose and came over to kiss the top of Jenny's head. "Good to see you again, kiddo." He mentioned having a report to finish and disappeared into his library office.

Her mother lasted somewhat longer, until she remembered she needed to pick out a formal gown from her wardrobe upstairs for her next big function. "Come with me," she said, coaxing with her eyes. "Help me choose it, won't you, dear?"

Seldom had Jenny been invited into the vast walk-in closet—*"the wardrobe paradise,"* as Mom had once called it. Shoes and purses were lined up according to color and style—casual, day wear, and evening wear. While staring at the abundant options, Jenny thought of how the old Amish houses didn't even have closets—just a row of wooden wall pegs.

Even though she craved some alone time, overwhelmed by her mother's astonishing passion for opulence and excess, Jenny made herself stay. She wanted to show interest and attempt to connect. And after far longer than Jenny hoped it might take, she confirmed her mother's choice of a gown, which brought a smile from Mom. It was important, Jenny now knew, to demonstrate how much she cared. Had she always held her family at arm's length? Was she partly at fault for the distance between them all these years?

Later, when she'd patiently waited for Mom to choose her accessories, Jenny asked permission to go to the large guest room closet, where she'd left behind a few of her clothes. Then, needing some air, Jenny borrowed one of her mother's casual jackets and walked down to her former workplace to talk with her friend, the owner, who said she'd gotten her voicemail, and yes, she could offer Jenny twenty or so hours a week to start.

Strolling along the lovely main street, Jenny looked forward to getting her bearings in Essex again, needing to put the hapless situation in Lancaster County behind her. She wondered most of all if Andrew had read her letter. Did he think poorly of her? She was actually glad she'd stayed long enough at the springhouse to explain herself so that she hadn't appeared to simply vanish . . . as she had initially from home.

When Jenny returned to her parents', her hair was white

with fluffy snowflakes. Mom came into the large entryway to meet her for the second time—and she rather liked the attention. "Your Amish friend Marnie Lapp called a few minutes ago. You just missed her, dear." Evidently Marnie wanted Jenny to call her sometime this weekend and had given the number for the phone shanty. "She said you can leave a voice message if she's not there to pick up."

"Did she say what time I should call?"

Mom smiled brightly. "You know, I believe she did. After supper on Saturday night—yes, that's what it was."

"Denki . . . er, thanks."

"And, dear, sometime when you're ready to talk about it, I'd like to know more about your Amish experience," Mom said, a soft expression on her pretty face.

Jenny caught her breath. "How about now?"

Her mother motioned her toward the kitchen, walking back to an open cookbook. Jenny followed into the grand kitchen and sat on the barstool, observing her. "What would you like to know?"

Mom shook her head. "I have no idea."

"Well, I can tell you that, while I practiced repeatedly, I never managed to make a successful loaf of bread like Rebecca Lapp. Yet it's something Amishwomen do frequently."

Mom raised her eyebrows and pursed her lips.

"Have you ever made bread?" Jenny asked.

"Sure, just not recently. Years ago, I made fresh bread every week."

"Would you teach me how, Mom?"

"Well, why not now?"

Jenny smiled at the sudden sparkle in her mother's eyes.

··· ➤ ➤ ···

311

When she returned to the family's guesthouse, Jenny took time to hang up her Amish clothing, putting the dresses in the far back of the large closet before closing the door. Her time in Hickory Hollow had turned out to be shorter than she'd ever expected, an experiment meant to have a different outcome. "Nothing more," she whispered sadly.

Then, brushing her hair, Jenny was surprised to see that her bangs came all the way down to her nose. She moved to the floor-length mirror and fluffed them a bit. "Well, what do you know . . . one small triumph!"

··· ≻ ≺ ···

After a formal dinner the next evening, Jenny made a point of sitting with her father in the den to show him the newly published Pennsylvania Dutch Bible. He thumbed through to various Old Testament passages and into the Psalms. He asked her to read to him, and she did, surprised at how much she'd learned in such a short time. He even asked for the translation of certain words, and she brought up her dictionary. She waited for him to create an excuse to leave, but he didn't, at least not for a solid hour, which pleased her.

He did ask, though, before she headed to the guest cottage, if someone by the name of Andrew Lapp was a friend of hers from Amish country. Curious, she asked where he'd seen the name. "Well, here." He pointed to the second page, the one following her name and the date, which she'd already seen.

The pages had evidently been stuck together when Andrew presented it to her. There, in Andrew's own strong hand, were the words *Delight thyself also in the Lord: and he shall give thee the desires of thine heart.* ~ Psalm 37:4

Andrew had also written a note saying the verse was a favorite and signed his name.

"That's an interesting book—can't say I've ever seen a whole volume in Pennsylvania Dutch before." Dad peered at it more closely.

She nodded and smiled as she looked up Andrew's reference to the Proverb to see the translation, then read it aloud in Deitsch.

"You enjoy studying this language, don't you, Jenny?"

"It wasn't easy for me, despite my classes in German, and I don't have your patience for such detailed work."

Dad chuckled, folding his hands and making eye contact. "Tell me about Amish life. What things stand out most to you?"

She explained how chores were broken up along clear gender lines. "There's a specific hierarchy in Amish culture: Men and women have very defined roles, even from childhood. I was surprised at how much time I spent in the kitchen, for instance—it takes a lot of work to keep up with all those hearty appetites, but Amishmen expect nothing less of their womenfolk."

Dad smiled. "*Womenfolk*, Jenny?"

"That's what we call ourselves. Well, what *they* call themselves." And now Jenny was smiling, too.

Rebecca looked out when she heard the clatter of a carriage that evening. Her pulse sped up when she saw it was Bishop John—surely he'd heard of their Christmas Day reunion. She'd held her breath, waiting for this dreadful moment, but was in some ways relieved to be confronted at last.

Samuel was sitting near the stove in the kitchen in his stocking feet when the bishop knocked on the back door. "Willkumm, bishop," he said, rising and going to shake John's hand. His expression showed no trace of concern as he pulled up another chair, giving up his rocker for the man of God. "Have a seat," he said.

They exchanged particulars—mostly about the weather and two upcoming farm auctions. Rebecca offered hot coffee and some cookies, and the bishop accepted them, which surprised her a little. Was this not to be a serious visit after all?

At last, though, he began to share what was on his mind. "I heard Katie and her husband were over for Christmas dinner."

Samuel gave a quick nod, his eyes serious. "Was there anything wrong with that, bishop?" he asked respectfully.

The silence grew lengthy as Bishop John studied the coffee cup in his hands. "Well, in my thinkin', there's nothing wrong with a God-fearing man having a visit from his grandchildren. Might be a blessing."

Rebecca thought her heart might stop. "No, but something else is wrong, Bishop," she admitted, wanting—*needing*—to come clean.

Samuel frowned. "Rebecca?"

"I'm talking 'bout what *I've* been doing . . . in secret." She unloaded her burden right then and there, revealing her numerous nighttime visits to see her shunned daughter. "I just couldn't stay away from my grandchildren," she confessed. "My family."

The bishop ran his fingers through his beard, appearing far more flabbergasted at this admission than did her own Samuel. And before the bishop could say a word, Samuel said he wished John had been on hand to see his young grandson Sammy being granted his "dearest Christmas wish." Samuel was as calm yet determined as she'd ever seen him with any of the ministerial brethren, and his composed demeanor made her fall in love with him all over again.

Amazingly, the bishop did not pursue the topic of her breaking the ordinance, though he did not offer to forgive Rebecca, either, just kept his face turned toward Samuel. "Mercy has an important place in our community," John said quietly, his expression serious. "I daresay it's been a long time comin'." This most of all astonished Rebecca. Did John Beiler mean what she thought he was saying?

Rebecca wanted to clap her hands. No, she wanted to give her husband a sweet kiss, and she would do just that the minute the bishop left, which he did much sooner—and more calmly—than she or Samuel might have imagined.

"He didn't condemn my visits to Katie," Rebecca said in wonder as the two of them watched their neighbor head to his waiting horse and carriage.

"Come here, my dear woman," Samuel said, drawing her to himself. "You have nothin' to fear. Jah?"

"Thank the Good Lord," she said, taking the opportunity to lean in and stand on tiptoes. But Samuel kissed her first, before she could even pucker.

Chapter 48

J enny never dreamed her sojourn home would amount to
  such pleasure on not just her part, but her parents'. And
Kiersten, too, had come around a couple days after Jenny's
return, wanting to stay longer than just to drop by and say
"hey," actually asking questions about Plain life.

To her family's thinking, Jenny hadn't been gone very long.
In fact, she assumed they had hardly noticed . . . and here
she was back already. Still, Jenny felt almost doted upon by
them, and also by Kyle Jackson, who'd taken her to one of
her favorite spots—a walk along the Connecticut River in
Essex, where Main Street ended at the rushing water's edge.

She asked Kyle if he would purchase the land in Kentucky
for himself, if the two of them weren't together as a couple.

"No, probably not," he said, honest as always.

Then why do it? she wondered but didn't want to shoot
him down.

"Why do you ask, Jenny?"

"Just curious."

Kyle bypassed that topic and went on to inquire about her
stay at the Lapps' farm. Jenny felt more comfortable now and

ready to tell Kyle what had transpired there. She even shared about the practice of social avoidance called the shunning, explaining that Rebecca's ties to her daughter had seemed to take precedence over the strict church ordinance, although she did not reveal Rebecca's forbidden visits.

Jenny also recounted her time with the Old Wise Woman, and the many hours working together with Rebecca in her kitchen, as well as quilt making and baby-sitting at the bishop's big farmhouse. "Lots of domestic chores," she said, moving on to describe Marnie's and Naomi's plights. Then she described how reserved and soft-spoken Samuel Lapp had been, "until he talked my ear off, showing me how to hitch up the pony to the cart." That had Kyle laughing, saying he'd like to have seen her go flying up Hickory Lane in the pony cart. She did not divulge her calamity with Josie and the pony cart, however. Nor did she say a word about Andrew Lapp.

"Do you know how impossible it is to see the stars here at night?" she suddenly blurted out. Kyle looked bemused, then suggested it was mostly because of the bright city lights. And in that moment, Jenny was glad she'd returned the call to Marnie Lapp, though Marnie had sounded so sad, missing Jenny yet giddy to talk to her again. *"We'll stay in touch, like before,"* Marnie had promised.

Jenny had quickly agreed, certain things would never be the same but relieved Marnie wanted to remain friends.

She did not permit her mind to wander back to Andrew, though. Dwelling on him was a mistake, knowing as she did the great emptiness she felt—sometimes nearly a lack of air in her chest—when she allowed herself to return to him in her sweet memories. Jenny guessed she might feel that way for a very, very long time.

By leaving Hickory Hollow, she'd lost Andrew Lapp forever. Their precious friendship was a closed book.

The distant sound of firecrackers punctuated Rebecca's dreams, and later, in the wee hours, when she was fully awake and plodded downstairs to the bathroom, she realized she had tears on her face. Had she been dreaming of Jenny Burns again? Or was it Katie?

Samuel had warned her she would miss the daughter figure she'd found in naïve Jenny. Rebecca had indeed begun to mourn this new and unexpected loss, wishing there was a way to let the former seeker know there were no more secrets to be kept. Samuel was now quite sure the bishop would simply turn his head to their visits to Dan and Katie, and vice versa.

Rebecca was compelled to go and look in Jenny's room, thinking how odd it was that she'd lost both girls. *And both to the English world.* So the fancy life won out, when all was said and done, and yet she loved them both. *I put Jenny at risk by going against the Ordnung and hoping she'd turn a blind eye,* she thought. *When I was supposed to be her mentor!* Sorrowfully, Rebecca realized she'd done much the same with Katie by withholding another secret.

"Haven't I learned my lesson yet?" she whispered, remembering how Jenny had flitted from room to room while living here, so taken with the trappings of Amish life: the wringer washer, the smooth bone of the crochet hook, and the comforting livestock in the stable. Yet she was not able to embrace it long enough to make it her own.

Rebecca lifted the heirloom quilts and slipped into the bed where both Katie and Jenny had rested their heads, said their silent prayers, and longed to be accepted. A new year had come on swift wings just hours before, but Rebecca did not care to sleep. No, it was time to pray. "Dear Lord in heaven, be with all of our family this night. Keep them ever in thy loving care. I pray this, too, for Jenny Burns, who is also thy child. In Jesus' name, amen."

··· ➤ ◄ ···

Marnie was shocked to see Roy arrive by van following breakfast New Year's morning. She was helping Mamm redd things up in the kitchen, her younger siblings sitting now at the table, looking at the cute cards they'd made for each other before Christmas.

She went running outside to greet Roy, not bothering with a coat or shawl. "Happy New Year!"

"You, too, Marnie." He was all smiles and she thought he might reach to kiss her cheek, but they did not embrace. "I have *gut* news for you. Had to come in person to tell ya."

"That *gut?*"

He nodded, his eyes alight. "But first, go an' get your coat and scarf so we can walk right quick."

"Let's go to the barn, where it's warmer," she said, liking the thought of being with Roy on this first day of the year. She hurried inside and pulled on her work boots, coat, and scarf, then donned her black candlesnuffer-style outer bonnet. She looked for her mittens and smiled when she found them pushed into her next youngest sister's coat. "I'll be right back, Mamm," she called into the kitchen, not waiting for an answer. Oh, the joy of seeing her beau again!

She listened carefully as she and Roy walked slowly across the backyard to the barn, where she knew they'd have privacy.

Making their way inside to the stable, Marnie could scarcely believe what Roy was saying.

"You're mighty sure?" she said, wanting to be sure she had it right.

"Jah, your bishop and I had a long talk early yesterday morning. He sought me out, said it was all right in his opinion if I take you to gatherings with others who are seeking to understand God's Word."

Marnie found herself shaking her head, amazed.

"I was surprised by John Beiler. I honestly liked him, Marnie. He seems to understand where I'm comin' from—that I love God and want to learn as much as I can from Scripture before I become your husband."

"So he knows that, too?"

Roy reached for her mittened hand. "I'm actually thinkin' of joinin' church over here in Hickory Hollow."

"Wha-at?" Now, this was a surprise! She leaped up and Roy caught her, embracing her and planting a warm kiss on her cheek. "Oh, this is the best news ever!"

"I thought you'd say so." He held her near and removed his black felt hat, then gave her the first-ever kiss on the lips. He explained that he truly thought the bishop was taking a few steps back from the youth who were in Rumschpringe, letting them choose baptism without so much coercion.

This was as astonishing as Roy's tender kiss.

"Can ya stay for dinner?" She looked up at his handsome face. "Perty please?"

He grinned his answer and pulled her close again.

"This has to be the happiest day for us, jah?"

"Well, I can think of a better day yet . . . next fall, ya know."

She smiled. Their wedding day would top this moment, no question on that.

"'Course now there's no need for you to move to Dan and Katie's," he said.

She'd nearly forgotten with all this rush of news. Goodness' sake, was she ever relieved. "Kumme mit—we must talk to my parents, 'specially to Daed."

This will be the best gift ever for my father!

Chapter 49

I think I've learned a tough lesson," Jenny told Pamela and Dorie at the noisy eatery in Hartford days later. "Silly me . . . I have to accept who I am, not what I wish I might've been."

Pamela shook her head. "Sounds philosophical, Jen . . . something your father might say."

"I can't believe you're back," Dorie said. "I mean, you looked so at home in Amishville. We talked about this on the drive back here."

"I agree with Dorie; you seemed really settled there . . . despite your crazy Plain costume." Pamela cringed. "Don't hit me!"

They laughed together, and when their lunch order arrived, Jenny dismissed their remarks, ready to enjoy her salad and crab-cake sandwich. Dorie smiled at her apologetically across the table from behind a mound of fries.

Pamela suggested they pray silently, which they often did when eating out together, but Jenny's mind flew to the dozens of times she'd watched Samuel purposefully bow his head in reverence, with Rebecca doing the same. Jenny still wished she knew what words they prayed—surely it was a learned rote prayer, as was the bedtime prayer. But she'd never asked.

Another regret.

"It's so great to have our little trio together again," Dorie said as she reached for the ketchup.

Jenny took note of the busy place. The walls were lined with posters and other paraphernalia, and it wasn't long before her thoughts were in Hickory Hollow, where Rebecca's home was anything but frenzied and overdecorated. Tidy, simple . . . that was the Amish approach to interiors.

"*A house is a home because of the people who live and love there,*" Ella Mae had once said.

"Jenny? You look wistful." Pamela leaned near, studying her. "You okay, hon?"

"Of course." Jenny reached for her soda and took a sip, yearning for the unusual taste of Rebecca's homemade root beer.

Later in the week, Kiersten talked Jenny into meeting at an upscale strip mall in Hartford, where they shopped for most of the afternoon, Jenny mostly observing what her sister bought. They capped off the outing with supper. "I'll bet you miss home-cooked Amish food," her sister said, juggling her many purchases as they sat down.

"Well, Mom's the best cook ever."

"So is that a no?" Kiersten probed.

"Food is food, right?"

Kiersten laughed. "You haven't changed at all. I thought you'd return all geared up for our modern ways . . . the ones you looked down on most of your life, remember?"

Jenny listened, trying to get a grasp on Kiersten's perception of her. It was unnatural for sisters who grew up under the same roof to have to go through these kinds of maneuverings. "You must have thought I was checked out, even when I was a little girl. Everyone did."

Kiersten didn't come right out and agree, but it was clear what she thought. "Oh, you know."

"No, really, I'm sorry if I shut you out." She paused. "I must have."

Kiersten waved it off, bringing up Cameron. "Talk about checked out—our brother is crazy in love with Lexi." She explained that he and his new girlfriend saw each other several times a week, and even hauled Lexi's kid along. "Totally surprising."

"So if they marry, he'll be an instant daddy."

"Who knew?"

Jenny smiled. Cameron had been too busy to see her since she'd landed back here. But she could easily overlook that. Things were pretty much the way they had always been between her and her brother—nebulous. *Don't bother me, and I won't bother you.* Still, she hoped to change that, too.

"Do you want to drive up to Mystic with me sometime?" Kiersten said she'd read online about an amazing boutique there. "Or are you still clinging to the pure and simple life?"

Jenny glanced down at her navy blue skirt and cream-colored sweater. "Guess some things never change."

"Why *did* you come home, sis?"

Jenny sighed, not comfortable with the idea of rehearsing the whole excruciating mess. Besides, she was sure her sister was just filling the spaces, uneasy with natural silence. Kiersten wasn't the type to be interested in old souls. She was all about the next cool dress shop or casino restaurant—anything "hoppin' or hot."

"Maybe it's more about why I ever left," Jenny said bravely.

"Okay."

"And sure, I'll go shopping with you in Mystic."

Kiersten squinted her eyes. "You *will?*"

"Name the day," she said, committing to stepping out of her comfort zone. It was about time.

··· ➤ ➤ ···

That evening, an unexpected call came in from Rebecca Lapp. Jenny was delighted to hear from her—Rebecca's voice was sweet music to her ears. They exchanged a bit of small talk before Jenny asked about Marnie and Naomi . . . and Ella Mae.

Then Rebecca's voice turned tense. "Things happened so abruptly when ya left, I never had a chance to say a proper good-bye." She wanted to let Jenny know that things had worked themselves out. "Ach, my dear girl, I couldn't bear thinkin' you'd left here because of me." She sounded pitiful. "It wasn't your fault . . . not at all." She paused for a beat. "Honestly, I put you in an awful tough situation, askin' you to keep what you knew from the brethren."

"Rebecca, I—"

"No, listen . . . I failed you in doing so—didn't measure up as your mentor." She continued, explaining that she never should've gone against the Bann. "I've made things right with the bishop; I wanted you to know."

Jenny realized once more how painful this had been for both of them. "I'm so glad you called." She didn't go on to tell her how much she missed talking to her, or any of that. *Best not,* as Rebecca might say. *Besides, what's the point?*

She changed the subject and mentioned how busy she was now with her family, and that she'd started working again while living at her parents' place. "Please tell Marnie hi for me, and Samuel, too."

"I'll be glad to do that. But just so ya know, things ain't the same here without ya. All of us miss you!"

"You're so kind. Thanks for calling, Rebecca. Denki, I mean."

They said good-bye and hung up.

··· ➤ ➤ ···

More than a week later, Jenny received a letter from Andrew Lapp. He wrote that he was still praying for her, and that he understood why she had to leave so quickly. *If you truly believed you wouldn't pass your Proving, you figured you might as well not wait around, jah?*

Reading his considerate words brought her a strange comfort. And she was relieved that, despite his disappointment at her going, he did not seem upset. She knew it was so when she read the last line of his letter: *I pray earnestly that you will be happy in the English world, if that is where God wants you to be, my dear Jenny.* The idea that he still considered her "his" on any level took her by surprise, and she found her thoughts returning to him many times throughout that day and the days that followed. She felt astonished that Andrew was so selfless, releasing her back to the modern world without him. His unexpected letter was a soothing salve for her heart . . . yet she could not help wishing she had not left so much behind in Hickory Hollow.

··· ➤ ➤ ···

The Monday after St. Patrick's Day, a new shipment of antiques arrived at the shop where Jenny had begun working full-time again. Her boss was over in the corner talking to the dealer when Jenny happened to overhear a mention of Lancaster County, and she made a mental note to look through the items, just for fun, before heading home that evening. If she saw anything she liked, she might use her employee discount.

She finished helping several more customers, finding it curious how fashionable the sleek look of the '50s and '60s was to young couples—pole lamps and Danish furniture in particular. It was fun for her to snatch up the occasional find, as well, thinking how nice it might look in a new apartment, since she'd sold everything. She'd had her eye on one residence in particular for the past week or so, but wanted to be frugal rather than impulsive.

Near the closing hour, Jenny took her time to study each of the antiques from Lancaster County—sideboards, corner hutches, and an assortment of unmatched cane chairs. She turned over one of the chairs and saw the name *E. M. Zook*, and for a split second wondered if Ella Mae had perhaps passed away. But there were so many Zooks in Amish country. *"Oodles,"* Rebecca had mentioned early on, also listing some of the other popular surnames—Stoltzfus, King, Fisher, Beiler, and Lapp.

Thinking again of Ella Mae, Jenny was sure Marnie would have said something when they last talked by phone, weeks ago. Surprisingly, her friend had not moved to Katie Fisher's, telling instead of Roy's friendly conversation with Bishop John. *"This changed everything for us,"* Marnie said, sounding so happy. She and Roy were looking forward to taking baptism classes together next summer, prior to their November wedding. *"We're joining church here in Hickory Hollow, of all things!"*

Jenny decided to purchase one of the old chairs, and her

dad agreed to pick it up. And all the rest of the evening she wondered what E. M. stood for. *Eli Mathias? Ephraim Marcus?*

In the end, she preferred to think the chair had somehow been linked to the Old Wise Woman. The beautiful chair, along with the wall hanging Marnie had sent her and Andrew Lapp's cards, notes, and gifts were her only keepsakes. *Along with my unforgettable memories.*

Chapter 50

Another two weeks passed, and Jenny was happy to keep her hands and mind busy while her heart journeyed here and there. *Well, not really*, she thought. *Only to one place.*

She tried to keep her focus on her present surroundings the Friday after Easter, when her father had planned their first ever father-daughter outing. They settled in at an inviting restaurant, Skipper's Dock on Water Street, in beautiful Stonington Borough. It was an hour before sunset, and Dad must have pulled strings to get a perfect harbor-side view for their leisurely meal.

She felt relaxed enough at this rare event, having taken her mother's suggestion to wear one of her own long, white sleeveless dresses from *the* wardrobe. It was a comfortable yet dressy outfit, complete with a black bolero with white piping. Mom had remarked that she looked like a million bucks. *Oh yes, exactly what I was going for*, Jenny thought, laughing at the paradox.

Her father was impeccable in navy slacks and a white oxford shirt and tie with a tan sports jacket.

"I've been thinking about this evening for quite a while," he said over appetizers of stuffed Stonington clams swimming in butter.

She leaned back in her chair, taking in the waterfront, the piers dotting the fading red sky, and the wail of seabirds. It was hard to imagine being in such a lovely spot, let alone with her dad.

What's gotten into him?

"It's been wonderful having you home," Dad said, his eyes searching her face. "And I think you'll be surprised when I say this, but I'd like to apologize for letting my work crowd out my time with you, Jenny."

"Dad—"

"I'm serious."

He smiled, but there was a hint of something else, something other than joy. Momentarily, he looked toward the wharf, as if second-guessing, then back at her. "I don't think you're all that happy here."

She was surprised he'd picked up on her private reveries. "I'm sorry," she said. "I didn't—"

"Jenny, no . . . don't be. More than anything, I want your happiness, just as your mother does." He paused again. "And you know what, honey? I think you might be right about the Amish . . . the appreciation you've always had for the culture. I really don't think you belong here, in this crazy, modern, stress-filled world."

Jenny considered this as the waiter came to remove their small plates, then left. "You must think I'm still Plain inside."

"Aren't you?"

She didn't want to spoil this special evening. "You must love me a lot, Daddy," she whispered, not fully realizing it until now.

He reached across the table and took her hand. "Enough to let you go, if we must."

Dad's words reminded her of Andrew's first letter after she returned home.

"There's something else," her father said, glancing toward the water. "In many ways, losing you from the family for those two months opened my eyes."

"Dad, I . . ."

He shook his head and reached for his water glass, and she knew he wasn't interested in belaboring the point. He'd said what was on his heart and she appreciated it.

When the main course arrived, Jenny and her father ate heartily, enjoying the scrumptious seafood. And Jenny had much to ponder, realizing again that she had been too impulsive, leaving Lancaster County so quickly. Yet it wasn't as if she could simply return there whenever she wished.

Or could she? Her heart beat faster at the exhilarating thought.

Marnie flew down the stairs to the kitchen, filled with the rich aroma of baking chocolate pies. Her sisters were still playing on the lawn this springtime Saturday, making themselves scarce while Marnie and her mother finished setting a pretty table. Afterward, they chopped onions for the baked ham supper. It wouldn't be long now and all their guests would be arriving.

Feeling like a flibbertigibbet, Marnie dashed back to the sitting room near the large kitchen and ran her fingers over the sideboard's surface for the second time. She smoothed the checkerboard-patterned afghan on the back of the upholstered chair in the corner and glanced out the window.

Her heart leaped and she leaned closer, her nose nearly bumping the windowpane. "Quick, Mamm . . . tell Daed she's just arrived! Ask him to bring Posey along, too, on a leash! Oh, Mamm, she's here!"

Jenny stepped out of the taxi, paid the cabbie, and left her suitcases there on the driveway. She had no idea how well she would be received by the Amish community as a whole, if at all, although Marnie had clearly rejoiced when Jenny had written with her decision.

Presently, she spotted Marnie dashing around the side of the house to come this way, a bright smile on her sweet face. And then Peggy, her mother, appeared, accompanied by brawny Chester and Posey, who barked and wagged her spunky tail.

"Hullo, *liewi Freind!*" Marnie called as she flung her arms around Jenny.

Dear friend . . . Jenny felt the same about Marnie.

Stepping back, Marnie looked her over with delight. "Well, aren't you the cutest Amish girl in Hickory Hollow! All you're missin' is the prayer Kapp, ya know."

Jenny smiled, catching her meaning. "I brought my entire Amish wardrobe back with me."

"Oh, Jenny! Everyone's been fussing 'bout you since we heard you were returning—I mean just *everyone*." Marnie grinned, tilting her head and shielding her eyes from the sun. "But it was my idea to have a gathering here tonight. Hope that's all right."

Chester greeted Jenny warmly, shaking her hand and holding

the golden Lab up to show how much Posey had grown. "Seems you've been gone a long while, Jenny. Willkumm back."

Jenny accepted a hug from Marnie's mother, all dressed up in her for-good dress and matching apron.

"I hope you're hungry," Peggy said. "We're havin' Easter dinner all over again, or so says Chester." She laughed and looked up at her husband. "And some of your friends will be here . . . comin' very soon."

Jenny could not believe the warm reception and assumed Marnie's parents had humored their daughter with the plans for a special meal. *Like Ella Mae did for me last Thanksgiving.*

"And someone else is here to see ya," Marnie whispered and grinned, pointing toward the barn, where Andrew Lapp emerged. "Well, I guess I'd better leave ya be . . . for now."

Marnie followed her father, who had picked up Jenny's suitcases and was carrying them up the driveway. Posey scampered along, close behind, and Marnie and her parents hurried toward the house as Andrew came to greet Jenny.

"Quite a nice doin's, jah?" He removed his straw hat and she saw the old mischief in his eyes. "Nearly everything but the fatted calf."

He's right, she thought. *I am a prodigal.*

The earthy fragrance of freshly plowed soil and the feeling of serenity she'd sorely missed swept over her. Once again, she appreciated how very special a place Hickory Hollow was. *And always will be,* she thought, enjoying the bright yellow forsythia bushes in full bloom.

"Not much has changed since you left," Andrew said. "But on the other hand, there *are* some surprising things happening."

She wondered what he meant. When he didn't volunteer more, she let it go. Was he courting someone—was that the reason for the awkwardness between them? Or was he offended by her silence after she'd left? She hadn't replied to his letters because she felt it was unfair and didn't want to lead him to hope she was ever returning. Besides, she hadn't the right to expect he'd wait for her, anyway. The fact that Andrew was even here this evening, welcoming her back as a friend, was a real surprise.

Marnie wasn't kidding. Nearly every Amish friend Jenny had made last fall came to supper that evening. Even Emmalyn Lapp appeared, a blend of beauty and skepticism, while they all milled about in the front room, waiting for the meal to be served. But it wasn't long before Emmalyn came over to talk to Jenny. "I wondered if we'd scared ya off." Emmalyn looked chagrined. "Well, if *I* did."

Jenny assured her otherwise. "I guess I had to return home to see how deeply Plain I really was."

Emmalyn gave her a smile. "Well, you sure weren't here long enough to know for sure, were you . . . *last* time?"

Jenny nodded agreeably. "Things will be different now; you'll see."

Soon, Rebecca Lapp wandered over and gave Jenny a gentle hug. "You have no idea how I hoped and prayed you'd be back again, Jenny. And just so ya know, your room's all redded up and waitin' for you."

Jenny thanked her, grateful for the chance to reconcile their relationship during the rest of her Proving. "It meant so much to me when you called some months ago. And now . . . well, we're on new footing, jah?" she added, and Rebecca nodded and smiled.

Following the meal, the bishop and Mary lingered after everyone left, spending time alone with Jenny in the kitchen while Marnie and her parents and younger siblings scattered about the house. Bishop John read the Bible in English for Jenny's benefit, and later prayed with her and Mary. It was comforting to receive this second welcome, unexpected as it was.

Later, when it was appropriate, Jenny slipped in a comment about Katie Lapp Fisher. "She once told me that she was born fancy, considering her English genetic roots." Jenny paused. "But Katie pointed out that while I was born to Englishers, my heart was naturally Plain, so to speak. I know this might sound strange, but—"

"Not at all." Mary shook her head. "I think I understand what Katie meant. And ya know, I believe she just might be right."

After a while, Marnie came into the kitchen and brought out more cake, but the bishop declined, saying they had to get home to relieve their niece Naomi, who was evidently more settled in the community, too. And Jenny was glad to hear it.

After the Beilers headed home, Marnie offered to walk with Jenny down to Lapps', helping to carry one of the suitcases. Jenny so enjoyed the sound of springtime insects. She smiled when Marnie forgot and slipped into Deitsch occasionally without thinking.

Jenny was very surprised to hear that the bishop had recently permitted Katie Fisher to visit their own home. Not for a meal, but Katie and Mary had sat out on the porch and sipped iced meadow tea together. "I can't tell ya what a turnabout this is," Marnie added. "Nearly a miracle, really."

Jenny realized she'd missed out on quite a lot during a few months. "A very special reunion of true friends, jah?" she said, and Marnie wholeheartedly agreed.

"Oh, Jenny, I'm ever so happy you've returned," Marnie said as they observed the extravagant sunset and the way the clouds reflected the sprays of color.

Slowly, as the brilliance began to fade, Jenny's memory of the touching father-daughter dinner overlooking the harbor, and her father's perceptive remarks, rose up in her mind. She embraced *that* particular sunset, too.

Looking at Marnie, she blinked away tears as they turned into the Lapps' lane. "It's so wunnerbaar-*gut* to be back."

Chapter 51

A waking to darkness, Jenny yawned, and her first conscious thought was of being back at her parents' guest
cottage in Connecticut. Sleepily, she ran her hand over the
embroidered edging of the pillowcase, wondering if it was
the one she'd bought as a girl to surprise her mother. But her
awareness kicked in when she heard the wonderful *clip-clop-
clip* of a horse and buggy going up the road.

Ah yes . . . jah! She stretched, raising her arms high over
her head and bumping the headboard as the handmade quilt
slipped away from her. Then she heard stirring in the hallway,
and wanting to assist Rebecca with the hot breakfast, she
rejected the urge to lie there between the crisp white sheets
under the cozy bed coverings. Tossing them aside, she got
up and fumbled for her slippers, remembering how chilly
the wooden floor planks had been last December. But it was
midspring now, and summertime hovered in the wings.

I'm where I belong, Jenny thought, hearing the horse and
carriage as it moved up Hickory Lane toward Cattail Road.

Later that morning, Jenny surprised herself by making her
first-ever perfect loaf of bread. "Thanks to a few tips from my

mother," she told Rebecca, who beamed with happiness when she shared how she'd connected with her family.

"Ach, now, this makes me wonder if you weren't s'posed to return to them for a time."

"I believe you're right." Jenny set aside the loaf to cool.

"Sometimes the Lord leads us to make amends in situations." Tears sprang to Rebecca's eyes. "In His own time . . . and way."

Jenny didn't bring up Katie and Dan, or anything regarding Rebecca's confession to the bishop. There was no need to. But she completely agreed with Rebecca and smiled warmly at the tenderhearted woman.

Later, when their morning chores were finished, Rebecca recited off a list of flowers and other gardening items she wanted to purchase at an Amish greenhouse. "The owner, Maryanna, is expecting me today, and I daresay it's 'bout time you saw her charming place for yourself."

They headed out to greet the balmy day and to hitch up Star. Jenny helped Rebecca, remembering more than she'd expected to, though Rebecca said nothing to point it out. And then they were off.

Jenny was helping to carry flats of fluffy golden marigolds to the back of Rebecca's enclosed buggy when she saw Andrew Lapp coming up the driveway. Not certain she should catch his eye, she wondered if he was headed to the greenhouse, too.

But he came right up to her, made a comment about the wonderful weather, and then asked if she might go for a walk with him later. "Once you're back at Samuel and Rebecca's," he said with a serious look.

She glanced over her shoulder, glad Rebecca was still talking with Maryanna at the entrance to the greenhouse. The two women were obviously unaware of Andrew's presence.

"Sure, I'd like that, Andrew."

His smile was so broad, so endearing, it took Jenny's breath away. "There's the prettiest little springhouse pond just down the road," he said, leaning closer. "I'd like to show ya." He winked at her.

She played along, her heart beating hard. "Sounds nice."

Then, taking her by surprise, he led her around to the other side of the buggy, and when they were completely obscured from view, he reached for both of her hands. "Just so ya know, all that prayin' I was doing back when . . . well, it wasn't just that you'd pass your Proving, Jenny."

She frowned, trying to comprehend what he meant. Then, seeing his familiar twinkle, she smiled. To think he'd waited for her!

"You know what I'd really like to do right this minute," he said, his voice soft. "I'd like to take you in my arms and never let ya go."

Jenny knew she must be blushing—even more so when he raised her hand to his lips and tenderly kissed it, his gaze never leaving hers. "I think you stole my heart that very first Preaching service."

"When you admonished me about snitchin' the ministers' food?"

"Ah . . . so you *do* remember?"

Warmed by his sweet admission, Jenny longed to walk and talk with him more privately, as he'd suggested. And soon!

"So, Jenny Burns, how long do ya 'spect to be stayin' with us *this* time?" he asked, still holding her hands.

She smiled up at him. "How's forever sound?"

Epilogue

The following May, more than a year after my return to the People, the deacon approached me about possibly joining the church. He did so on behalf of all the ministerial brethren. "Do ya feel you're ready?" By now, I was speaking the language fairly fluently and could even hitch up a horse to a buggy—on my own! Even my sock darning improved after Tessie Miller took me under her proverbial wing and taught me a couple tricks.

So, from May to August, I will attend baptismal instruction every other Sunday morning, prior to the September baptismal service. I'm expected to acquaint myself with and understand the *Dordrecht*—the Confession of Faith—as well as meet individually with the ministers on Preaching Sundays.

"Remember," the deacon warned, "it's best never to take this holy vow than to make it and break it later on."

After he left, I thanked God for allowing me to learn and understand the Old Ways. But most of all, I was grateful for the opportunity to live among people with whom I can relate. The topping on the cake is Andrew Lapp, who officially proposed marriage to me the week after the deacon's visit.

We'll wait to marry until after I'm baptized, sometime in the middle of November, Andrew says. My parents and Kiersten and her husband are talking about coming, even though I've informed them of the long service and the hard benches. Dad says he'd like to take another look at my Deitsch Bible, which is heartening. Oh, and he wants to meet Andrew, of course. I'm just glad my family is interested in seeing Hickory Hollow for themselves. Who knows, it might help them understand why I'm so drawn to the place.

At any rate, I've never been so happy, or so settled. What I feel for Andrew Lapp, and he for me, isn't just a special kind of love. Plenty of couples think they have a corner on that sort of thing. We, however, believe God drew us together for a reason, and our love belongs to Him first. Andrew says our love is all wrapped up in a firm and precious faith—"*our foundation's gut,*" he likes to say. And when he winks at me, my heart flutters nearly out of control.

Although Marnie is my first choice for a bridesmaid, I can't choose her to stand up with Andrew and me because she and Roy married last fall, and an Amish bridesmaid is required to be a single young woman. I'm honestly leaning toward Emmalyn, although she doesn't know it yet. It seems like the right thing to do.

Naomi's second on my list, as she and I continue to be close friends. Tessie Miller's a good choice, as well, as are several of Marnie's younger cousins.

All of us get along so beautifully . . . it's like having a dozen or more sisters!

Ella Mae said months ago that she truly suspected—well, no, she was quite positive I would return here, after I left for home. She also insisted that Rebecca's confessing her former secret was the best thing that could've happened. *"Because sometimes when you tell the truth, you can start a fire,"* she said, and I think I understand what she means.

As for Rebecca and Katie, there is even more cause for rejoicing, with another grandson, little Leon Matthew, celebrating his first birthday soon. Samuel declares he's the spitting image of Elam and Annie's son, Daniel—Dan's sister's only child.

Rebecca's confided in me that she still prays for Katie's and her husband's return to the Amish church. But she no longer believes she has thwarted the helpful effects of the Bann on them. If anything, she is more accepting of their earnest faith, as is the bishop. And while the baptized People still aren't permitted to go to the Fishers' to visit, Katie and Dan are sincerely welcomed here in Hickory Hollow.

What Katie once told me is true: A person grows best spiritually when exploring God's Word, letting it get rooted and planted in the soil of the heart. There is no substitute for that for anyone, Plain or not.

And I've discovered that Hickory Hollow is not the ultimate place, no more than any community is perfect. But I *do* know that when the Lord puts a desire in your heart, you'll know it . . . and if you allow Him to nurture it, that yearning will blossom into a *brechdiech Gaarde*—magnificent garden—of blessing and grace.

Author's Note

For the very first young woman who wrote to me years ago, pleading to know what it would require to become Amish, I offer a special thank-you for planting the seed of this book in my thinking and in my heart. This story belongs to you! *The Secret Keeper* seeks to bring to life the heart's cry of many thousands of readers who yearn for the Old Ways or who wish to live with an Old Order Amish family somewhere near Hickory Hollow.

I am sincerely blessed with devoted readers, as well as the extraordinary people who edit and publish my novels. Thanks to each of you, especially to David Horton and Rochelle Glöege, ever astute and encouraging—two of my greatest joys.

I also wish to pay tribute to the many unsung heroes of my research, assistants who tirelessly check and double-check my fact gathering, including Amish and Mennonite friends and family, and my own dear Dave and our grown children, Julie, Janie, and Jonathan.

My great appreciation also goes out to the growing number

of prayer partners, especially my wonderful friends at Bethany House, who take praying seriously—a real blessing to this author!

For all of you who kept my "secret" (the storyline for this book) while I delved into the journey of Jenny Burns's Proving time, I am truly thankful. And for those who prayed so earnestly when I fell and broke my right wrist just *three short days* before the book's deadline, I am forever grateful.

Hank Hershberger, Pennsylvania Dutch linguist and former Amishman, was always there for me and graciously answered numerous questions regarding *Deitsch,* not to mention how to hitch up horses and ponies to buggies and carts. Thanks so much!

I'm also indebted to the superb writings of John A. Hostetler and Donald Kraybill, the spokesman for the Lancaster County Amish community . . . and to the good folk at the Lancaster Mennonite Historical Society.

It is my ongoing delight to create stories that touch your heartstrings and somehow make a difference in your life or others'.

Soli Deo Gloria!

Beverly Lewis, born in the heart of Pennsylvania Dutch country, is the *New York Times* bestselling author of more than ninety books. Her stories have been published in eleven languages worldwide. A keen interest in her mother's Plain heritage has inspired Beverly to write many Amish-related novels, beginning with *The Shunning,* which has sold more than a million copies. *The Brethren* was honored with a 2007 Christy Award.

Beverly lives with her husband, David, in Colorado.

Don't Miss

The Last Bride
From Beverly Lewis

Nineteen-year-old Tessie Miller is the youngest of five daughters—and the only one yet to marry. She has her heart set on Amishman Marcus King. Come wedding season, they plan to tie the knot and start a family together… until Tessie's father forbids the marriage.

Impetuously, Tessie and Marcus elope to exchange their vows in the English world. After a secret honeymoon, they return to their community to live as singles, hoping that, in time, they can convince her father to give their love a chance. But when the unthinkable happens, Tessie faces the biggest challenge of her life—and the almost-certain censure of the People.

Can anyone offer hope for Tessie's desperate plight?

The Last Bride
The fifth book in the HOME TO HICKORY HOLLOW series

Available April 1, 2014

Don't Miss the Rest of the HOME TO HICKORY HOLLOW Series!

To learn more about Beverly and her books, visit beverlylewis.com or find her on Facebook.

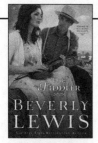

When Amelia Devries, thoroughly modern and equally disillusioned, takes a wrong turn during a rainstorm, she unexpectedly meets an Amishman—and a community—that might just change her life forever.

The Fiddler

Joanna Kurtz is so far proving the adage "always the bridesmaid, never the bride." Yet despite appearances, she has a beau who is secretly courting her from afar. Will her hidden passion for writing and his duty to his family keep them forever apart?

The Bridesmaid

Mystery surrounds the lost little girl Jodi Winfield finds along the road one morning. Do the answers lie within the cloistered world of the Lancaster Old Order Amish?

The Guardian

BETHANYHOUSE

More From *NY Times* Bestselling Author Beverly Lewis

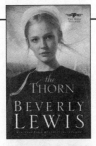

As two Amish sisters find themselves on the fringes of their Lancaster community, will they be forced to choose between their beloved People and true love?

THE ROSE TRILOGY: *The Thorn, The Judgment, The Mercy*

Now a Hallmark Channel Original Movie!
All her life Katie Lapp has longed for forbidden things, but will her dreams come at a price too dear to pay?

THE HERITAGE OF LANCASTER COUNTY: *The Shunning, The Confession, The Reckoning*

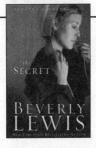

When her mother's secret threatens to destroy their peaceful Amish family, will Grace's search for the truth lead to more heartache or to the love she longs for?

SEASONS OF GRACE: *The Secret, The Missing, The Telling*